DRAGON OF GREYWOOD

By: Beverly J. Remmer

Beverly J Remmer

ISBN 978-0-9783717-0-8

www.dragonofgreywood.com

Printed in Canada

Blitzprint Inc.

ACKNOWLEDGEMENTS:

I would like to thank the following people: My husband for his business advice and help; my sister Karen, for being Dragon of Greywood 's first reader and my staunchest supporter; my former students for being my inspiration; my family, friends, and colleagues for their encouragement; the grade five students of Horsholm International School for being my first audience; my editor, Heather, and Blitzprint for their expertise. I would also like to thank my children: Jason for being official keeper of the files, Michelle for her enthusiastic response to my story and offering to share it with her grade five students, Patricia for being so proud of me, and David for his amazing dragon artwork.

DEDICATION:

To my grandchildren; Mason, Anna, Seth, and Marius. Thank you for the wonder and magic you bring to my life. I will love you forever and always.

ABOUT THE AUTHOR:

Beverly Remmer is a retired teacher and vice-principal. She has also been a freelance writer, and has published an article on guinea pigs in Club Connection, a children's magazine. Beverly lives in Calgary, Alberta. *Dragon of Greywood* is her first novel.

*****

The time had finally come. With a sigh, Durkin slowly got to his feet and stretched to his full height of four feet. He rubbed one warty hand across his knobby brow. He made the sign of fourfold over the magical pool and whispered the closing words of acknowledgment: "My deepest gratitude for allowing me to be your voice, Tawyn. I shall deliver your message." With his right thumb, the small man touched his head, his heart, and each cheek as he murmured, "Abra, Vishni, Marah, Wello." Staring into the water, he respectfully backed away from the oracle pool. He then looked toward the sun to break the spell.

"At last, Griswold and my people shall be free," Durkin said aloud. He limped over to a well-worn stump and carefully lowered his ancient body.

Visionary times with Tawyn always left him weak and light-headed. He also needed a few minutes to decide who should get the news first - the dragon or the king. He truly didn't want to cope with King Ulric's many questions and ponderings while he waited for His Majesty's permission to visit the dragon. Griswold was in great pain and would not live much longer. With the help of Rhiannon, Magical Maiden, he could get to the dragon's lair before it was too late.

Using his gnarled walking stick to get to his feet, Durkin slowly shuffled through the forest in the direction of the magic maiden's hut. He had made his decision. The dragon would be the first to learn the news. Hopefully, he would be able to set things right with the king when he returned.

CHAPTER ONE

“This place is massive,” Morgan said as he got out of the car.

“Wow!” replied his identical twin brother, William. They both stared up at the huge, old house built of stone. It was two stories high and had a partial third floor that was shaped like a tower. Morgan noticed a small curtained window in the tower. For a moment, he thought he saw the curtain move. He shuddered and turned to his brother.

“Kind of a creepy old house isn't it, Will?”

“Yeah,” his brother replied, “I can't wait to explore.”

“No one is exploring until we've unpacked and had dinner,” said their mother. “Let's go inside and see your great-grandmother." She turned to their fifteen-year-old sister. "Katie, you and the boys help Dad carry the bags. I'll go and find Grandie."

The trip from Vancouver, Canada, was finally over and they had arrived safely at Tintagel, Cornwall in the south western part of England. They had come to stay with their great-grandmother, so that their mother could help her run 'Adney House Bed and Breakfast'. Katie and her mother had spent the previous summer at Adney House helping with the guests, but the thirteen-year-old twins had never been to Tintagel. They had last seen their great-grandmother in London, two years earlier.

Living in England for a year was definitely going to be a big adjustment for everyone. Luckily their father, Dr. Paul Hanford, would be able to work at a small hospital in the town of Wadebridge, where the children would also attend school in September.

The family fell over each other trying to fit themselves and all of their bags into the front foyer. The boys kept turning around in circles trying to see everything at once. There was a library next to the entrance hallway. Morgan was immediately drawn into its dark recesses. He quickly began scanning the rows of very old books. William, on the other hand, was halfway up the circular staircase when their great-grandmother came to greet them.

"Welcome to Adney House," Grandie said, smiling broadly. "I have been most anxious to get all of you together in one place, and now I have you here for at least a year." She hugged Katie and looked up the stairway as William clattered down to greet her. "Oh my! Look how you've grown. Suddenly I feel very small," she said, reaching up to ruffle his curly blonde hair. "Now tell me, where is your brother?"

"He's probably in there," William said, pointing to the library.

Grandie laughed when she spotted Morgan on the top rung of the wooden ladder. He was surveying some very old leather-bound books.

"Morgan, I see you still have a fascination for old books. You've found the oldest ones in our entire collection. I don't think they've even been dusted since your great-grandfather died. He was very fond of the leather ones too. Please come down here and give me a hug."

Morgan reluctantly placed the book he was holding back into its niche and climbed down to embrace his great-grandmother. "My goodness, you boys seem to look more alike every time I see you. How will I ever tell you apart?"

"William's a bit taller than me, but I'm the good-looking one," Morgan teased. Then he added, "I'm sorry for snooping Grandie, but I just had to check out the library. Do you mind if I read some of these books?"

"Of course you may dear, but let's get everyone settled first," she replied, leading him to the stairway. "I'm hoping you boys will like the rooms that I have chosen for you. I'm putting you in the old nursery on the third floor, away from the guests and from the rest of the family as well. I thought you might like some space of your own."

Grandie was able to get around very well in spite of her age, and she easily managed to lead the family upstairs to the second floor. The children's parents were taken to the master suite just down the hall from Grandie's rooms. Katie was given a beautiful room with large, shuttered windows that overlooked the rose garden.

"Oh Grandie, this is the same room I had last summer. I love it," she exclaimed.

"I'm glad you approve, dear," replied her great-grandmother

"We want to see our room," William said impatiently.

"Up those stairs to your left," laughed Grandie. The boys rushed up the narrow staircase and waited outside a locked door for the others to arrive.

"When the cleaning staff got the rooms ready, I didn't realize they had locked the door again. Luckily, I always carry keys in my apron," she said, as she handed William a large key ring. "See if you can find the one that opens the door to your new residence."

The boys gasped as they stepped into the tower room. Old books filled wooden shelves that had been built to exactly fit the curved shape of the wall. A skylight in the domed ceiling scattered rays of light across the hardwood floor. At one end of the room, there was an eating area with a sink and a small refrigerator. In the centre of the room, three oversized leather chairs faced a big wooden cabinet. Grandie opened the cupboard doors, revealing a large television. The boys were speechless.

"I had things rearranged a bit so it wouldn't seem like an old nursery anymore," Grandie said, smiling at their reaction. "Now, let me show you the bedroom."

They all followed her into a large room with curved walls and shelves similar to what they had seen in the main room. Tall captains' beds had been placed on either side of a wood-trimmed window seat. Heavy drapes covered the window.

There was a wooden desk at the foot of each bed and a huge wardrobe at the far end of the room. A telephone rested on a small table by the door.

The boys climbed up on the window-seat and parted the heavy drapes. "What a great view!" Morgan exclaimed. "Is that a castle down the hill?"

Grandie nodded. "Yes, dear, that is the famous King Arthur's Castle."

"Wow, let me get a look at that," William said, pushing Morgan aside.

"Let's move on boys," Grandie said. Everyone followed her out of the bedroom. "The toilet and shower are next to the kitchenette. The room next to the lavatory once belonged to our nanny, but now it's just full of old furniture. The wiring and heating were upgraded a few years ago."

"This is the coolest part of the whole house," William said excitedly.

"It will be perfect for us," Morgan added, completely forgetting about his earlier apprehensions when he had looked up at the tower window.

Their mother was less enthusiastic. "Are you sure they'll be okay so far away from the rest of us?" she asked.

"Of course they will," Grandie replied. "The

boys are thirteen years old and there are two of them. I spent most of my childhood up here with my twin brother. We had a wonderful time in these rooms. However, if the boys would rather be on the second level, they can move into the room across from Katie." Grandie offered. She turned to the twins. "Would you like to see that room before you decide?"

"No," William assured her. "We definitely want to be up here don't we, Morg?"

"Definitely," Morgan agreed. "Don't worry about us, Mom."

"Well, alright. But you boys have to keep everything very tidy," their mother said.

"We know, Mom," William groaned.

"Now, let's go down and get the bags," their father said. "Most of our things will be delivered later this week. For now, we all have clothes to unpack."

"Oh my, it's almost half-five. I have guests to feed," Grandie said. "You must all be feeling a bit peckish too. Come down and join me in the family area next to the kitchen in forty minutes." She turned to Katie. "And after we've had tea, I'll show you a special part of my studio that I've fixed up for you. I'm hoping we can create some masterpieces together. Do you still enjoy painting?"

"Oh yes, Grandie. I can't wait to see what you've done," Katie replied eagerly.

'Tea' turned out to be supper. It included something called 'Cornish pasty', – an interesting folded meat pie that reminded Morgan of pizza pockets. The boys were also introduced to the Adney House dessert special – 'sticky toffee pudding'. It was a small sponge cake surrounded with custard and covered with sweet toffee syrup. Morgan decided that he would gladly eat sticky pudding every day.

After dinner, the boys had hoped to go exploring among the famous cliffs of Tintagel. However, it had begun to rain, so their father said they would have to go exploring in the morning. Morgan was just as happy with that. He wanted to search through every nook and cranny of the old nursery. William was disappointed that they had to stay indoors, but he agreed to check out the third floor with Morgan.

By nine o'clock, the boys had given their rooms a good 'going over'. William wanted to rename the nursery, 'Room of Doom', while Morgan wanted to call it 'The Tower' because of its shape. William reluctantly agreed. He settled down in front of the TV, while Morgan began scanning the shelves for books about King

Arthur. With such an amazing historical site nearby, Morgan wanted to learn all about the area before they went exploring in the morning. He finally located a promising book – *Arthur and Merlin,* by Orson Terrill.

"Hey Will, look at this old book I found about King Arthur. Want to see what we can find out about the castle before we go exploring tomorrow?"

"Sure, why don't you check it out?" he replied absently, his eyes glued to the television. William had never shown much interest in reading. Whenever he had to do book reports for school, he always chose a book that had been made into movie. He'd do his report on the movie and never actually read the book. He had always managed to get away with it too. Morgan, on the other hand, loved to read, particularly books about knights, warriors, castles and magic. Throughout their school years, Morgan had always done very well academically. Science and sports; especially soccer, basketball and archery were William's main interests. Both boys were excellent swimmers.

Morgan decided to read in bed. He stripped down to his boxers and crawled under the feathery quilts of his new captain's bed. Propping himself up with several pillows,

Morgan was just getting into the book, when he began to feel drowsy. He tried hard to concentrate, but he soon fell asleep in spite of the interesting book.

A few hours later, Morgan awoke and it was pitch-dark in the tower. He could hear William snoring in the bed next to him and was angry that his brother hadn't left a light on somewhere. Morgan had to use the toilet; there was no question about that, so he slid out from under the cozy quilts. When his feet hit the ice-cold floor, Morgan began hopping around in the dark, searching for his socks. He finally found them on the chair by his desk. He didn't dare turn on the light and risk waking William. His brother had been known to throw things, or leap up and choke anyone who woke him up for no good reason. Morgan remembered that he had a flashlight in his backpack, which was under the desk. He felt around in the side pocket until he located it.

Closing the bedroom door quietly, Morgan headed for the washroom, clad only in his boxers and white socks. The steady beam of his flashlight helped him find it quickly. He attended to his needs and was getting so cold that he decided to wash his hands in the morning. He opened the door and shone the flashlight across the room to gauge the distance as he prepared to sprint to the bedroom.

Suddenly an odd noise startled him – two noises actually. The first one was a tapping noise coming from the wall behind the books. The other noise was an intermittent shuffling sound, as though something heavy was being dragged across the floor. Morgan stood in the doorway, trembling.

"Okay, the first noise is probably the heating pipes," he reassured himself. "The other noise sounds like a curtain flapping in an open window...but there are no open windows up here!" A cold shiver shot through him. Then the tapping noise started again. "That's definitely heating pipes. I can handle that...I don't hear the swishing noise anymore."

Morgan shone the flashlight around the room. He saw nothing out of the ordinary, so he decided to make a run for it. He dashed across the sitting room and was just about to open the bedroom door when he heard the shuffling noise again. A cold draft hit his back. Slowly he turned and shone the flashlight around the room. His blood turned to ice.

A strange, grey fog was enveloping the room! There was an unmistakable sound of heavy breathing, and a foul stench emanated from the vaporous mass. Morgan stood pressed against the bedroom door, gripping the flashlight. His heart was pounding and his knees were shaking. From within the dense fog, he heard something heave a great sigh, and then he heard the shuffling, dragging noise again.

Suddenly the fog vanished as quickly and mysteriously as it had appeared, and the sitting room seemed to be normal again. Morgan slowly let out his breath and cautiously turned to grasp the doorknob. He jerked the bedroom door open and quickly slammed it behind him. He raced over to his bed, and dived under the covers. He still held the flashlight in his hand and was grateful for its steady glow.

William moved around restlessly and began to wake up. "What's going on?" he mumbled. "Bright light..."

Morgan's constricted throat muscles relaxed at the sound of his brother's voice.

"It's just my flashlight," he said hoarsely. "Go back to sleep."

"Idiot," William muttered as he rolled over. He was snoring again within seconds.

*****

Rhiannon had taken him quickly and invisibly to the lair. Durkin could feel Griswold's relief when he visited the dragon's thoughts and gave him the message. Steam rose from the creature's nostrils as he let out a tired sigh. Scaly lids closed over the ancient yellow eyes. Durkin hoped the news would keep the dragon alive until the visitors arrived.

Once he was back at Greywood, Durkin went directly to the king's chamber. The ancient little man approached the throne and was given permission to speak.

"Sire, I have a message from Tawyn," Durkin said, kneeling before the king

"Stand and speak of it Messenger," Ulric ordered. "And be exact in your delivery."

Durkin rose and recited clearly. "The time has come. Two as one, shall cross time and distance, so the Mighty One may sleep."

"Griswold must be told," the king said. "Go now."

After an awkward pause, Durkin quietly stated, "He already knows, Majesty."

"You dared to go to the dragon without permission?" boomed King Ulric. "Explain!"

"Given his present state of ill health, I felt the

Mighty One had to be told at once. This humble servant begs forgiveness," the messenger replied nervously.

Suddenly, a bolt of electrical energy tore through Durkin's body, terminating in his feet. Black smoke rose from his leather shoes and the acrid smell of burning flesh filled the room. The pain was excruciating, but Durkin dared not cry out. He had suffered the wrath of the king and he knew that he was lucky to be alive.

CHAPTER TWO

Morgan could see a small sliver of daylight through the window where the bedroom drapes met. He had tossed and turned all night, his thoughts alternating between fear and curiosity about what had happened to him. He looked at his watch and saw that it was ten o'clock. William was still asleep. Morgan had decided that he wasn't leaving the bedroom until his brother woke up. He was afraid of what he might find on the other side of the bedroom door.

William finally yawned and stretched. Looking over at his brother, he asked, "If you're awake, why didn't you go down for breakfast?"

"I was waiting for you. I didn't want to go down there by myself," Morgan said. "Grandie might spot me, and decide that I should eat with her B&B guests," he added, blurting out the first excuse that popped into his head.

"I'm going to the washroom," William said as he got out of bed and searched for his clothes. "Man, it's cold. We'll have to ask Grandie for more heat up here."

Morgan was grateful that nothing out of the ordinary happened when his brother opened the door. Still, he didn't want to be alone, so he leaped out of bed, grabbed his clothes, and followed William.

"Hey, I have dibs on the 'loo'," William challenged as he ran toward the washroom.

"I know that. It's cold in the bedroom, so I'll just get dressed in the sitting room," Morgan said casually.

After he was dressed, Morgan looked warily around the room. Everything seemed to be in order. He didn't see, smell or hear any of the oddities from the previous night. He walked over to the bookshelf where he had heard the tapping. All of the books were tightly in their places. As he walked toward the locked nanny's room, he noticed a stain on a small scatter rug near the door. As he knelt down near the spot, he felt it with his hand. It was damp! Morgan brought his hand to his face and sniffed. There was a faint reminder of the disgusting odour that had filled the room when the fog had appeared. Stunned, he got to his feet, only to be roughly pushed back to the floor.

"I guess you just couldn't wait," William teased, letting go of Morgan's neck. "Who's going to clean up the mess you made on the rug?"

"I didn't do anything. I noticed this spot and wondered what it was," Morgan retorted.

"Sure you did," William said sarcastically. He grabbed the damp rug and tossed it at his brother. Morgan jumped back and the rug landed in a crumpled heap on the floor.

"I'm telling you, it wasn't me," Morgan argued. "There's probably a leak in the ceiling or something. Forget about it. Let's go downstairs."

"Maybe you should go to the 'loo' before we leave," William said grinning, as he continued to torment his brother.

"I don't have to go," Morgan yelled. "Let's just get out of here."

"You seem kind of tense this morning," William hinted.

"I – I didn't get much sleep," Morgan admitted gruffly. "I'm just tired and hungry."

Without any further discussion, the boys headed for the family dining room. The cook served them large helpings of 'bangers and mash'. Just as they were finishing up, their father walked into the room.

"Well, you two seem to be over your jet lag," he commented. "Looks like a great day to go exploring."

"Are you coming with us to the castle, Dad?" asked William.

"I have to go to Wadebridge later this afternoon, but I would like to go up to Arthur's Castle with you, this morning," his father replied. "How soon can you be ready?"

"We'll just grab our shoes, "Morgan said, jumping up from the table.

"Meet you outside in five minutes," added William.

Soon the three of them were walking down the hill to the main path that led up to the legendary birthplace of King Arthur. They went down about fifty or sixty slippery stone stairs, and then ascended as many on the other side to get to the entrance. The castle had been built high up on a jutting cliff that overlooked the sea on three sides. The boys could feel the salty spray on their faces. Morgan wished he had brought a jacket to ward off the wind.

"Hey, Dad, this isn't much of a castle," declared William. "There's no roof or rooms or anything; just a few walls and a stone floor."

"Yes, but this is the original stonework," his father said. "It was initially a monastery that was built about 400AD. It is believed to have been the birthplace of Arthur, around 460AD. Supposedly, he lived here with the monks, until 480 AD when he became king. Centuries later, around 1300, the monastery became a duke's castle."

William ran over to the entrance wall. "Were these holes in the wall for shooting at the enemy?" he asked.

"Probably at some time or other," his dad replied absently. "Now, this first area was the main hall when it was both a monastery and a castle, so you can kind of imagine the floor plan."

"It's hard to believe that this structure has been here for more than sixteen hundred years," Morgan said.

His father nodded in agreement. He had brought along a pair of binoculars, so they were able to see far out to sea on two sides and down into a bay as well. Across the bay, William spotted several caves and many more paths and stone walls. "Look at those caves," he said handing the binoculars to his brother. "Let's go over there and explore."

"We should finish looking around here first,"

his father suggested. “When we get over there, we can walk straight across the moor to Adney House.”

That seemed logical, so the boys and their father continued along the path to the point of the peninsula and they were surprised that the sea was so far below them. Morgan remembered something he had read the night before.

“Dad do you know anything about Merlin having a cave somewhere near this castle?”

“Yes, it was down in the bay, directly below us,” answered his father. “Some people believe there once was a way to get to his cave from up here. They claim that there used to be a grove of oak trees near the monastery and, if you knew where to look, you could find an entrance to the cave. Apparently that was how Merlin and Arthur would meet.”

“Do you think Merlin was real?” William asked.

“I think he was a real teacher, but I’m not sure that I believe he was a magician,” his dad replied, breathing in the brisk air. “I love it here. I’ve always had a keen interest in British history and folklore.”

“Me too, it’s pretty cool to actually see where it all really happened,” Morgan agreed.

“Is this where Arthur lived when he became

king?" William asked.

"No, his castle was near Camelford, not too far from here," Paul stated.

"What do you know about the knights of the round table?" William continued.

"Actually, they started out as 'knights of the round stones'. When Arthur was made king, a meeting was held at Stonehenge with the knights that supported him as their leader. And I've read that he had a lot more than twelve allies."

"I remember reading about Stonehenge. I also saw a special about it on TV," Morgan said. "It's a powerful, mystical circle of gigantic stones that couldn't have been placed there by humans. I think the narrator said the bluestones that make up the circle, had to have been imported from Wales because they aren't native to England. Have you ever been to Stonehenge, Dad?" he asked.

"Yes, your mother and I went there several years ago," his father replied. "But we should all go to Stonehenge soon. It's a very interesting place."

"Let's get back to the knights," William said. "Were Arthur and his men defeated?"

"Eventually, but they won many battles as well. England had twenty years of peace during his reign, for the first time since the Roman invasion. Arthur's final battle happened not far from Camelford in 516 AD."

"Did he really have a sword called Excalibur?" William asked.

"Yes, although, it may not have always been called Excalibur," his father said. "I think a writer named Tennyson, gave it that name."

William continued to fire questions at his father. "What was the original name? Did Arthur really pull it from a stone? What happened to his sword when he died?"

"No more questions," his father moaned. "You can read all about Arthur in Grandie's books or look it up on your computer when it arrives. Let's move along. Do you want to go to the other side now? We can see Merlin's cave from over there."

"Sure," the boys said in unison. "Can we go into the caves?" William asked.

"We can explore a few of the old mining caves," his dad answered. "I know that some areas are out of bounds, but let's go down and see."

The boys discovered that they were able to walk quite far into many of the caves.

"Too bad we didn't bring our flashlights," Morgan said.

"We'll be sure to bring them next time,"

William stated.

Looking over at Tintagel Castle, Morgan asked his father which cave had belonged to Merlin. His father explained that it was the large one that was directly under the castle.

"Let's go down there," William said.

"No, that area is definitely out of bounds. It's blocked off and there is a 'no entry' sign," his father pointed out. "I don't want you boys to get any ideas about going in there," he warned. "It's obviously not safe. Do I have your word that you won't go into Merlin's cave?"

"Yeah," Morgan agreed reluctantly.

"But ...." William began.

"No 'buts'! You cannot go in there," their father emphasized.

The three of them continued to explore the cliffs until it was lunch time. As they walked across the moor, Morgan was making a mental list of all the things he wanted to research about King Arthur and Merlin.

Their father went into the garage at the back of the house. The boys declined his offer to go with him to his clinic in Wadebridge.

As they walked around the house toward the front veranda, Morgan complained to his brother that he was lost without his computer. "Do you think the tower is wired for Internet?" he asked.

"Probably," William replied. "What do you need it for?"

"I want to look up some information on Arthur and Merlin," Morgan replied. "I guess I'll have to use Grandie's old books until our computers arrive."

"We need to find a way to get into to Merlin's cave," William said.

"That won't be easy. The area is blocked off and probably guarded by park staff or dogs or something," Morgan said.

"Guarded," William scoffed. "Are you kidding? They just fenced it off so they won't get sued if someone falls or gets lost in the cave. You're obviously scared to go down there. C'mon admit it."

"I'm not scared, but we did promise Dad," Morgan said.

"You promised," William clarified. "I didn't. Besides, he'd never have to know."

"I don't see why you're in such a big hurry," Morgan said. "I think we should find out more about the area first. I want to explore the cave too, but we have to be cautious."

"Nice stall, Morg, but you're probably right. We don't get want to get caught," William admitted grudgingly. "But we aren't going to waste too much time thinking about it. School will be starting soon and I want to have some major fun before that."

"I agree, but let's just plan things carefully. We might only get one chance to..."

Morgan stopped mid-sentence when he saw their sister sitting on the veranda with her feet up on the rail, polishing her toenails.

"Plan carefully? Might only get one chance?" Katie repeated. "What are you two plotting? We've only been here twenty-four hours. You'd better not be cooking up any wild adventures," she cautioned.

"We're not cooking anything up," Morgan said defensively.

"Don't get into it with her," William said. Leaning over the rail, he added, "Katie, what we do is none of your business."

"It will be if I make it my business," she insisted. "I don't really care what you're up to, but here's a little warning. Tintagel is a small place and Grandie knows everyone. You won't get away with anything." With a knowing smile, she gathered her polishing supplies together and clomped into the house on her heels with bits of tissue sticking out from between her toes.

"You won't get away with anything," William repeated sarcastically. "She is so annoying. Let's go up to the tower where we can talk without worrying about Little Miss Dumbo Ears."

"Yeah, let's go," Morgan agreed. "Wait, I want to check something first."

"What?" William asked.

"You'll see. Come out to the driveway," Morgan replied mysteriously. "I want your opinion about something I noticed when we arrived." The boys went to the end of the driveway and Morgan pointed up to their tower. "See that small window?" he asked.

"What about it?" William asked.

"Well, when we got out of the car and were looking around yesterday, I noticed that window. I thought I saw the curtain move, but I wasn't sure because it's so high up,"

"So, do you think someone is locked up in the tower?" William teased.

"My question is this," Morgan remarked, refusing to be affected by his brother's harassment. "Did you see a window like that anywhere in our tower?"

"Didn't notice, but I still don't see what you're getting at. Clue me in, Sherlock."

"I've been thinking about it, and there's only one place where that window can be – in the old nanny's room," Morgan said. "That door is locked and I think it's about time we found a key."

"Very good idea," William agreed. "I've been wondering why it's locked."

The boys ran into the house and up the two flights of stairs, nearly crashing into a maid's cleaning cart that was in the hallway by Katie's room. Once in the tower, William slid his wallet under the door of the locked room, and the boys ran back down to the second floor to find the maid.

The maid was just coming out of their parents' suite. Morgan told her who they were and she said her name was Jally. William said that his wallet had gone under the locked door in the old nursery. Jally said she didn't have time to go up to the nursery right then, but assured them she would get the wallet when she cleaned their rooms.

"But, my brother and I are planning to go to the store right away," William lied.

"Do you think we could borrow your key, Miss?" Morgan asked politely.

"Aw right, lads," she said in a very thick accent. "Mind you bring 'em back right quick. The Missus'll 'ave me 'ead, should I lose me pass keys."

"Of course," Morgan said, as she handed him

a ring of keys from her pocket. "I'll bring them back in just a few minutes. Thank you, Miss."

The boys ran back to the tower rooms, and quickly unlocked the nanny's door.

While William retrieved his wallet, Morgan returned the keys to the maid. When he got back to the tower, he heard his brother rummaging around in the nanny's room.

"Find the window?" Morgan yelled as he ran through the sitting room.

"Yeah, I found the window and something else too," his brother answered from some far corner of the room. "Come in here and see."

Morgan shivered as he stepped cautiously over the damp stain on the carpet. He stood in the gaping doorway, not sure if he wanted to go inside.

*****

"Be gone," the king said coldly. In spite of his incredible pain, Durkin bowed respectfully and stumbled out of the king's chamber. Leaning heavily on his walking stick, he hobbled down the road to the healer's cottage.

Asa helped Durkin to a cot, and began cutting the leather shoes from his charred feet. Pieces of leather had burned right into his flesh. "What did you do this time my small friend?" Asa asked, while removing pieces of embedded leather from Durkin's feet.

"I g-gave a mess-age to Griswold be-fore the king," Durkin stammered, painfully.

Asa shook his head; there was nothing more to say. He was able to soothe some of Durkin's suffering by applying a powerful poultice of elder bark, betony, calendula, and comfrey. After wrapping the small man's feet, Asa gave him several sips of a strong herbal infusion to heal his body, and allow him some relief from the pain.

Within a short time, the messenger was asleep. The healer knew that his wounds would heal, but he also knew that Durkin would have to face King Ulric again.

Asa looked up and saw a slender girl standing in the doorway. It was his apprentice,

Camilia. She always seemed to know when she was needed. He motioned for her to come to the cot. She touched Durkin's forehead and then looked at Asa.

"He just received a warning from the king," he whispered. "I must leave for awhile. Please stay with Durkin. Bathe his brow with burdock water. When he awakens give him a few sips of the herbal infusion. I shall return in a few hours to change the dressings." Camilia nodded. After putting several vials into a leather bag, Asa left.

CHAPTER THREE

"What have you found?" Morgan yelled from the doorway.

"A couple of things," William answered in a faint voice from deep within the room.

"Why is it so dark?" Morgan asked, still standing in the doorway.

"The bulb is burned out. I have my flashlight, but we could use more light. Go get yours. And hurry," William said.

Morgan dashed to the bedroom and searched through his backpack for the flashlight. It wasn't there! Then he remembered having it in bed with him after his terrifying experience the night before. Morgan shook his head to get rid of the dreadful memory. He grabbed the flashlight and ran back to the nanny's room.

"Are you still in there?" he asked as he shone the light into the room.

"Of course I'm still here," replied a muffled voice.

Morgan's intuition was telling him not to go into the dark, cluttered room. "Where are you?" he yelled at his brother. "I can't tell where your voice is coming from."

"I'm back here," William answered, aiming his flashlight at the ceiling. "Do you have your flashlight?"

"Yes, but there's too much junk in the way, I'll just wait here," Morgan said.

"Get in here," William ordered. "Turn on your flashlight, go around the big dresser and the boxes, and come over here."

Morgan knew that he had run out of excuses. He took a deep breath and waded slowly through the maze of junk, carefully lighting his way to the far corner of the room.

"Okay what have you found?" Morgan asked as soon as he saw his brother.

"Well, for starters, there's your little window," William replied, as he shone his flashlight on the wall behind them. Morgan walked over to the window, parted the ragged curtains and looked out.

"Yeah, this must be it," he said. "I guess I couldn't have seen the wind moving the curtain since the window is nailed shut. I wonder if...."

William cut him off. "Follow me. I've found something much more interesting."

The twins made their way through the stacks of boxes and old furniture. William stopped by an old bedstead that was leaning against the wall.

"Hold my flashlight and shine yours over here so I can move this bed out of the way," William said. "There's a small door behind it."

"Probably just a closet," Morgan suggested.

"I don't think so. It's too low for a closet," his brother replied haltingly as he tried to force the bed into an already crowded space.

Suddenly the bed frame fell forward against the boxes, knocking both flashlights out of Morgan's hands. There was a crash as the bed hit something metal and a groan from William somewhere in the darkness.

"Will, are you alright?" Morgan asked, groping around for the flashlights.

"I'm pinned under the bed," William muttered. "My head hurts. Find the flashlight and get me out of here."

Morgan found one on the floor by his foot and hoped that it wasn't broken. He shook it and the light came on as strongly as ever. He beamed in on the crash sight and tried not to laugh. William was all tangled up in the bed. His face was pressed against the frame, one arm was sticking out of the springs, and his shoe was twisted around another spring. The front end of the bed was propped precariously against some boxes.

"Get me out of here," William demanded.

Morgan placed the flashlight in the hand that was sticking out of the bedspring. "You could help out a little," he said, with a chuckle. "Shine the light back here so I can figure out how to lift the bed." After a lot of grunting, pulling, and lifting, Morgan managed to set his twin free. William seemed fine, although he had a small lump on his forehead where the metal frame had hit him.

The boys carefully set the bed against the wall and Morgan located the second flashlight. It worked too. They shone their lights on the small door and William turned the knob slowly. It opened easily. The boys looked down a steep, narrow set of stairs.

"Let's see where they go," William whispered, as he ducked his head and started down. As they descended, Morgan mentally counted the number of stairs. When he got to fifty-two, they came to another door.

"Don't open it yet," Morgan cautioned. "We

don't know what's on the other side."

"So?" William snapped as Morgan pushed him away from the door.

"We don't want to burst into a room full of people," Morgan whispered. He put his ear against the door and listened carefully. William put his ear against the door too.

"Sounds like banging metal and running water," William said.

"It must be the kitchen," Morgan deduced. "Let's turn off our flashlights and I'll open the door a bit so we can see what's out there." He cautiously opened the door a crack and the twins peeked out, one blonde head above the other. Then Morgan quietly pulled the door shut and they both turned their flashlights on again.

"Cool," William whispered. "We just found a secret route to the kitchen." A mischievous grin spread across his face. "This will come in very handy."

"Yeah," agreed Morgan. "I wonder who would ever have used this steep, narrow staircase."

"Who knows? Who cares?" William answered. "I'm just glad we found it. It's also a great way to get in and out of the house. Let's go back up and make sure we plug the door lock, so we can come down here whenever we want."

"Good idea!" Morgan agreed. The boys ran quietly up the stairs and listened at the top for any indication that the maid was cleaning their room. Nothing! They closed the small door and quickly wove their way around the boxes to the doorway that led into their suite.

"Do you have any gum on you?" William asked.

Morgan began rummaging around in his pockets. He came up with a small green gumball. He handed it to William, who quickly chewed the gum, then stuffed it into the strike panel of the doorjamb. Once it was firmly in place, he carefully closed the door. The knob was in the lock position so it wouldn't turn, but when he pushed on the door with his shoulder, it sprang open.

"Perfect," William said proudly. "No one will ever notice. Do you want to look around in here anymore?"

"Maybe later," Morgan replied. "Let's look through some of the books to see what we can find out about Merlin's cave before we go exploring," Morgan replied.

"Okay, I'll help you in a few minutes," William said. "First, I'm going down to the kitchen to get us a snack. While I'm there, I'll see where the secret door comes out and make sure that no one in the kitchen is suspicious."

"I'll come with you," Morgan suggested.

"No, you start looking for some books. I'll be right back," William said as he ran out and slammed the door behind him.

Morgan stood in the middle of the room, wondering if he should run after William.

Shrugging off his silly apprehension, he walked over to the bookshelf and began looking for titles that related to Merlin or Arthur. He quickly found three books; *Legends of Arthur*, by A.J. Haynes, *Magick of Merlyn*, by Selwyn Drucker, and *Excalibur*, by G. Williams. Morgan felt sure the third book would be of interest to William. He was so absorbed in his quest for books that he forgot his fear of being alone in the tower.

Suddenly he heard a noise outside the door. In came Jally, the same maid that had let them borrow the keys.

"Well then, are you back so soon?" Jally asked.

"What do you mean?" Morgan said, glancing quickly at the door to the nanny's room. He was relieved to see that William had remembered to close it.

"Your trip to the shops," she replied. "Did you go to Granny Wobbly's Fudge Shop?"

"Oh!" Morgan suddenly remembered their plot to get the key. "Actually, we haven't gone yet. We decided to look at some books about Merlin first."

"Merlin is it then? So you're already getting caught up in the goings-on," she said.

"What goings-on?" he asked cautiously. She had his full attention now.

"Why, the mysteries of the area. This hillside has its own stories to tell, lad."

"Can you tell me about..."Morgan began.

At that moment, William backed into the room with a tray of snacks, babbling away. "Apparently it's high tea time. Grandie wanted me to bring up tea and biscuits, if you can imagine, but I talked her into cola and chips. No one down there is suspicious so everything is okay." William looked up and saw the maid. "Oh...hi," he said lamely.

"Well lads, I'll be leavin' you to your tea then. I'll come back and do up the rooms later," Jally said, quickly pushing her cleaning cart out of the room.

"Great," Morgan muttered. "She was just about to reveal the secrets of Tintagel."

"What secrets?" William asked. Morgan told him what the maid had said.

"Should I go after her and see if I can get her

to come back?" he offered.

"Forget it, I could tell that she regretted bringing it up, anyway. We'll talk to her about it later. Let's look through the books I found," Morgan said, settling into one of the big leather chairs. "Here, I found one for you about Arthur's sword."

The boys ate their snacks and had been searching through the books for about thirty minutes, when they heard a knock at the door.

"Come in," Morgan said absently. It was Katie.

"Hi twins. I'm so bored," she moaned, flopping into a chair beside them.

"So why are you telling us?" William asked.

"Well, I thought you might want to go for a hike or something. I could show you around Tintagel since I've been here before," she suggested.

"Where would we go?" Morgan asked, looking up from his book.

"Where do you want to go?" she asked.

"To Merlin's cave," William answered quickly.

"You know very well that we can't go down there," Katie said.

"Then we don't want to go hiking with you," William said rudely.

"What about you, Morgan?" Katie inquired.

"No thanks," he answered, turning back to his book.

"You guys are no fun! Why am I wasting my time with you?" Katie grumbled. Her brothers were ignoring her, so she reached over and grabbed Morgan's book.

"Hey," he complained. "Give it back."

"*The Magick of Merlyn'*, she said, reading the front cover. "What kind of book is this? Magic with a 'k' and Merlyn with a 'y'? Selwyn Drucker couldn't even spell."

"That happens to be the ancient spelling of 'Magic' and 'Merlin'," Morgan said as he snatched the book from her.

Completely bored, Katie sighed and stared up at the ceiling. "Okay, I give up," she finally conceded. "If Merlin's cave is the only thing you're interested in, I guess we could go down there."

"Seriously?" asked William.

"Seriously," she repeated. "But we can't actually go inside." The boys groaned. She'd lost their interest again. "What if I were to tell you that I know a short cut that takes you right to the bay in front of his cave?" The boys looked up at her.

"A friend took me down there last summer,"

she continued. "We looked for a way into the cave, but the entrance is blocked by huge boulders."

"Then what's the point of going?" William asked.

"Because it's something to do," she said. "Besides, there are tide pools full of interesting sea creatures."

"Okay, I'll go," Morgan said.

"Might as well, she's obviously not going to leave us alone," William muttered.

"No one is forcing you to come," Katie said. "We'll go without you if you have something more interesting to do."

"Let's go," Morgan urged. William reluctantly followed them downstairs.

Katie and the twins were soon scrabbling down the rocky cliffs. The sun was shining and it wasn't foggy, which was a pleasant change from the dreary weather they'd had since their arrival. Katie's shortcut took them quickly down to the entrance of Merlin's cave. The three of them stood on the sandy shore of the small bay and Katie could see that her brothers were impressed with its quiet beauty. William immediately ran over to the cave and began searching for a way to get in.

"Who is the friend that brought you down

here last summer?" Morgan asked Katie.

"His name is Russell," she said, bending down to pick up a stone. "He lives in the village and he'll be going to Wadebridge School with us."

"Why hasn't he come to see you yet?" Morgan asked.

"He's in London at football camp, which is like socc..."

"Yeah, I know it's similar to soccer," her brother interrupted. "So when will he be back? How old is he?"

"Why are you so interested in my friends?" Katie asked suspiciously.

"Because I didn't know you had any friends here. Maybe he has a brother our age."

"He'll be back next week. He's sixteen years old and is quite tall with brown hair. He has one sister, about twelve or thirteen years old. Now stop bugging me and go look for some shells or something."

"I was just curious," Morgan said. Katie put her hands on his shoulders and turned him toward the water. "Go," she said, laughing.

Morgan started walking toward Merlin's cave. He turned back to Katie and yelled, "Just for the record, Will and I aren't interested in meeting his sister. Not ever!"

"Whose sister?" William asked when Morgan

climbed up on the rock beside him.

"Oh, just a friend of Katie's," Morgan replied. "I see you found out that the cave really is blocked off, just like she said."

"Yeah, but I've been looking it over, and I think we can get around those big rocks to the right."

Morgan looked where he was pointing. "Maybe, but it would be a tight squeeze," he observed. Then he jerked his head around to face William. "You aren't seriously thinking of doing that are you?"

"Not today," William said. "We'll come back again... without Katie."

"Oh great," Morgan groaned. "You and your stupid ideas! Someone could see us or we could get stuck in there."

"Stop whining," William interjected. "Sometimes you sound just like Katie."

"Very funny," Morgan retorted. "C'mon, let's go look at some of the tide pools." The boys headed toward the small seawater puddles among the rocks. They weren't very interesting, so they decided to climb the cliff above the cave.

"Get down from there right now," Katie yelled when she spotted them. The boys continued to climb higher. "If you fall and break your arms, I'm not taking the blame," she warned them, as she walked toward the cliff. "Come down!" she shrieked. There was still no response from the boys. "Okay, I'm going home."

"Go then," William yelled, standing on a rocky ledge. He looked down at his brother, who was carefully making his way up the cliff. "C'mon Morg, there's a tide pool up here that you have to see."

"Come down, please," Katie pleaded.

"We won't go any higher," Morgan promised, as he joined his brother on the ledge. "We're just going to look at something and then we'll come down."

"Don't tell her that," William hissed. "We can do whatever we want." The boys looked down and saw their sister stomp over to a big rock and sit down with her back to them. William grinned at his brother. "It's so easy to drive her crazy," he giggled.

Morgan smiled and then turned to look at the rocky basin of water. "Look, the water is blue," he said.

"Probably just a reflection from the sky," William said, looking into the small pool.

"I don't think so," Morgan argued. "Otherwise all the other pools would be like this."

Shoulder to shoulder, the twins looked into

the water and saw two identical faces staring back at them. They stuck their tongues out at their reflections.

Suddenly the water rippled and they saw something very strange. As the water stilled, a grotesque face began to appear. The boys stared at each another in disbelief.

"What's that?" William gasped.

Morgan shrugged. He was speechless! The twins slowly slid to squatting positions on the rocky ledge.

"What did you see?" William whispered hoarsely.

"I-I saw a troll face," Morgan stammered. "What did you see?"

"Same," William replied, looking at Morgan's chalky white face. "He had a big nose, beady eyes, and a warty forehead."

"Yeah, and his face was all wrinkled," Morgan added.

"But who was that?" William asked, after a few minutes.

"I don't know, but he sure was creepy," Morgan answered.

"Should we see if he's still there?" William asked.

"I guess," Morgan replied shakily.

Cautiously the boys stood up and turned simultaneously toward the pool of blue water.

*****

Durkin slowly opened his eyes and saw that Asa was removing the bandages on his feet. He tried to sit up, but was gently pushed back to the cot.

"Welcome back Friend," Asa said. "You are healing very quickly, considering..."

"How long have I been here?" the small man asked.

"Sennight," the healer replied.

"Seven nights? I must go," Durkin became very agitated. "Please help me up."

"You must rest," Asa said calmly. "Your burns are just beginning to heal."

The messenger flailed his arms around wildly, as he tried to get up. Sighing, Asa helped him to a sitting position. Durkin swung his feet over the side of the cot. He almost fainted from the pain as the blood rushed to his feet. He took a deep breath, and waited for the agony to pass.

"Tawyn," he said shakily. "You understand. I must go now."

"You cannot possibly walk on those feet yet," Asa stated firmly.

"I...I have no choice," Durkin argued. "Help me, or I'll go there by myself."

Because of Durkin's determination, Asa gave

in and proceeded to prepare him for the journey. He rubbed the swollen feet gently with wintergreen, bandaged them, and carefully wrapped them in leather. He hauled Durkin onto his back and they set off for the magical pool in the forest clearing.

When they arrived, Durkin insisted that Asa leave him on the stump by the pool. Durkin hobbled painfully to the water's edge, and gratefully sank to his knees. He made the sign of fourfold, and looked into the pool, awaiting a message from Tawyn.

CHAPTER FOUR

The boys' identical faces stared back at them from the rocky basin of water.

"Let's go," Morgan whispered.

They climbed down to the sandy shore and glanced around nervously, not knowing what else to expect, but everything was the same. In fact, Katie was still sitting on the same rock by the water.

"Did we just imagine that?" William whispered.

"I don't think so," Morgan replied thoughtfully. "It was very real and we both saw the same thing. Should we tell Katie?"

"No!" William answered emphatically. "We don't tell anyone!"

"Okay," Morgan agreed.

Katie and the twins hiked back up to Adney House.

When they were safely in the tower, the boys sank into the big chairs and tried to figure out what had happened on the cliff.

"It doesn't make sense," William insisted. "I just can't believe that we saw that creepy face in the water.... but both of us saw the exact same thing."

"I know. It was so weird," Morgan agreed. "No matter how much I try to rationalize it, there is no explanation."

William nodded and turned on the television. Morgan picked up one of the books he had found and was just getting into it, when the telephone rang. William went to the bedroom to answer it and returned within a few minutes.

"That was Dad calling from downstairs," he sighed. "The trucks have arrived with the rest of our stuff and he wants us to come down and help unload."

"Oh rats," Morgan groaned. "That'll take up the rest of the day."

"I know, but at least we'll have our bikes and skateboards," William said.

"Plus our computers," Morgan added, as they headed downstairs.

For the next few days, the boys were involved in unpacking and organizing. Once they could get around on their own, they spent the daylight hours exploring the village of Tintagel on their bikes or skateboards. At night they fell into bed, exhausted. Morgan woke up each morning relieved that his night had been uneventful. There had been no more unusual sounds or disgusting smells since that first night in the tower.

While biking one day, they met two brothers, Tag and Jack Randall, who had lived in Tintagel all their lives. Jack was going into seventh grade and Tag into eighth at the same school that the twins would be attending in Wadebridge. Morgan and William enjoyed hanging out with them. It was good to finally meet some boys their own age.

One hot afternoon, after riding around in the hills for several hours, the four boys sat down by a stream. They removed their socks and shoes and dangled their feet in the water to cool off. Morgan was thirsty, so he leaned over to scoop some water into his hands. When he looked into the stream, he remembered the troll face that he and William had seen in the tide pool. He sat back on the shore and turned to Jack and Tag.

"I've heard that sometimes strange things

happen around here," he said, trying to sound casual. William jerked his head up and looked directly into his brother's eyes, warning him to drop the subject.

"What're you going on about?" Jack asked.

"I'm not really sure, since no one will tell me much," Morgan replied vaguely. "I guess I mean things like voices, ghosts, elves, trolls, things that go bump in the night."

"My brother's crazy," William said, laughing. "Just ignore him."

"Are you talking about the *piskies*?" Tag asked Morgan.

"The wh-what?" Morgan stammered. He hadn't expected that response. "The pixies, or as we call them – piskies. They're well known around here," Jack said.

"Everyone has a story about piskie mischief," Tag added. "Children are warned by their folks not to follow them. They say the piskies will pack them off into the bogs, and they'll never be seen again."

"C'mon, that's stupid," William snickered. "Don't tell me you believe in that stuff."

"I didn't used to believe in them," Jack said. "But Tag should be the one to tell you about the piskies." Tag shot his brother a furious glare.

"So don't keep us in suspense, tell us what

you know," William urged.

"There's nothing to tell," Tag insisted. "Jack's just going on about nothing..."

"No, I'm not," Jack said defensively. "Tell them about the night you heard the music and saw the piskies." Tag's face turned red and he stared angrily at his brother.

"Please tell us," Morgan begged.

Tag sat quietly staring across the stream. Finally, he turned to Morgan.

"Here's what I saw," he began. "One night last fall, when we had a full moon, I woke up at midnight, because I heard music and merriment coming from the woods behind our house. I looked out the window, but I couldn't see much, so I got dressed and went outside to see what was going on. I'm always up for a good time, so I thought I might join in. I walked through the trees as quietly as I could, thinking I'd sneak a look before charging in, uninvited. As I got to a clearing, I saw light from a wee fire. I crouched behind a thick bush and parted the leaves so I could see. What I saw was no ordinary sight." He paused and looked at his new friends.

"What did you see?" Morgan asked. His throat was dry with anticipation.

"Well, I saw about twenty or thirty wee, ragged people sitting in a circle. Some of them were smoking pipes; some were drinking from small cups. Others were playing odd instruments, and dancing around the fire in the middle of the circle. I could hear their voices, but I couldn't understand what they were saying. They spoke some kind of daft nonsense. I stayed crouched behind the bush and watched them for a long time. I knew right off that they were piskies because of all the stories I've heard about them. Suddenly one of them started coming straight at me, carrying a stick wrapped in burning rags. The fire on the stick was glowing so bright, I could see him clearly."

"What did he look like?" Morgan interrupted.

"He was a bit bigger than my hand. He had messy red hair, a long turned up nose and squinty, green eyes. He wore a raggedy green shirt and trousers, and he had an evil grin on his face. He looked right into the bush where I was hiding. He was small, so I wasn't scared and didn't run off. Besides, I didn't want to leave without proof that I had seen a real piskie. I thought I might grab him when he got close enough." Tag paused and glanced at his brother.

"Go on," Jack coaxed.

"He came closer and closer," Tag continued. "Soon he was within my reach, so I stuck my hand out real slow like and grabbed him around the middle. Right off, the piskie started screeching in a high-pitched voice and he threw his firebrand into my face. The pain was intense, so I dropped him and put my hands to my face. He jumped to his feet and ran back to the group; yelling words that didn't make any sense. I decided I'd better get out of there. Fast. But as soon as I stood up, all the piskies had surrounded me. They kicked me and shoved their firebrands at me until they knocked me to the ground. I landed flat on my back and hit my head on a rock.

Before I knew what was happening, piskies were climbing all over me, tying me down with some long pieces of string. Two of them forced my mouth open, while another one tied a string around my tongue. All the little blighters kept wrapping me tighter and tighter with that string. Then they all jumped to the ground, joined hands and danced around me singing and laughing. Suddenly one of them shouted in English, 'Away! Away! I smell new day.' They immediately stopped dancing and ran off. I was left in the woods completely tied up, unable to move. I couldn't call for help, because my tongue was tied with string, so I just lay there..."

"How did you get free?" William asked.

"While I was lying there, unable to move, I got to thinking that the strings were pretty thin, so they mightn't be that strong. I tried really hard to free myself, but it was useless, I couldn't move. I waited and listened for the piskies to return. It was dead silent though. I heard nothing but an owl hooting somewhere. Suddenly out of nowhere, a huge black bird descended on me. He was diving straight at me. I was completely at his mercy. Then he landed right on my chest, and I saw that it was a huge black raven. He cocked his head to one side and looked right into my eyes. I felt I was in a weird Greek myth and was sure that he was going to peck out my eyes like poor old Prometheus. Instead, he jumped to the ground and paced around me, pecking at my hair and clothes. Thinking he might be able to untie me, I started making noises to attract his attention. But he ignored my attempts at communication. He jumped back onto my chest and let out a shriek that sounded just like the noise the piskie had made. I thought he was calling them back to finish me off, but the piskies didn't come. Next, the raven threw his head back and squawked really loud, and then he flew off." Tag leaned over the stream to scoop a handful of water into his mouth before continuing with his story.

"I was alone again," he said wiping his mouth with his shirt sleeve. "With my teeth, I pushed against the string in my mouth, trying to bite it so I could call for help." Tag paused and ran his hand through his short dark hair, the memories obviously upsetting him. The other boys shifted their positions on the grass and waited for him to go on.

"It was impossible to loosen the string on my tongue," Tag went on. "So I tried to wiggle some part of my body, but I couldn't move at all. Before long, the bird was completely out of sight. I was doomed! Blood was running from my mouth from biting my tongue. I could also feel a wet spot under my head, so I knew it was bleeding too.

I must have fallen asleep or passed out for a bit. When I woke up, I turned my head and brought my hand up to my mouth. Then I realized my hands were free. I tried moving my legs, and sure enough, I was able to break free. I don't know who untied me. As I untangled myself from the string, I noticed that it felt sort of like cobwebs, only thicker.

Aching and bleeding, I got up and stumbled back to the house. I let myself in and went to the loo to clean some of the blood off my face. I looked in the mirror and noticed a big red blister on my cheek. When I stuck out my tongue, I saw that it was all cut up, but the bleeding had stopped. Then, I went to bed," Tag said, ending his story.

"Are you saying all of that really happened?" William asked doubtfully.

Tag didn't answer, so Jack took over from where Tag had left off.

"The next morning, Tag stayed in bed so late that I finally pounded on his door to make sure he was all right," Jack began. "He didn't answer so I went in to check on him. Tag was sleeping on his back. There was dried blood all around his mouth and a big red blister on his cheek. He groaned when I shook him. I said, 'Tag, wake up. What happened to you? You look like you've been in a fight.' He sat up slowly, holding the back of his head and he mumbled, 'I guess you could say I was in a bit of a fight.' His voice was scratchy and he talked like he had just come back from the dentist. Slowly, he told me the whole story. I didn't want to believe him, but with the condition of his tongue, the burn on his cheek, and the bump on his head, I was soon convinced that it had happened."

"So, did you tell your parents?" Morgan asked.

"Nah, Mum was at work and Dad was in Camelford that day," Tag replied. "Besides, I just wanted to forget about it, so I didn't tell anyone.... until now."

"Did either of you ever see any piskies again?" William asked.

"No, but you can be bloody sure that I won't be going out at midnight during a full moon again, especially if I hear music," Tag said emphatically.

"Wow," Morgan whispered, shaking his head in disbelief.

Without saying any more, the boys put their shoes on and picked up their bikes. They rode together to the Randall's turnoff. Tag and Jack started heading up their lane, when Jack suddenly stopped and looked back at the twins.

"By the way, there are lots of stories about piskies living up your way," he said.

"What?" Morgan and William shouted.

"It's true," Tag confirmed. "The piskies used to hang out in the caves when the men were working the mines years ago. Apparently, they still live around there." Before the twins could say anything, the Randall boys were gone.

They rode toward Adney House in silence. When they were almost home, William stopped his bike and turned to Morgan. "What do you think about Tag's story?"

"After what we saw in that tide pool, I'll believe anything," Morgan replied.

“Well, if pixies, or piskies, or whatever they’re called, really do exist and are known to live near us, then I think we better go find us some proof,” William suggested.

“Are you crazy?” Morgan asked, alarmed. “You heard what happened to Tag when he tried to get proof. I’m not going out in the middle of the night to find pixies.”

“Calm down,” William said. “We wouldn’t be stupid enough to try to catch one like he did, but we could take a picture with Dad’s digital camera.”

“One flash and we’d be toast,” Morgan replied.

“Maybe we wouldn’t need a flash if there was a full moon and the piskies had a fire,” William said thoughtfully.

“So, who cares about a picture of some ratty old elves?” Morgan grumbled. He was getting nervous. William’s hair-brained schemes usually got them into all kinds of trouble. This scheme could put them in very real danger.

“We care, because one picture of those ratty old elves could make us very rich,” his brother said dramatically.

“What do you mean?” Morgan asked.

“Look, no one has ever been able to prove that they exist,” William said. “So, you and I get a picture and then we find some newspaper to buy it. Within days, reporters will be all over us. Just think of the possibilities."

"The reality is, even if we were to find the piskies, we could get caught and tied up or...or... even killed. Remember Tag's little adventure?" Morgan retorted.

"Don't be such a wimp!" William snapped. "The possibilities far outweigh the dangers and if we don't try, you know very well that we'll both regret it."

"I'm not a wimp," Morgan protested. "I'm just trying to be realistic. I don't want to end up as a trophy on some piskie's wall."

"Come on, Morg, you know you want to see if they're real as much as I do," his brother coaxed. "All I'm asking for is one, just one, picture. Now let's go home and see when the next full moon is."

Morgan sighed. He hated that William could always convince him to do whatever he wanted. He hated his inability to stand up to his brother. But what he hated more than anything else was that William was absolutely right. Morgan did want to see if the piskies were real.

The boys pushed their bikes the rest of the way up the hill to Adney House. Just as they got to the veranda, they heard someone calling them.

"Yahoo," a shrill voice shouted excitedly. "Are you the Adney twins?" A thin girl with long copper-coloured hair caught up with them.

The boys stared at her without saying a word. She jumped onto the veranda just as William reached for the door handle.

"I said," she repeated. "Are you the Adney twins?"

"Nope," William said bluntly.

"Well that must be who you are since you are obviously twins, and you are going into Adney House," she said.

"Adney is our great-grandmother's name," Morgan explained. "I'm Morgan Hanford and this is my brother, William."

"Hi, nice to meet you," she said pleasantly. William ignored her.

"Who are you?" Morgan asked.

"Oh sorry, I'm Janey Burrows. My brother Russell knows your sister, Katie. Didn't she tell you that I was coming up here to meet you today?"

"No, she certainly didn't," William said rudely. "We have to go in now. Bye-bye." He went into the house and up the stairs. Janey turned to Morgan.

"Your brother is in a bit of a mood, isn't he?" she said, frowning.

"He gets cranky when our sister plans things and doesn't tell us," Morgan replied.

"Will you be going to school in Wadebridge?" she asked.

"That's the plan," he said.

"Me too!" she exclaimed. "I could show you around and introduce you to..."

"Thanks, but we're going to meet up with Tag and Jack Randall," Morgan said quickly. "I really have to go in now. Maybe I'll see you at school next week."

"Hold on," Janey said. "Are you going into second form?"

"I don't know what that is, but we'll be in eighth grade," Morgan answered.

"Brilliant!" she squealed. "I'm so looking forward to school now. My friends will be gob smacked when they see the two of you. Well, I must be off now."

"Gob smacked?" muttered Morgan, shaking his head as he went into the house. He ran into William, coming out of their father's office, on the second floor.

"Are the computers ready?" Morgan asked.

"Dad's is running. Let's go and see if ours are hooked up," William said.

When they walked into the bedroom, they saw their two laptops on the desks at the foot of their beds. Morgan turned his on to make sure they had Internet in the tower.

"Yes!" he shouted. "Finally, I can go online and do some research."

"What kind of research?" William asked.

"Tintagel, King Arthur, Merlin, piskies," his brother reminded him.

"Oh, speaking of piskies," William said. "I just checked Dad's calendar and there's a full moon tonight, so I guess that makes this 'Proof-of-Piskie Night'."

"Tonight?" Morgan said. "No way!"

"Yep, we go at midnight," William declared. "So, let's get ready to roll."

*****

The healer sighed as he changed the dressings on Durkin's raw, swollen feet. The stress of the trip to Tawyn's pool had opened the wounds again. Just as he finished the bandaging, Camilia gently tapped on the door. Asa motioned for her to enter.

"Durkin has been summoned by the king," she said. "He is to go there at once."

"He can't even walk yet," the healer snapped. "Ulric will have to wait."

"I-I'll be fine," Durkin protested. "H-Help me up, I must go to the king."

Asa said nothing as he put new leather shoes on Durkin's swollen feet. He handed him his walking stick, and Durkin boldly walked down the lane, barely limping.

Durkin was taken to the king's chambers. He bowed before King Ulric.

"Messenger," the king said sharply. "Do you have word from Tawyn?"

"Yes, Majesty," Durkin replied. The king motioned for him to speak.

Durkin repeated Tawyn's latest message. "Across time and distance, come the two as one, at dusk on Alban Vine." He bowed respectfully and waited.

"Alban Vine...less than one lunation," mused the king. "Go now. Bring Osdruan to my chambers at sunrise. He will be taking care of the lads." Durkin nodded.

"Messenger," the king shouted. "I trust I am the first to receive Tawyn's message."

Durkin bowed and walked out with his head held high.

Once outside, he almost fainted from the pain he had been hiding from the king. He looked at his blood soaked shoes. With every ounce of his remaining strength and willpower, Durkin regained his composure and hobbled down the lane, leaning heavily on his walking stick.

CHAPTER FIVE

Late that evening, the twins gathered their things together. William had the digital camera in his backpack, along with a flashlight and both pairs of binoculars. He had instructed Morgan not to bring anything. However, Morgan had carefully tucked his pocket knife in his jeans, just in case he had to cut any piskie strings.

Fifteen minutes before midnight, the boys were making their way down the secret staircase in the nanny's room. They listened for any sounds of activity when they reached the kitchen. Hearing nothing, they opened the door and dashed across the room. Morgan made sure the back door was unlocked before closing it quietly behind them. Secretly he hoped they wouldn't see any piskies, so that the trek across the moor in the dark would be over very quickly.

William led the way down the hill. “It sure looks different at night,” he said.

“Yeah,” Morgan agreed nervously. “Are you sure we’ll be able to find the spot where they might hold their meeting?”

“If we hear music and see a fire, I think that’ll be where they are,” William pointed out. “We have to stop talking now, we’re getting close. There’s a clearing down by the mine caves, which is probably where they’ll be. Let’s find a place to hide.”

The boys crept quietly downhill, toward the caves, trying not to trip over any rocks or debris. William stopped abruptly and Morgan ran into him, nearly knocking both of them to the ground. William quickly turned off his flashlight.

“Look,” he whispered. They could see surprisingly well by the light of the full moon. There, on the sandy shore by the caves, a small fire glowed softly. Morgan gasped when he saw the fire. William pulled him down, behind an outcropping of rocks.

“Well, look at that,” William murmured. “This is the right night after all.”

“I see the fire, but I don’t see any piskies,” Morgan whispered back.

William quietly took a pair of binoculars out of his backpack and looked toward the clearing. "Here they come!" he announced. "They're marching in a long line."

Morgan grabbed the other binoculars, and quickly put them to his eyes. What he saw was amazing! Piskies by the dozens were emerging from the cave. Each one carried a sack and a stick wrapped in cloth. They looked exactly as Tag had described them; very small, scruffy clothes, red hair.

Each tiny person walked up to the fire, turned, walked exactly ten paces back, and stuck his stick in the sand. Then they all ran about, setting things up. Cooking pots, musical instruments, and other odds and ends were unloaded from their sacks. Everything was set up very quickly and quietly. They had obviously done this many times. Then, each piskie stood next to an upright stick in the sand. They had formed a perfect circle around the fire.

Once everyone was in position, a portly little piskie picked up his stick, walked into the middle of the circle, and stuck the cloth-wrapped end into the fire. When it had ignited, he went to the edge of the circle and stood before one of the piskies, raised his firebrand into the air, and shouted "Bodaway!" Immediately, his torch turned a brilliant indigo colour. A flash of blue light seared the night air and lit the bound stick in front of the first piskie. He then went to each piskie in turn and repeated the ritual. When all of the sticks were glowing brightly, the entire group began chanting and waving their small arms in the air, while the portly piskie did a lively dance inside the circle.

Suddenly, the dancing piskie began changing size and shape, until he became an orange dragon with green, glowing eyes. Flames shot from his nostrils, licking the night air briefly, and then sizzling into the cool, damp sand beyond the circle. The chanting slowed to a hum, and the dragon slowly transformed back to a chubby little piskie. He returned to his spot in the centre of the circle and everyone sat down.

Morgan and William had not moved or spoken during the entire performance they had watched through the binoculars.

The whole scenario had been too much for Morgan. Breathing heavily, he put his binoculars down and leaned toward his brother. "I'm going home," he murmured.

"Just wait, let's see what they do next," William whispered.

"I don't care what they do next," Morgan hissed angrily. "I'm leaving!"

"Alright," William agreed, as he dug the digital camera out of the backpack. "Just let me get a picture and then we'll go." He was already focusing on the scene below.

"NO! If they see or hear us, we're dead!" Morgan warned.

"I won't use the flash, and there's no way they can hear the click of the camera," William argued.

"They obviously have powers we can't even begin to understand," Morgan whispered nervously. "They probably already sense that we're here. Let's just go."

"Okay! You put the binoculars away and grab the flashlight," William said.

Morgan quietly gathered their things together. Just as he was getting up, he saw a flash and heard the digital camera click twice.

"You idiot," he muttered fiercely.

Before Morgan could say anything else, William grabbed the back of his jacket and pushed him forward. The two of them scrambled out from behind the rocks and stumbled up the hillside to Adney House, not daring to turn on the flashlight or look back.

Once they were in the tower, Morgan switched on the light and turned to face his brother. His cheeks were red with rage. He clenched his fists angrily and began to tear a strip off William. "What were you thinking down there? You may not value your life, but I value mine. You could tell from what we saw, that those piskies know some powerful magic. If they had discovered us, they would have shown us no mercy. We saw a ceremony that we were not supposed to witness. I can't believe you risked our lives for a few stupid pictures." He was so furious that he wanted to punch William. Instead, he slammed his fist into one of the leather chairs, sending it toppling over.

William looked at Morgan's red, angry face and watched him gasping for air. Never had Morgan been so upset. He righted the chair and began pacing back and forth.

"Morg, I'm sorry I took such a chance tonight," he apologized. "I didn't mean to put either of us in danger. It's just that I really wanted to prove that the piskies exist. I knew that I would regret it if I didn't take a picture – if only to prove to myself that the piskie event really happened."

"Oh, it happened alright! Just like Tag's story and the troll in the pool," Morgan retorted. "You didn't need proof – I saw it too!" He threw himself into one of the chairs, struggling to control his anger.

William sat down beside him. "I know you saw it too," he said quietly. "I just wanted some proof. I'm having a hard time believing that all of the weird things that have been happening are real."

"Yeah, me too," Morgan agreed. He had begun to calm down. He decided this was as good a time as any to fill William in on the one event that he hadn't been able to tell him about. "Something else happened the night we arrived," he said quietly. "When I tell you about it, I think you'll see why I was so freaked out tonight."

"Our first night in the tower? Why didn't you tell me before?" William asked.

"Because I wasn't sure it had really happened at first. Plus, I was pretty sure that you wouldn't believe me. But, after everything that has happened since then…"

"Just tell me," William said impatiently.

Morgan told him every detail of his adventure on the first night; the tapping noise, the grey mist, the presence in the room, the dragging noise, and the stench. When he was finished, he looked at his brother, waiting for his reaction.

William stared past his brother, deep in thought. Then he asked a few questions and eventually came to the same conclusion as

Morgan. It had really happened. "But why?" he wondered aloud.

"I don't know the answer to that yet," Morgan admitted. "I just know that I had a feeling that the 'presence' was trying to tell me something, but I couldn't understand it."

"Have you seen or heard anything like that since?" William asked.

"Well, there was that wet spot on the carpet by the nanny's room when we went to the washroom the next morning. I remember that you accused me of having an accident."

"That's when you should have told me what had really happened," William said.

"I couldn't. I knew you wouldn't believe me," Morgan stated.

"You're probably right," William admitted. He looked thoughtfully at his twin.

"Is there anything else that you haven't told me?" he asked.

"I just thought of something," Morgan said. "The last few nights, I've had this strange dream. When I wake up, I can't remember anything, but I have this odd feeling - like I'm supposed to get out of bed and go somewhere, or do something. I don't get up though, because I don't know where to go, and also because I'm scared," he confessed.

"There's some crazy stuff going on around

here," William said, running his fingers through his hair. He paused for a moment and then added, "Do you think the piskies had anything to do with what you saw that first night?"

"I don't know," Morgan admitted. "I sure hope not."

"I just wonder what's going to happen next," William said. "And how do we get ready for it?" He sat quietly for a few minutes and then turned to his brother. "Listen Morg, next time you get that feeling and you think you know where you're supposed to go, wake me up and I'll go with you."

"Thanks," Morgan said. He was relieved that William seemed to believe him. The two boys got up and went to get ready for bed.

"By the way," Morgan said as he began to undress. "I'm sorry I overreacted tonight, but that whole piskie thing really freaked me out."

"I get that now," William said. "And I'll try not to jump into stuff without discussing it with you first. And, let's promise that we won't keep secrets from each other. Whatever happens, we're in it together, just the two of us."

"Okay," Morgan agreed. Then, he grinned up at his brother. "Should we see if your pictures turned out?"

"Are you sure you want to?" William asked.

Morgan nodded, and they went over to William's computer. He downloaded the pictures and they both stared at the monitor, waiting for the first image to appear. A blank screen stared back at them. William tried the second picture. There was a faint outline of the caves and the shore, and a blur of light from the ceremonial fire, but no piskies were visible.

"It didn't work," William complained. "We'll never get another chance."

"Probably not," Morgan agreed, with a hint of sympathy in his voice. "But look at it this way – now you don't have to decide which newspaper gets the pictures."

William slammed his fingers down angrily on the keys, and erased the photos. "Let's just go to bed," he muttered.

That night, Morgan slept a little more soundly. He was comforted by the fact that William was going to be there for him, if anything else should happen during the nights ahead.

*****

It was almost midnight when the exhausted healer finally returned from visiting his patients. He tripped over a lumpy mass in the doorway of his hut. He shone his torch on it and gasped. The lumpy mass was Durkin. Asa carried the messenger inside and laid him gently on a cot. He lit several candles and stared in horror at the blood-soaked body. Durkin moaned as Asa began checking his vital signs. Suddenly his eyes flew open and he began thrashing around. The healer gently placed his hands on Durkin and spoke to him quietly and calmly.

"You are safe now, my little friend. Lie back and let me see what I can do for you."

Durkin sighed with relief as he recognized Asa's voice. He lay back on the cot. "Are you getting tired of patching me up?" he asked, breathing heavily.

"Yes," Asa said, smiling. "Can you tell me what happened?"

Durkin began his story slowly and laboriously. He was in a great deal of pain.

"Coming...from king...four men...attacked in forest...said...kill me if...I didn't tell...why I was...with the king. Made no sense...I...said nothing...Hit me...head...and stabbed...I fell...

kicked me... Said, this was w- warning...All I ...remember."

"Where you are hurt?" Asa asked gently.

"Head...chest...can't breathe." With that, Durkin lost consciousness.

Asa removed the small man's clothing. He discovered a deep stab wound in his left side near his ribcage, and another stab wound in his abdomen. Dark bruises covered his back, and there was a large, bloody lump on the back of his head. The healer sighed, hopelessly. Durkin could not possibly live through the night.

CHAPTER SIX

At ten o'clock the next morning, the telephone rang. Morgan stumbled out of bed and picked it up on the fourth ring.

"Are you blokes still planning to meet us at the caves at half-eleven?" a voice inquired. It took Morgan a few seconds to realize that it was Tag on the line.

"Oh, hi... I guess so. I'll call you back in a few minutes. We're just waking up."

"Who was that?" William asked sleepily, as Morgan climbed back into his warm bed.

"Tag," his twin answered. "I don't remember telling him that we would go exploring down at the caves today."

"I do," William said. "When are we supposed to meet them?"

"Apparently we said 11:30," Morgan replied. "I told him I'd call him back."

"We can probably be ready," William said, yawning. "Call him back and tell him we'll meet them at Merlin's cave. I'll ring for the maid and see if she'll bring us some cereal or something."

An hour and a half later, the twins were hiking across the moor. As they approached the edge of the cliff, they could see two dark-haired figures sitting on rocks by the cave.

"Looks like Tag and Jack are already here," Morgan said.

"Remember, not to tell them anything about the piskies we saw last night," William reminded him.

"I know," Morgan snapped. "And let's not mention the face in the tide pool, or the fog, or the stain on the rug either."

"We've been waiting here for bloody ever," Jack said impatiently, as the twins clamoured down the rocks to join them.

"We were still in bed when you called," William stated.

"Were you out partying last night?" Tag teased.

"Yeah, that's it," Morgan replied

sarcastically.

"There's only one week of holidays left, so we plan to sleep as much as possible before we have to start getting up at six in the morning," William said.

"Well, you're here now," Jack said. "What say we try to get past the barricade and explore old Merlin's cave?"

"Sure," William replied eagerly. "Lead the way."

"Not me," Jack said. "You two are a lot smaller than we are, so one of you will have to squeeze through first and find another way for us to get in."

"And if there's not?" William asked.

"Well then, I guess you'll have to come back and let us know," Tag said bluntly.

"What if we get stuck?" Morgan said nervously. "There's no way either of us can fit through that little crack."

"You're not giving up that easily. C'mon, you can at least try," Tag urged.

"Alright, I'll go first," William said.

"No, send Morgan in," Jack said. "He's smaller. Morgan, get in there."

"I said I'll go first," William insisted. "Now let's get on with it." He began climbing over the cement barrier. Morgan was right behind him.

"You don't have to do this," he whispered to his brother. "I'm smaller, I'll go in." William pushed him back, sucked in his breath, and forced himself through the narrow space between the barricade and the cave wall.

"Are you okay?" Morgan asked, peering into the darkness that had just swallowed his brother.

"I need some light," William's voice echoed from the blackness.

Jack quickly handed Morgan a flashlight, which he passed to William.

"Do you want me to come in now?" Morgan asked.

"There's no room. I'm standing on a small ledge," William replied. "There are huge boulders everywhere. I'm trying to find a way around them."

"What's he found?" Tag asked.

"Nothing yet," Morgan answered.

Tag muttered impatiently. "William, I'm coming in," he yelled.

"No!" William said, emphatically. "There's no room on this ledge and you won't fit through the opening. I barely squeezed through. Have you got another flashlight?"

"Hang on, I'll get ours," Morgan yelled. He scrambled down to the shore, grabbed his knapsack and hurried back to the cave entrance.

Tag took the flashlight from him, turned it on, and stuck his arm and head through the narrow opening. He shone the light around, searching for William. "So, what do you think?" he asked William, when he spotted him on the ledge. "Is there another way in?"

"I don't know yet," William grunted. "I'm going to climb around those two big boulders and see what's on the other side. Shine that flashlight on the rocks so that I can find my way down."

Morgan was trying to get a look into the cave by standing on the cement barrier just above Tag's immersed head and leaning over him. He couldn't see much, but he could hear William's heavy breathing as he climbed among the rocks. All of a sudden, there was a crashing sound followed by a moan.

"William! What happened?" Morgan yelled. He yanked Tag back and snatched the flashlight from him. He shone it into the cave, but couldn't see or hear his brother. "Will! Answer me!" There was a muffled groan from somewhere in the darkness.

Tag roughly pushed Morgan aside again and tried to squeeze through the opening. There was no way that a boy of his size could get through. He grumbled angrily when he realized that he was stuck. It took Morgan and Jack several minutes to pull Tag out.

Morgan picked up the flashlight again. "I'm the only one that can fit through," he said to the Randall boys. You guys go and get help."

"Are you daft?" Tag shouted. "If anyone finds out we've been nosing around in there, the cops will call our folks."

"Then what do you suggest we do?" Morgan demanded angrily. "My brother is stuck in that cave and we have to get him out."

"Don't get all spun out," Jack said reasonably. "Here's what we'll do. Morgan, since you're the whidden of the group, you take the torch and go into the cave. Tag and I'll go over to a mine, across the way, where we once saw some old ropes and cables. We'll bring some stuff back that we can use to haul your brother out."

Tag nodded and turned to Morgan. "Will you be okay until we get back?"

"Yeah, I'll be fine. How far away is the mine?" Morgan asked.

"Just on the other side of the cliff," Tag explained.

"Okay, but don't be gone too long," Morgan said. "Hand me the backpack and flashlight when I get in there." He took a deep breath and squeezed through the opening. When he reached for the backpack, he asked, "What's a whidden?"

"A runt," Tag chuckled.

"Oh," Morgan said. He looked seriously at Tag. "Please hurry back."

"We will, mate," Tag assured him. "C'mon Jack, let's go."

Morgan shuddered as he stood on the same shelf where his brother had been. He panned the dank cave with his flashlight. When he shone the light upward, he saw hundreds of bats hanging upside down. When he looked at the rocks below, he noticed pools of muddy water and massive boulders blocking most of the cave.

"William," he whispered hoarsely. He cleared his throat and yelled louder, "Will!"

He heard a distant moan. He directed the light toward the area where the sound had come from. Inching his way along the ledge, he tried to catch a glimpse of his brother. He thought he saw something move on the cave floor. He aimed the flashlight at the spot and saw a shoe and part of one leg. "Don't move! I'm coming down," Morgan shouted.

He settled the backpack securely on his shoulders and got a good grip on the flashlight. Carefully, he made his way to the end of the ledge. After slipping and sliding on damp rocks most of the way down, he finally arrived safely at William's side. His twin was lying face down in the mud. Morgan put his hand on his brother's back and was relieved to find that he was breathing. "Are you okay?" he asked quietly.

"Morgan, are you really here?" William muttered hoarsely.

"Yeah, where are you hurt?" Morgan inquired.

"My head... my leg," his brother groaned.

"I'm going to try to turn you over," Morgan said.

"Okay, but be careful of my leg."

Morgan shone the light on William's head and saw dried blood near his ear. He crawled down to his feet and shone the light on his legs. "Which leg hurts?" he asked.

"Right one... my ankle," William cried out in pain as he tried to lift his head.

Morgan pulled up his brother's pant legs so he could look at his ankles. The right foot was already very swollen.

"It's going to be hard to turn you over without causing you a lot of pain. If I hold your feet, can you turn the top part of you?" Morgan asked.

"I think so," William answered.

"On the count of three then," Morgan said. "One...two...three..." William's screams echoed through the cave as Morgan helped him turn over. Once William was lying on his back, Morgan saw that the entire front of him was covered with mud. He was breathing heavily and his body began to shiver violently. Morgan grabbed the backpack, dumped everything out, and covered his brother with his jacket. Carefully, he placed the backpack under William's head and wiped some of the mud off his face with the front of his own shirt. Morgan was getting really worried. He tried to recall everything their father had told them to do if one of them was injured. He knew that William's shaking meant that he was going into shock.

Morgan tried to sound confident as he spoke to his brother. "Tag and Jack have gone to find some ropes. Do you want a drink of water?" William nodded.

The water bottle had rolled into a puddle when Morgan had dumped the backpack.

After cleaning it off, he offered his brother a drink. William drank awkwardly as Morgan held his head up. After settling him down again, Morgan looked around for some sticks to make a splint for the swollen ankle. He couldn't see anything that would work. He leaned over William and was relieved to see that he was no longer shaking.

However, his face was very pale and he

looked like he was in a lot of pain.

"I'm going to look for some sticks to splint your ankle," Morgan said, adjusting the backpack under William's head and offering him another drink.

"No, don't leave me here in the dark," William spluttered as he choked on the water.

"Where's the other flashlight?" Morgan asked.

"I don't know," his brother replied.

Morgan shone his light around until he caught a reflection from the metal casing of the flashlight. It had rolled into a crevice between two big boulders. Morgan lay on his side and wriggled and stretched until he was able to reach it. He wiped some of the mud off with his shirt and flicked the switch but the light didn't come on. Propping his own flashlight so that he could see, Morgan unscrewed the cap and adjusted the metal clips around the batteries. He tightened the cap and tried again. It worked!

"Here's your flashlight. It seems to work okay," Morgan said, as he handed the torch to his brother. "You hang on to it. I'll be back as soon as I find some sticks."

Morgan carefully made his way around the huge rocks and was surprised to see a clear path leading to the inner parts of the cave. He shone the light ahead of him. The darkness seemed to go on forever. Morgan realized that it could be a lengthy hike to another exit, and a long walk certainly wouldn't be an option for William. He focused the light on the ground, so that he could search for splint material. Finally he spotted a fairly sturdy stick and took it with him to the spot where he had left his brother. Morgan became concerned when he saw that William had drifted off to sleep. He remembered his father telling him not to let a person go to sleep after a blow to the head.

He woke William and offered him some more water, but he moaned and refused to drink. Morgan talked to him, trying to keep him awake. At the same time, he moved down to the injured ankle and began to prepare the splint.

"I found a really good stick that will make a perfect splint. I'm going to have to snap it in two, so don't be surprised at the noise." He stepped on the middle of the branch and it snapped loudly. "The sticks are a perfect length. What should I use to wrap them around your ankle?" he asked, trying to force his twin to stay alert.

"I don't know, maybe a belt?" he replied.

"I'm not wearing one," Morgan said.

"Me neither. Can you tear off part of my shirt?" William suggested.

"Yeah, that will probably work. Let me try to tear mine. It's cleaner than yours," Morgan said. He took off his shirt and examined it carefully. The back seemed to be fairly clean. He tried ripping the shirt, but the fabric wouldn't give. He searched his pockets for his knife, but he couldn't find it.

"Did you bring your pocket knife?" he asked William.

"Yeah, I think so." He fumbled around in his front pocket. "Here it is," he said, holding it up.

Morgan managed to slash two strips off the back hem and put the rest of the shirt on again. He placed the sticks in his brother's shoe on either side of the injured leg. William moaned painfully as Morgan tied the cloth strips tightly around the two sticks to hold them in place. "Now we wait for Tag and Jack," he said with a satisfied grin. "Do you want to try sitting?"

"I guess so," William said, trying to pull himself up. "Oh man, I'm so dizzy," he said as he started to fall over. Morgan grabbed him and gently helped him to a sitting position.

"I'm going to drag you back a bit, so you can rest against the rock," Morgan offered.

"Okay," William said, shakily. Soon, he was propped up and looked fairly comfortable. "How long do you think we'll have to wait for Tag and Jack?"

"Not much longer," Morgan assured him. "Are you feeling okay?"

"My ankle doesn't hurt as much now, but my head is pounding." William paused, breathing heavily. "I think I might throw up." He lay back against the rock and closed his eyes. A few minutes later, he lifted his head up and said, "I'm okay now. I've been thinking, Morg. I don't see how I'll get out of the cave. I'll never be able to climb back up to the opening where we came in." He paused again. "Did you see another way out of here when you were looking for the sticks?"

"I saw a path that goes further into the cave, but it looked like it would be a pretty long hike to another exit. Don't worry though, we'll figure something out when the guys come back," Morgan said with more confidence than he actually felt. "Just take it easy until they get here. Do you want more water?"

"Stop giving me water every two minutes," William grumbled.

"Okay, just don't go to sleep. Remember what Dad said about concussions."

"I don't have a concussion," William said angrily. "I have a sprained ankle. Now, quit pretending you're a doctor."

"Don't yell at me," Morgan snapped. "I'm only trying to help."

“I know, I’m just worried about how I’ll get out of here,” William admitted, leaning against the rock and closing his eyes again.

“Should I go up to the opening and see if they’re coming?” Morgan asked.

“No, stay here,” William urged. “I don’t want to be alone.”

“Alright,” Morgan said. “I think we should just have one flashlight on at a time, to save on batteries, in case we’re here for awhile.”

“Good idea,” his twin agreed. “I’ll turn mine off.”

The two boys got as comfortable as they could, and settled in to wait for the others to return. Within a short time, they both fell asleep, sitting side by side against the boulder. A sudden noise startled them.

“Did you hear something?” William whispered.

“Yeah, it’s probably Tag and Jack,” Morgan said, getting up. He swung around and shone the flashlight into the cave. There was a rhythmical, tapping sound coming from deep within the dark cave. Morgan ducked behind the rock.

“Are Tag and Jack coming?” William asked hopefully.

“No, it can’t be them,” Morgan said. “That noise is coming from inside the cave.”

"Maybe they found another way in," William said, struggling to get up.

Morgan reached down and helped him to stand up. He propped him against the rock. The injured twin winced as he accidentally put weight on his ankle. He repositioned himself so that he could lean on Morgan. They both stared expectantly into the darkness. Soon a strange glow became visible in the distance.

"Quick, turn off the flashlight," William whispered. His brother clicked the off switch. In total darkness, the two of them continued to watch the glowing light getting brighter. The tapping noise seemed to take on a more distinct pattern – tap, shuffle, shuffle, - tap, shuffle, shuffle. Morgan shuddered as he remembered a similar rhythm he'd heard in the tower a few weeks earlier.

"I highly doubt that light is coming from Tag and Jack," William murmured.

"Yeah," Morgan said hoarsely, his throat dry with fear.

"Hello," said someone with a very deep voice. The glowing light materialized into a gigantic, bearded man bathed in pale blue light. He used a walking stick that tapped rhythmically against the cave floor as he walked toward them. The glow seemed to emanate from the stranger, but as he got closer, Morgan realized that the light actually came from a blue crystal ball that was attached to his walking stick.

The stranger was at least seven or eight feet tall. Thick tangled hair covered his head, which almost touched the cave ceiling. His long beard hid the upper part of his full-length, belted robe. He wore leather thongs on his feet. The boys were speechless as they stared at the unusual man.

"Gemini," the tall man said. His deep voice resonated through the cave. The two boys shifted closer together.

"Well lads, can you speak?" he asked with a touch of humour in his voice.

"Y-yes sir," William answered hoarsely.

"You have found your way into my caverna, even after I blocked it," he mused.

"We d-didn't mean to dis-disturb you, Sir," Morgan stammered.

"Disturb me," said the stranger, "An interesting choice of words." Adjusting his walking stick, he went closer to the boys. "I cannot have anyone in here, so you must leave immediately."

"W-we would like very much to leave, but my brother is h-hurt," Morgan said.

"Please stop stammering. You have no

reason to be afraid." He turned to William.

"What is your name, and what injuries have you incurred?" he asked.

"I fell from the ledge up there," William said, pointing in the general direction of where they had come in. "I hurt my head and my ankle."

"And your name?" the tall man repeated.

"My name is William, and this is my twin brother, Morgan," he said.

"Yes, gemini...idem eadem idem," the man mused.

"Identical twins," Morgan said, pleased with himself.

"Well done," laughed the man. "You know some Latin."

"Not much," Morgan admitted. "But I like to decipher codes and play word games."

"Ah," the man nodded. He turned again to William. "When are you planning to vacate my humble caverna?" he asked, changing the subject.

"Very soon," William assured him. "We have friends searching for ropes to help get us out. They should be here any minute."

"That would be very interesting to watch, if I had time to wait for their return, which I do not," the cave dweller said. "Therefore, I suppose I must be the one to help you." He shuffled around the stone and stood towering over the boys. “Which one of you lads is the physician?” he asked, looking down at William’s ankle.

“I made the splint,” Morgan said. “Our father is a doctor and he showed us some basic first-aid so that we could help each other if we ever got hurt.”

“You have used your knowledge well,” the man commented, as he examined the splint and the patch of dried blood on William’s head. “You lads speak in a strange, clipped manner. Where are you from?”

“We just arrived from North America about a month ago,” Morgan explained. “We live with our great-grandmother at Adney House, just above the caves.”

“Adney House...how very interesting,” the stranger said, thoughtfully. “Well now, we must move along.” Without another word, he bent down and picked William up and put him on a large, flat boulder. He proceeded to examine his injured ankle more closely. William was too startled to protest.

Surprisingly, Morgan was beginning to lose his fear of the gentle stranger. His amazing height and odd appearance were no longer so intimidating. And he welcomed the luminous energy that bathed the dark cave in soft, blue light.

"I will take the pain from you, temporarily," the giant said to William, "You will be more comfortable. Then I am going to take you up to the place where you came in."

He placed both of his hands above William's swollen ankle and, without warning, a flash of light arced from the man's palms to William's foot. The boys gasped in surprise.

"Wow!" William exclaimed. "How did you do that?"

"An energy exchange," the man answered simply. "Do you still have pain?"

"No," William replied.

"Are you Merlin?" Morgan asked, looking up at the stranger.

"Why would you think that?" the tall man inquired.

"Because of that energy exchange that you just did, and because I thought this cave belonged to Merlin," Morgan replied.

"You may call Broleus," he said, smiling. Without any further explanation, he picked William up in his arms and started going toward the huge boulders where the boys had entered the cave. He stopped and looked back at Morgan. "Bring all of your belongings and follow me, quickly. We don't have much time."

Morgan grabbed the flashlights, the jackets, and the water bottle. He stuffed it all into the backpack and caught up to the others. He still had so many questions for their new friend. "Why are we in such a hurry?" he asked.

"Because I must leave, and you must get out quickly, before…" Broleus paused.

"Why can't we stay a little longer and talk?" Morgan rattled on.

"No more questions," Broleus said firmly. "Watch your step, the stones are slippery."

Within a few minutes, they were at the cave entrance. Morgan could see a shaft of light shining through the opening. The giant placed William on the ledge. He bent down and lifted Morgan up beside his brother.

"Let your brother lean on you," he said to Morgan. "Help him slip through the gap. I have enlarged it slightly, so you will get through more easily this time."

"I didn't see or hear the stones move," William said. "How did you make the opening bigger?"

"The same way I blocked the entrance in the first place," he answered, matter-of-factly. "Go now. You will soon be safely on the other side."

"But there is still so much I don't understand," Morgan began.

"Well, here is something that you must understand," Broleus said firmly. "You will not tell your friends about our meeting, or anything that happened here. And, you will not come into my caverna again. Morgan nodded. "Go quickly now," Broleus urged.

With his brother leaning on him, Morgan helped William through the opening, and eased him gently to the ground. He went back and looked into the cave. The mysterious man was still standing there. "Thank you for helping us, Sir. It was an honour to meet you," Morgan said.

"It was also a pleasure to meet you," Broleus said, smiling. "One more thing – when the time comes – carpe diem." He turned and vanished into the darkness.

The opening the boys had just crawled through narrowed slowly, until it was a thin crevice. Morgan repeated the giant's final words in his head as he climbed down to join William on a nearby rock.

"Broleus was so cool," William said.

"Yeah, I really liked him," Morgan agreed. "That energy transfer thing he did to you was amazing. Did it hurt?"

"No, it just felt kind of warm and prickly, and then the pain was gone. But, now it's really starting to hurt again," he noted.

“Tag and Jack should be here soon,” Morgan reminded him. “You can probably get a ride on one of their bikes.”

“We better decide what we’re going to tell them about how we managed to get out of the cave,” William suggested.

“Too late,” Morgan said, as he looked up. The Randall boys were already scrambling over the rocks with ropes across their shoulders.

*****

Asa slept fitfully in a chair by Durkin's side. He awoke to the sounds of thrashing and moaning. The healer was shocked. It was morning and the dwarf was still alive. "Lie still," Asa said when he saw fresh blood oozing from Durkin's wounds.

There was a loud rap at the door and a soldier boldly marched into Asa's cottage.

"What do you want?" the healer asked sharply.

"The king demands to see the dwarf. I was told he is here," the soldier stated.

"The messenger cannot go to the king. He has been mortally wounded," Asa said.

"What happened to him?" demanded the soldier.

"He was attacked by thugs in the forest last night," the healer said.

"A likely story," sneered the armed man.

"See for yourself, and then tell the king whatever you wish," Asa said calmly.

The soldier glanced at Durkin, sniffed arrogantly, and strode to the door. As he was about to leave, he turned to Asa. "Bring him to the king at midday."

"I will not," Asa stated firmly.

"You have been given an order!" the soldier said coldly.

"Durkin will die if he is moved," the healer said. "If the king wishes to see him, he will have to come here. That is my final word. Now leave!"

"I will tell the king of your refusal," the soldier said smugly. "You had better hope your healing powers are strong enough to counteract the king's wrath." He marched out, chuckling to himself.

Asa stared nervously at the empty doorway.

CHAPTER SEVEN

When they saw the twins sitting on the shore, the Randall brothers stopped and stared, their mouths hanging open.

"What...How?" Tag stammered.

"We're okay," Morgan said, walking over to them. "William hurt his ankle when he fell, but I wrapped it for him and helped him out of the cave."

"But...how?" Jack asked. Without waiting for an answer, he ran over to William. "Can you walk?"

"No, I can't. Morgan had to practically carry me out of the cave," William said. "But, I really want to go home now. Do you think you can give me a ride on your bike?"

"Sure, but we'll have to get you up the cliff, first," Jack said.

The three boys pushed and pulled William up the side of the hill, using the ropes as a sling. William moaned and grumbled as he bumped against the rocks. When the three boys managed to get him to the top, Jack helped him onto the seat of his bike and walked him back to Adney House. Morgan ran ahead and caught their father as he was pulling into the driveway.

"Dad, Dad, William is hurt!" he shouted. Their father ran to meet them. He lifted William off the bike and carried him into the house. Morgan thanked the Randall boys and went inside to help William face the inevitable questions from the family.

Their father's immediate concern was his son's ankle. After a quick examination, he told everyone that he would have to take William to the clinic for an x-ray. The two women bustled about cleaning the mud off William, and helping him to change his clothes. Morgan insisted on going with his brother to the clinic.

During the ride to Wadebridge, Morgan had expected to be severely grilled and reprimanded for what had happened. Surprisingly, Dad didn't really ask a lot of questions. He seemed to think that they had been in the mine caves just below Adney House and didn't even mention Merlin's cave. Of course, the boys didn't volunteer any information either.

Looking at the x-ray, their father said that the ankle was badly sprained, but not broken. William seemed relieved to be fitted with a removable splint, rather than a cast. But when Dad told him that he would be on crutches for the next week, William scowled angrily. Morgan knew that his brother would hate to spend the remaining days of summer vacation hobbling around on crutches.

When they arrived back at Adney House, Grandie, Mom, and Katie all helped to get William seated comfortably in a large chair in the library. The women began fussing over him and asking questions about the results of the x-rays.

"His ankle isn't broken," Dad said. "He should be walking on it by the weekend and ready to start school on Tuesday."

"Oh goody," William said sarcastically. "I'll be able to start school on Tuesday."

"Now, now, don't worry about school just yet," Grandie said soothingly. "I think we should put a bed in here," she added. "It would be very quiet and convenient for you."

"No, I'll be fine in the tower," William

argued.

"But you can't go up and down the stairs," his mother pointed out.

"I'll help him," Morgan offered. "Once we're in the tower, I'll take care of him."

"I have to agree with Morgan," his father said. "It's much quieter up there, and I'm sure the maids won't mind delivering meals to them for a few days."

"Well, I guess that would be best," their mother agreed. "But, what if he needs something and Morgan isn't there?"

"We can hook up the old bell system that runs from the nursery to the kitchen," Grandie said. "Then he can ring the staff if he needs something."

"And I'll check on him several times a day," their father said.

"We can all check on him," Katie added. "We'll take turns. I'll make a schedule."

"No, I don't need a bunch of nursemaids," William groaned.

"I'll be with him all the time," Morgan promised. "We also have a phone in our bedroom. Besides, Katie's room is close by, so she can help if we need her," he added, remembering how hurt she had looked after William's comment about nursemaids.

“I think we should take William upstairs now,” Dad said. “I’ve given him pain medication and he needs to rest.”

“Why don’t you use the lift in the hallway?” Grandie suggested. “It only goes to the second floor, but then you have only a few stairs to the nursery.”

“Great idea,” Morgan said. “Will you be okay on the crutches?”

“I guess,” William answered doubtfully. “I’m just not sure if…”

“Why don’t you use my push chair?” Grandie interrupted. “I certainly don’t need it.”

“Thanks Grandie,” William said, yawning sleepily.

“Morgan, you come with me to get the chair,” Grandie ordered. “Katie, you go to the kitchen and tell the maid, Jally, that William will need some milk and juice.”

Within half an hour, William was settled comfortably in the tower. His mom had rigged up a daybed by pulling the ottoman up to one of the leather chairs and covering it with quilts and blankets. As soon as William had begun to doze off, Morgan shooed his parents out of the room, insisting that everything was under control and he could take care of his brother quite competently.

While his brother slept, Morgan sat beside him, deep in thought. He mulled over what the mysterious stranger had said and done. He thought about Broleus' final words: When the time comes, remember carpe diem. He went over to the bookshelf and located a Latin dictionary. Quickly, he found what he was looking for; carpe diem – seize the day.

Morgan tried to understand the significance of what the tall stranger had said to him. Carpe diem? When the time comes? What time? What did Broleus mean? He put the dictionary on the desk by the bookshelf, and decided to search for a book that might somehow explain who Broleus was, or some information about events that had taken place in Merlin's cave in the past.

Once again, Morgan climbed the ladder and searched through the books. He found one that looked promising. Just as he took it from the shelf, the ladder slid out from under him and he crashed to the floor. He sat there, a bit dazed. When he reached for the book he had dropped, he noticed a small green book on the floor beside him. He picked it up and turned it over. It looked like somebody's tattered old journal. He was barely able to read the faded hand-written words on the cover, A Moment In Tyme.

"Yeah, quite a moment in time for me,"

Morgan said aloud.

"What's going on?" William asked. "I heard a crash. Are you okay?"

"I'm fine," Morgan assured him. He stood up, placed the little green journal on the table and picked up the Merlin book. "I fell off the ladder when I was getting a book."

"What book?" William asked, crawling out from under the mountain of quilts.

Morgan showed the book to William. "This book may give us some information about Merlin's cave. I'm hoping that Broleus, or blue lights, or energy transfer may be mentioned."

William yawned and stretched. "I was just dreaming about Broleus. "Do you think he could really be Merlin?"

"Probably not, but he seems to be living in Merlin's cave," Morgan said, glancing through the book. "Maybe it's a long shot, but let me look at the chapter titles to see if there's anything of interest. Here's a chapter that might be of interest, 'Caves of Cornwall and Anglesey'." Morgan quickly flipped to that chapter and began reading aloud. "Merlyn had several cave dwellings, but the most interesting and most studied ones are at Tintagel, Cornwall, and at Anglesey, formerly called Druid's Isle. It is believed that..." He was cut off by a sudden loud noise across the room.

Surprised, both boys turned and looked over at the wall of books. The ladder shot down the length of the shelves and crashed against the wall. A small green book flew through the air, and skidded across the floor. It landed at Morgan's feet.

William looked at the book and then at his brother. "What was that?" he whispered.

Morgan leaned over the side of the chair to get a better look. "That's the book I saw when I fell off the ladder. Should I pick it up?"

"Wait, let's see if anything else happens," William said, as he wriggled closer to Morgan. They both watched the book for several minutes, but nothing happened. Cautiously, Morgan reached down and picked up the book.

"I guess somebody wants us to read that book instead," William suggested.

"Okay then, let's have a look at it," Morgan agreed, laughing nervously. He opened the book to the first page. He was startled by the odd appearance of the text. "This book has been handwritten," he stated.

"Do you think it's someone's diary?" William asked.

"I don't know. Since it was handwritten, I'm sure I won't find a publisher's name," Morgan suggested. He looked inside the cover and discovered only an author's name and a date. "It was written by Farold Tyme, in 1651, no, 1657," he said, squinting to read it.

"Wow, that's old," William said. "So, is it his journal?"

"I'm checking. Oh, here's a dedication: For the twains, Victor and Nevin, who found the ...bridge." Morgan looked up at William. "This is really faded. I can't read the name of the bridge. See if you can figure it out."

William took the book from him and studied the page carefully. "I can't read the bridge name either," he said, flipping through the pages. "Do you think these guys were old relatives of Grandie's?"

"I'm not sure, but if they were, that means they were relatives of ours too," Morgan reminded him. "Maybe Grandie has a family tree or some records that we could study. Should I go and ask her?"

"Sure, but let's try to find out more from the book first. Here," William said, handing it back to Morgan. "I can't read his writing."

"I know. The writing is so illegible and faint. I'm going to see if I can find a magnifying glass. I think Dad has one in his office. I'll be right back." Morgan set the book on the table and started toward the door.

"Wait, I want something to eat first. Let's call down for pizza," William said.

"As if the maids will bring us pizza," Morgan chuckled. "We'll be lucky to get a cucumber sandwich and a pot of tea."

"Maybe our dear sister Katie will buy us some pizza," William suggested. "She seemed to want to take care of my needs, and what I need is a pizza. Call her and tell her I want pepperoni."

"Okay, I'll call her, but don't hold your breath. The pizza place doesn't deliver, so she would have to get a ride into town with someone," Morgan said. He went to the bedroom to phone, and returned shortly with a smile on his face.

"Well, believe it or not, Katie said she'd do it. Her friend, Russell is coming up to see her in an hour and she's going to ask him to pick up some pizza." Morgan sat down next to William and picked up the book about Merlin. "While we're waiting, I'm going to see if this book can tell me anything about tall giants with blue lights. After we've eaten, I'll get the magnifying glass so we can try to figure out what's so special about the UFB."

"UFB?" William repeated, puzzled.

"Unexplained Flying Book!" Morgan said

proudly.

"Oh that's a good one," William mocked. "Seriously though, Morg, did the flying book and the weird things that happened at the caves scare you as much as the stuff that you saw on the first night in the tower?"

"No, the fog incident was very creepy. Plus, I was alone and it was dark," Morgan said. "But the night with the piskies also freaked me out. Meeting Broleus in the cave was cool, though. I wish we could have spent more time with him. His size was kind of intimidating, but I really liked him. Maybe he represented..."

"Okay, don't analyze it to death. I just wondered if maybe we're beginning to accept these strange events as normal," William said.

"Or we're hallucinating, or we're being possessed by discarnate entities from some pagan era," Morgan stated dramatically.

"Why can't you use normal words?" William wailed. "I think you're possessed by some psycho Latin dude."

"Oh, that reminds me, when we were leaving the cave this afternoon, Broleus said something very odd to me, which is why I was looking for a book in the first place."

"What did he say?" William asked.

"He said, 'When the time comes - carpe

diem'. I looked it up in the dictionary and it's Latin for 'seize the day'."

"So what do you think he meant?" William inquired.

"I don't know," Morgan admitted. "I get 'seize the day' – enjoy, make the most of it."

"But 'when the time comes' is the part that is confusing."

"Maybe, it wasn't a message, just a good-bye kind of thing," William said.

"Oh, I think there was some sort of hidden meaning. Broleus chose his words very carefully. When he said something, it was important," Morgan said emphatically.

"Maybe, but let's get back to the weird things that are going on," William said. "I don't think we're imagining this stuff, so why is it happening?"

"Sometimes I think that we're supposed to learn something, or do something. But I can't put it all together yet," Morgan replied.

"Or, maybe this house is haunted," William suggested.

"That's a strong possibility," Morgan agreed. "Jally, the maid, hinted that it was haunted weeks ago, but we can't get her to discuss it with us. Maybe it's time to sit down and have a serious talk with Grandie. Weird things might have happened to her when she was a kid. Grandie and her brother played and slept in these very rooms."

"She can also tell us about the history of Adney House," William added. "Why don't we get her to come up and have a wee chat with us?"

"I'll go down and get her after…" Scuffling and voices in the hallway interrupted him.

"Quick, hide the UFB," Morgan whispered.

*****

Within an hour, a palace messenger arrived and handed Asa a note.

Please be advised
Due to present circumstances, His Majesty
Will arrive at the Healing Cottage
At half eight, this evening
To discuss certain matters with the Messenger
It is expected that Durkin will be present and alert
As ordered by King Ulric, Ruler of Greywood

Asa quickly scribbled a response, and gave it to the messenger.

After he had gone, Asa smiled as he tried to imagine King Ulric and his entourage holding a meeting in his cottage. The pompous king was truly amusing. He was a reasonably capable leader, but he had to fill the impossibly large shoes of his father, King Frederick, who had been the greatest leader of all time. Frederick had used his wisdom and powers effectively to gain support and respect of the people, and keep peace in Greywood. Ulric did not have the same level of support. Many doubted his leadership capabilities. So, King Ulric had chosen to gain respect by bullying.

Durkin began to stir. He opened his eyes and

smiled gratefully when he saw Asa.

"Well little warrior, your battle to stay alive is admirable," the physician said. "I am impressed with your self-healing abilities."

"It is your healing powers that saved me," Durkin whispered, hoarsely.

"Well, now we must combine our powers," Asa said. We are about to have a visit from our king."

Durkin stared at him in disbelief.

CHAPTER EIGHT

Katie and Russell came in, loaded down with pizza. "We've decided to eat with you," Katie announced. "Russell, these are my brothers, Morgan and William."

"So, you are the Adney twins," Russell said smiling. "I've heard all about you from my sister, Janey." William looked confused.

"The girl with the red hair who met us on the veranda," Morgan reminded him.

"She's your sister?" William laughed. "Does she ever stop talking?"

"Nah, she's a right windbag," Russell agreed. "She drives me mad with her constant yammering, but enough about my sister. I see you've wrenched your ankle. Were you down at the caves?"

"Yeah, I have to sit around here doing nothing 'til school starts," William grumbled.

"Your dad's a doctor, so you can't do much else, especially when your ankle is so gummy," Russell said.

"Gummy?" William repeated.

"Big…" Russell said.

"Swollen," Katie added. "C'mon guys, let's eat while the pizza is hot. Should we sit here, or go over to the table?"

"Here," the three boys agreed.

"Did you bring anything to drink?" Morgan asked.

"I have colas," Katie said, giving each of them a can.

Within minutes, the pizza was devoured and each of the boys burped appreciatively.

"So, what did you two do up here all day?" Katie asked. "Watch TV?"

"Pretty much," William lied.

"You're boring," Katie said, gathering up the boxes and pop cans. "Let's go, Russell."

As they were leaving, Russell looked around the tower. "Great flat you've got up here. I've always wondered what it looked like on the inside."

"We like it," William said.

"Thanks for the pizza," Morgan said, as Katie pushed Russell toward the door.

"Have fun watching TV," Katie teased. "Russell and I are going to Wadebridge to see a movie. "Too bad you can't come with us."

"Okay, see you later then," William said curtly.

After Morgan closed the door, the twins looked at each other and laughed.

"I think Katie has a boyfriend," Morgan said.

"Ooh, he's so handsome," William squealed, batting his eyelashes and pretending to feel faint. "Katie was totally showing off for Russell. I'm glad they're gone."

"Yeah, me too," Morgan agreed. "The pizza was good though," he added. Suddenly, he remembered their original plan. "I'm going down to get the magnifying glass from Dad's office. Should I see if Grandie will come up?"

"Sure, but just bring Grandie," William replied. "We don't need Mom and Dad getting into all this."

"I'll see what I can do," Morgan said. "Be back in a few minutes. Need anything before I go?"

"No, I'm fine. Just hurry," William answered.

Morgan raced down the stairs and found the magnifying glass on his father's desk. He shoved it into his pocket, and then went to find his great-grandmother. She was in her art studio off the kitchen.

"Hi Grandie," he said casually. "What are you doing?"

"I'm painting," she replied. "Good to see you, dear. How is your brother?"

"He's doing okay. Actually, he sent me down to get you. We're both hoping that you might have time to come up and talk to us."

"Talk about what?" she asked, surprised.

"Well," Morgan said, without looking directly at her. "We have a lot of spare time on our hands right now. We're curious about this old house and the people who have lived here, so we decided that you'd be the perfect one to tell us all about it." Morgan's face flushed as he realized how easily he had just lied to his great-grandmother.

She seemed pleased that she was being invited to visit with the boys. "Well I suppose I am the one who knows the most about the family history. This is a perfect time to have a chat with my favourite great-grandsons."

"We're your only great-grandsons," Morgan reminded her, smiling.

"And my favourite ones too," Grandie added,

patting his shoulder, affectionately. "I'll just clean my brushes and we'll be off."

"Let me help you," Morgan offered. He carried several paint pots over to the sink. "Grandie, do you have any books about our ancestors?" he asked.

"Yes I do. Our family record book is in the main floor library. We'll go there now," she said, wiping her hands after cleaning the last paint pot. "I know exactly where it is."

Within a few minutes, the two of them were on their way up to the tower with the family tree book tucked safely under Morgan's arm. To save time, they took the lift to the second floor.

Grandie was surprised to see William propped up in his make-shift bed, reading a small, green book. He quickly stuffed it under the quilt when he saw Grandie and Morgan. "Well, I never thought I'd see the day that you'd be enjoying a book," she said. "What has captured your interest?"

"Just a book from over there," William said. "I can't do much right now," he said, pointing to his injured ankle. "So I thought I might read some of the old books." Seeing the book under Morgan's arm, he asked, "What's that?"

"Our family tree," Morgan answered. "Grandie says it dates back to the 1600's."

"No wonder it's so thick," William said. "Let's see if our names are in it."

"Of course they are," Grandie stated. "We have always documented each birth, death, and marriage in this family. All of the information is current and very accurate."

"Good, then let's get started," Morgan said, handing the book to Grandie. "We want to know everything you can tell us about this family."

"First you must tell me why the sudden interest in this house and our relatives," their great-grandmother said, as she settled into the chair next to William.

The twins glanced at each other, as Morgan sat down on the other side of her.

"We love Adney House, especially this old nursery. We just want to know more about it. That's all Grandie," Morgan insisted.

"If you say so," she said, looking from one boy to the other. Neither of them said anything, so she continued. "Well, I'm proud to tell you about our family and I'm pleased that you want to know more about it, whatever the reason. Where shall we begin?"

"Let's start with us and work our way back," Morgan suggested. Grandie nodded and opened the heavy book to the last page of entries.

"There's our names and Katie's under Mom

and Dad," William noted.

"Yes. Going up the line, you can see that your mother, Bridget, is under her mother, Nan. You'll also see the names of two boys beside Nan. Those were my three children." Grandie paused for a moment and wiped her eyes with a handkerchief that she took from her apron. "The boys were identical twins born in 1945. Unfortunately, they died when they were only eight years old. So then, Nan, your grandmother, became my only child." She stared thoughtfully at the book. The boys waited for her to go on.

"Next you'll see my name on a line with my twin brother, Sterling. We were born in 1927. Sterling was killed in the war when he was only eighteen. Beside my name, you'll see my husband's name, Stewart Irving. He died when Nan was about your age, so Nan and I looked after Adney House and started the bed and breakfast business four years after his death."

"Didn't Grammy Nan go to Africa last year?" Morgan asked.

"Yes, she left just after Christmas," Grandie replied.

"Why did she go so far away?" William asked.

"Well, she had some friends there, and I thought it would help her get over the loss of her husband, Oliver, who was your dear grandfather."

"Men don't last very long in this family, do they?" William said bluntly.

"It's true, we've always been rather short of men," Grandie replied. "But the Adney women are of sturdy stock, so we've managed. However, our family is very lucky to have you boys and your father."

"Should we be worried about our longevity?" Morgan joked.

"Our longevity," William mocked. "You and your fancy words ..."

"Well, it was a good word to use in this case," Grandie said, smiling. "And no, I don't think you have anything to worry about, since you are all healthy and strong." Patting William's leg gently, she added, "Well, except for you at the moment, dear."

"Is Grammy Nan going to come back and help you with the B&B when we go home next year?" Morgan asked.

"I hope she comes back," his great-grandmother replied. "But I'd really like it if all of you could stay. I love having my family around me."

"We can't stay, Grandie. Mom has to go back to teaching," William stated. "She only has one year off."

"We'll just wait and see how it all works out," Grandie said. "Now let's get back to the family tree. Next in line are my parents, Robert and Anne, both born in 1897. Sterling and I were their only children. My grandfather had a twin brother too. Their names were Gregor and John."

"There sure seems to be a lot of twins in our family," Morgan noticed.

"Oh yes," Grandie said. "People from around here, have always teased us because there have been so many generations of twins. Some say we're bewitched."

"Why?" William asked.

"Well, they seem to think the piskies sprinkled some magical dust on us or something. That is a bunch of nonsense, of course. When people come upon something unusual, or something that can't be explained, they always blame the piskies. But we certainly have never given a toss about their silly gossip."

"Do you believe there really are pixies around here?" Morgan asked.

"I certainly do not," Grandie replied indignantly.

"Tag and Jack think they live in the old mine caves, down the hill," William said.

"Oh, I've heard that clap-trap too," she

admitted. "But I've never seen a single piskie in all my eighty-five years of living here."

"Grandie, aren't you only eighty?" William asked.

"Yes, I suppose I am. I guess it just feels like eighty-five," she said, smiling. "Now, let's get back to the business at hand. Do you boys want me to go through every generation, or is there something specific you'd like to know?"

"I'd like to know how many sets of twins there are," Morgan said.

"Then, let's explore that. We were at my grandfather and his brother. That's four sets so far. Let's go back further." With her finger, Grandie traced the many branches of their family tree, muttering to herself as she studied the entries. I count nine sets as far back as this book goes."

"That sure is a lot of twins for one family," William reflected.

"I don't imagine other families have had that many multiple births," Morgan added.

"We even had a set of triplets in 1718, born to the same family that had twins in 1716," Grandie added. "And according to these records, most of them lived to have children of their own."

"Amazing!" Morgan exclaimed. "How many of the twins were identical like us?"

"Well, my brother and I certainly weren't," she said with a chuckle. "Let me check.

Under some of the twins, I noticed the letters I - d - e - m, which means..."

"The same," Morgan interrupted. "From 'idem eadem idem' which is Latin for 'exactly the same'."

"Why, I had no idea that you knew Latin," Grandie said. "You are full of surprises."

"Oh he knows a lot about words, Grandie. He's a bit of a nerd," William said.

"He just has a different focus on things. We must learn to tolerate differences and appreciate each other's individuality," Grandie admonished.

"Yes, Grandie," William said quietly.

"I don't really know that much about Latin, just what I've learned from computer puzzles and games," Morgan admitted. "So, which twins were identical, Grandie?"

"There are nine sets listed here," Grandie said, returning to the book, "It would seem that besides you two, there were my dear little boys that died, plus my grandfather and his brother, and two more identical pairs; Wrighton and Marcus Adney in1744, and Victor and Nevin Tyme in 1645."

Upon hearing the names of the twins mentioned in the little green book, the boys glanced nervously at each other. Morgan gave William a warning glance, reminding him not to let on that they had already heard of the Tyme twins.

"Were all of the twins boys?" Morgan asked quickly.

"Of course not," Grandie said. "There were many girl sets of twins as well."

"Enough about twins," William said. "I'd like to know when Adney House was actually built."

"It was built by Wrighton Adney, and his identical twin brother, Marcus. The twins and their families moved into the house in 1772. Of course there have been additions and renovations over the years, but basically, it looks the same now as it did in the beginning. I've seen a photograph that was taken on the day they moved into Adney House. This house has always been occupied by Adney descendants," Grandie added proudly.

They were startled by a sudden knock at the door. Morgan opened it and the maid walked in with a dinner tray.

"My, how the time has flown," Grandie said, getting up. "What time is it, Jally?"

"Six, Ma'am," the maid replied, setting the tray on the table.

"Has the family gathered downstairs for tea, then?" Grandie asked.

"Not yet, Ma'am, they asked to wait 'til half six. The doctor hasn't come home."

"Well, I must make my way down to the kitchen to help get ready," Grandie said, gathering herself together.

"Wait, Grandie," Morgan urged. "One more thing before you leave..."

Motioning for the maid to leave, Grandie turned to Morgan "What is it dear?"

"When you and your brother stayed up here with your nanny, did it look the same as it does now?" Morgan asked.

"Yes, the rooms were the same, our nanny's room was over there," she replied, indicating the storage room that the twins knew very well.

"Did you, or your brother, ever… uh…hear any strange noises?" he stammered, not quite knowing how to broach the subject without evoking a lot of questions from her.

She searched his face thoughtfully. "Are you suggesting that Adney House is haunted?" she asked.

"No," Morgan said quickly. "It's just that this house is very old, and sometimes I hear strange noises in the night."

"I think you have an overactive imagination,

just like my brother had. He used to ask me if I had heard knocking in the walls at night," she said waving her arm toward the bookshelf. "Once," she continued, smiling, "Sterling tried to convince me that he had seen a ghost. I never saw or heard anything, nor did our nanny."

"Probably just your imagination, like Grandie said. Probably nothing more than that," William emphasized.

"Maybe," Morgan said. "So, the whole time you've lived in this house, nothing out of the ordinary has ever happened?"

"Not to me," Grandie said. "Over the years, a few maids have left, claiming the house was haunted. And the odd guest has asked me about ghostly shapes in the night, but I've never taken it seriously. However, if true, I think it would give the house character. Any house this old, and this close to the historical site of King Arthur's birth, is bound to stir the imagination of some, I would think."

"That's true," William agreed. "But it would be kind of fun to see our ancestors floating around here, checking on us every night."

"Oh, I'm quite sure they are keeping an eye on us, but I don't think they appear as ghostly apparitions," Grandie said. "However, if you are nervous about staying in the nursery, Morgan, you…"

"No, I'm not nervous," Morgan quickly assured her. "I guess I was just hoping that this old house 'had some character', as you've suggested."

"Sorry I couldn't offer you more," Grandie said. "Now I must go. Would you like to walk me downstairs, dear?"

"Sure," Morgan said, jumping up and grabbing the family album. "May we keep this for a few days?"

"Yes, but please remember that the book is very old and the pages are very delicate."

"We will," Morgan said, placing it gently on the desk by the bookshelf. As they were leaving the room, he turned to his brother. "I'll be right back, Will. Don't eat all the custard pudding."

"Then you'd better hurry," William teased.

*****

When the king and his guards arrived, Asa bowed respectfully and ushered them into his humble cottage. The king's eyes darted around the room, taking in the crudely nailed shelves crammed with bottles of all sizes and shapes. Rows of cots and medical paraphernalia filled the room. He sniffed disdainfully at the scent of lavender and eucalyptus, and seemed very uncomfortable in the healer's cottage.

"I will speak with the dwarf," King Ulric demanded. Asa led him to Durkin's cot. The king looked at his lifeless body. "Has he been drugged?" he asked accusingly.

"No, Majesty," Asa said quietly. "Durkin suffered near fatal blows from thugs in the forest. He was beaten and stabbed. I did not think he would survive the night."

"Thugs in the forest?" laughed the king. "Why would anyone rob him?"

"There was no robbery, Majesty," Asa said. "Four men savagely attacked him and told Durkin it was a warning."

"A warning! Of what?" Ulric spluttered in disbelief. There was a rustling of blankets as Durkin awoke. He began tossing and turning.

"Durkin," the healer said quietly. "His

Majesty is here." Durkin tried to sit up, but couldn't. He gasped and lay back painfully.

"What said these thugs?" the king asked, once Durkin was settled again.

"Asked... why I ... seeing Maj...esty again. I - I... said...nothing."

"Tell me of their appearance," said Ulric. "Was there enough light to see them?"

"Torches," Durkin gasped, painfully. "Tall...big noses...red hair...un...tidy."

"Piskies," muttered the king, angrily. "The shape shifters suspect..."

CHAPTER NINE

Shortly after dinner, the boys' parents arrived in the tower for a visit. Their father examined William's ankle and smiled. "The swelling is going down nicely. Do you want pain medication so you can sleep more comfortably?" he asked William.

"No, I'm fine Dad," he insisted.

"Have you been using the crutches to get around?" his father asked.

"Not yet. I haven't needed to get up because everyone is taking such good care of me," William said. Under his breath he added, "Too good."

"Well, I'd like to see you use them now," his father insisted. "Just in case you fall…"

"No, Dad," William moaned. His parents

obviously weren't leaving until he tried the crutches, so he managed to hobble back and forth across the room reasonably well.

"Good job," his father said.

"Would you boys like to come with us to the orientation meeting at your school this evening?" their mother asked.

"No, I can't walk that great yet," William said, quickly.

"What about you, Morgan?" she asked.

"No," he replied. "I should stay here with Will."

"Alright," their mother sighed. "Katie is going with us. We'll bring back information on your classes and instructors."

"Anything else we can do for you, before we leave?" Dad asked.

"No, we have everything under control," William said. "Enjoy the meeting."

Finally the boys were alone. Morgan took the magnifying glass out of his pocket and held it over the faint print in the green book. It didn't help much. Most of the writing had faded badly and Farold's writing was very hard to decipher.

"Too bad Old Farold didn't have a computer," William mused.

"It sure would have made it easier for us," Morgan said, leafing through the book, trying to find something he could actually read. "I think this book is an account of something that happened to his brothers. From one part, I was able to gather that it was a secret journey of some sort. Wait, here's something." He began to read, "Though they were mere boys, what they learned from crossing the..." Morgan adjusted the magnifying glass before continuing. "...from crossing the Oak Bridge... would raise the hair on the necks of scientists and historians alike."

"So, what's that supposed to mean?" William said impatiently.

"I'm not sure," Morgan said. "It seems like something happened to them that would have been hard to believe. But what was it? And what is the oak bridge?"

"Have you ever read about oak bridges or heard of one around here?" William asked.

"I don't think so," Morgan said, wracking his brain.

"See if you can find something in Farold's book that might explain it," William suggested.

Morgan continued to peruse the book, looking for readable passages. "Here's a legible quote from Farold's brother, Nevin," Morgan said excitedly.

'Twas a place we did not know
We know not how it came to be
That we two
were propelled by tempest winds
through cold and darkness
To a dense forest
where we lay terrored and alone'

"So where were they? What happened to them?" William asked.

"That's all it says," Morgan replied. "There is a big ink blob on the rest of the page."

"Maybe they were interrupted, and his brother spilled the ink," William said.

"Yeah," Morgan agreed, absently thumbing through the book. "I can't find anything else," he said putting it down. "Let's review what we know so far."

"First, this little book is pretty important," William said, holding up one finger. "It was written in the 1600's, before Adney House was even built."

"So, it was brought here and guarded for centuries," Morgan reasoned.

William held up two fingers and continued to relate the facts. "Second, we know that Farold and his brothers are real."

"Because, Grandie read their names from the family tree book," Morgan said.

"Exactly," his brother agreed. "Third, some of the Tyme descendants probably knew about their adventure and must have written things about it too. Are you sure there aren't any loose pieces of paper in the book somewhere?"

"No," Morgan replied. "There's nothing else. Here, look for yourself." William thumbed through it, shook it, and set it back on the table.

"Maybe there's a second book somewhere on the shelves," William suggested, reaching for his crutches.

"Sit! I'll go and look," Morgan said. "I fell off the ladder this afternoon. I don't think it's a good idea for you to try it." He picked up the green book and headed to the wall of books. He climbed up the ladder and returned the book to its niche. He checked several shelves, but couldn't find any other diaries or journals "Nothing!" he shouted across to William. He climbed down and walked back to the sitting area. "Let's forget it for tonight. I'm going to bed."

"What time is it?" William asked, yawning.

"Almost eleven o'clock," Morgan replied.

"Okay, let me use the loo first," William, said.

"Sure, I'll wait here, in case you fall or something," his twin offered.

"I won't fall," William said, thumping across

the room on his crutches.

The boys didn't bother to undress. They fell into bed, wearing their t-shirts and sweat pants. It had been an eventful day for both of them. Morgan had hoped to get to sleep first, to avoid his brother's snoring, but luck was not with him. He tried to make sense of everything that had happened. But, he was too exhausted to make sense of anything. He fell asleep in spite of William's moaning and snorting.

Shortly after midnight, Morgan bolted upright in bed. He had heard a crash in the other room. He sat very still, listening. Then he heard rustling and bumping noises like someone was moving books around on the shelves. Morgan was afraid to get up to find out what was going on, so he lay down and pulled his quilt up to his chin. Waiting, hoping that it would all go away.

Next, he heard a tapping noise. It was the same sound he had heard the first night in the tower. The tapping droned on continuously, pounding through every fibre of Morgan's being. He felt like he was losing control of his mind and body.

Suddenly, he was being pulled out of bed! He grabbed onto his headboard and tried to resist, but the force was too strong. Morgan was dragged to the floor. Using all of his strength, he crawled over to William's bed and hung onto the side.

"Will...Will, wake up," he begged.

"What?" William grumbled. "What's going on?"

"Move over," Morgan said, climbing into his brother's bed. "The tapping, it's happening again. Listen..."

"Probably the heating pipes," William mumbled.

"No, that's the same tapping noise I heard before," Morgan insisted. "And something just pulled me out of bed. What should we do?"

"Nothing," William mumbled. The monotonous tapping continued.

"Should we go out there?" Morgan asked nervously.

"No, I can't walk," William said.

"Oh, I forgot about your ankle. I have a strong feeling that I should go out there, but I'm too scared," Morgan admitted.

"Then don't go," William said, burying his head under his pillow.

Morgan listened and waited, but the tapping was not letting up. If anything, it was getting louder, and louder. He grabbed his head and moaned.

"What's wrong?" William asked, sitting up.

He was fully awake now.

"Hammering in my head..." Morgan stammered. "The tapping is inside my head. I can't stop it."

"I can still hear it, but I don't think it's as loud as before," William said.

"No, because it's in my head. I have to go out there," Morgan said desperately, rocking back and forth.

"Okay," William said. "I'll go with you. Can you get my crutches?"

At that moment, Morgan was yanked from the bed and hurled across the room. He moaned as he crashed against the door.

"Morg!" William shouted, scrambling awkwardly out of bed. He cried out in pain, as he put weight on his injured ankle. "Morgan," William yelled again. There was a groan, and the sound of movement from across the dark room. "Hang on, I'm coming," he muttered as he crawled across the floor. When he got to the bedroom door, William bumped into his brother's body. He got up on his knees and switched on the light. Morgan was lying in a crumpled heap, holding his head.

"Morg, get up. I can't help you, because of my ankle," William complained.

"The pounding! I can't stand it anymore,"

Morgan cried.

"You have to get up," William said, crawling over to his crutches. With his crutches under his arms, he hobbled back to Morgan. "We're going to go out there and put a stop to the pounding. C'mon, grab onto me." Morgan continued to moan and rock back and forth on the floor. "Get...Up...Now!" William demanded. The urgent tone of his brother's voice brought Morgan to his senses. Using the doorframe and William's arm for support, he struggled to his feet.

"Open the door, we're going out there," William ordered, switching off the light. Since the boys hadn't closed the drapes, they now stared into an empty room bathed in moonlight. "So what do we do next?" William asked.

Without a word, Morgan started moving forward. He was drawn to the tapping noise.

Like a zombie, he walked slowly and purposefully toward the books. William followed him; neither of them spoke.

When he got to the bookcase, Morgan grabbed the ladder and pushed it down the rows. Halfway across, the ladder stopped. Hypnotically, he began climbing the rungs.

The tapping noise ceased.

"Morg, what are you doing?" his brother

whispered into the eerie silence.

There was no response from Morgan. He took books from the shelf, one by one, and dropped them to the floor. William could barely see what was going on, so he hobbled over to the desk and turned on the lamp.

The light startled Morgan. He looked down at his brother and then at the pile of books on the floor. "What's going on?" he asked, confused. "When did the tapping noise stop?"

"I'm not sure," William replied. "You're throwing books. What are you looking for?"

"I don't know…let me think…"

"Can you come down here to think?" William asked. "You're making me nervous."

"Hey, I remember now," Morgan cried, suddenly coherent and alert. "There's something in the wall behind the books." He began searching frantically for a secret opening in the wall. All of a sudden, something clicked. "Bingo!" Morgan shouted.

What is it?" his brother wanted to know.

"A little door in the wall just opened. I'm reaching in…I feel something…I've got it!" Morgan withdrew his arm and began to carefully descend the ladder. In his hand, he was holding a small box wrapped in black cloth. When he reached the floor, he held it out to his brother.

"Look! This is what the tapping was all about."

"So let's open it," William said, reaching for the box.

"Not so fast," Morgan said, holding it against his chest. "After everything that has just happened, I want to approach this with a bit of caution."

"I want to approach this with a bit of caution," William mimicked.

"If you're going to mock me, then you can go back to bed," he said indignantly.

William glared at him, but didn't say anything.

"If you're interested in finding out what's in this box, follow me," Morgan said, walking toward the bedroom. William clomped along behind him.

Once they were both seated at his desk, Morgan carefully tugged at the string that held the black cloth. The fabric and string fell away and a small wooden box lay before them. Morgan rubbed his palms together. "Are you ready?"

"Just open it," William said impatiently.

Morgan undid the clasp and lifted the lid. Both boys tried to look into the box at the same time. "Move your head," Morgan said, pushing William aside. He reached in and took out a folded piece of paper.

"Is that all?" William said, grabbing at the box.

Morgan slammed the lid down on his brother's hand. "I'll check," he said.

"Quit acting so stupid," William growled.

It was after one o'clock in the morning. Tempers were short, and the twins were beginning to squabble like a couple of four year olds.

Morgan reached into the little wooden box once again. "Well, lookie here," he said triumphantly. Dangling from his fingers was a small leather bag. He set the bag on the desk, and untied the string. Morgan couldn't believe what his fingers touched when he reached inside. Very carefully, he took three clear crystals from the little bag.

"Wow!" William whispered, holding one up to the light of the desk lamp.

"I wonder where they came from," Morgan said. They are so beautiful."

"They're incredible," William added. "They must be worth a fortune."

"Maybe this note will explain everything," Morgan said, remembering the paper that had also been in the box. He unfolded it and smoothed it out. "It's dated 1758."

"What does it say? Who wrote it?" William

asked, peering over Morgan's shoulder.

"It was written by someone named, Wrighton Adney," Morgan said, thoughtfully. "Isn't that the name of one of the twins that built this house?"

"I think so," William replied. "Read the note. We'll sort out the who's who later."

Morgan began to read:

Omnis annus centum
Two shall go as one
Across time and distance
So the Mighty One may sleep

"What does that mean?" William asked.

"I have no idea." Morgan yawned and rubbed his eyes. "I don't understand anything that's happened tonight. He yawned again. I need to get some sleep."

"I agree. Let's set the alarm for ten," William suggested. "We'll sort it all out in the morning." He hopped over to his bed on one foot.

Morgan put the crystals back in the bag, tucked them safely into the box, and shoved it to the back of his desk drawer. He then turned out the light, choosing to ignore a warm glow from the lamp in the other room. He was too tired to worry about it.

*****

The strain of the king's visit had exhausted Durkin. He could feel himself slipping again into the welcome darkness where he would feel no pain.

King Ulric seemed deeply absorbed in thought. When he finally turned his attention back to Durkin, and spoke his name several times, there was no response from the small messenger.

"Healer, waken the dwarf," he demanded.

"Begging your Majesty's indulgence, Durkin must rest," Asa said quietly.

"I will speak with him," the king said angrily. The guards stepped forward. The king stopped their advance by raising his hand. "Waken him," he repeated.

The commotion caused Durkin to stir. The king leaned over him.

"Messenger, tell me one thing more, so I may take my leave." Durkin's eyes fluttered open and he tried to focus on the king's face. "Tell me again, exactly when do the visitors arrive?"

"Autumn...Equinox...dusk." Durkin replied groggily. He began to gasp for air.

"Durkin is very ill. I will not allow him to be interrogated further," Asa stated.

"You will not allow," sneered the king. "Must

we have a test of powers, Healer?"

"Forgive me, Sire," Asa apologized quickly. "I am just trying to save the life of your messenger and my friend."

"Humble, and dramatic as well," the king said rudely. "Guards, we are leaving," he shouted. At the door, King Ulric turned to Asa, "See that he lives Healer, or you shall pay the price."

CHAPTER TEN

A loud, banging noise jolted the boys awake. Morgan was already sitting up before he was completely awake. He sat in his bed, staring blankly at the wall.

William pulled the covers over his head. "Someone's at the door," he grumbled.

Morgan went to unlock the door. His mother came in with a basket of clean clothes.

"It's almost ten o'clock and you boys are still asleep," she said, bustling into the room. "You are in for a real shock when school starts. You'll have to get up at six-thirty every day, so you had better start preparing yourselves by getting to bed earlier."

"Good morning Mom," Morgan mumbled, as

he closed the door.

"Is William still sleeping?" she asked. She was already on her way to the bedroom.

"I'm up, I'm up," he muttered impatiently, reaching for his crutches.

"I hope you heard what I just told your brother," she began. "I find it appalling that you can't seem to get your act together. How you will ever get up at six…"

"Mom, you're making my head hurt," William groaned. "It's our last few days of freedom."

"You don't have to make it sound like a prison sentence, for heaven's sake," his mother said, stuffing clothes into drawers. "If you had come to the school with us last night, you would have seen that it is a very modern school with a new science lab…"

"That's great, Mom," William interrupted. "We'll see it in a few days. I'm going to the washroom." He lumbered out of the room on his crutches.

His mother was close behind him, still clutching the laundry basket. "William, don't brush me off, when I'm trying to talk to you," she demanded.

Morgan intercepted her in the sitting room. "Mom, come and sit down. You seem tense this morning."

"I'm not tense," she shouted at him. "I just feel that you boys are acting irresponsibly up here by yourselves; watching television until all hours, sleeping all day, and not joining the family for meals. I have a mind to move you down to the second floor with the rest of us. I should never have agreed to this arrangement in the first place."

"Hold on, Mom," Morgan interjected. "Grandie was up here visiting us yesterday. Katie and her boyfriend had dinner with us the night before that. Just because we didn't go to the meeting, that doesn't mean we aren't interested in the family or anything else. "So, tell me what you found out about Wadebridge School."

"I think you'll like it, Morgan," his mother said more calmly. She sat down and put the basket on the floor beside her. "You'll have five teachers. We met them all and they seemed very nice. Classes start at 8:30 and end at 2:30. There is a big cafeteria where you can buy hot meals every day."

"Do we have to take a bus?" Morgan asked.

"You can go into Wadebridge with your father most mornings. His office is only a few blocks from the school. But you'll probably have to take the bus home," she replied.

"Why can't we do home-schooling?" William asked, hobbling over to his 'chair bed'. "We're only going to be here for one year."

"Home-schooling isn't an option," Mom said firmly. "I can't look after your education and Grandie's bed and breakfast at the same time. Besides, it's time you met some kids your age."

"We already have," William said. "Tag, Jack, Russell, and let's not forget Janey."

"I saw her last night," Mom said, smiling. "She is a bit much isn't she?"

"You could say that," William agreed. "So what else did you find out last night?"

"Oh, I almost forgot," she said, reaching into the laundry basket. "I have your school uniforms." She handed each boy a folded bundle of blue clothing.

"Uniforms!" William exclaimed, handing his bundle back to her. "I'm not going to wear a uniform."

"You don't have a choice," his mother said. "Every school child in Britain wears a uniform. At least you don't have to wear short pants, or blazers and ties," she said, holding up a fleece sweatshirt imprinted with the school's logo.

"What else do we have to wear?" Morgan asked, unfolding his package.

"A sweatshirt, a long or short-sleeved t-shirt, navy blue cotton trousers, and black shoes. I have to pick up the shoes later today," she replied.

"This is so dumb," William whined. "We'll look like geeks."

"You'll look the same as every other boy in the school," his mother said. "But you will look like geeks if you aren't wearing uniforms. Just be glad that you don't have to wear a plaid pleated skirt and knee-high stockings. You can imagine how thrilled Katie is about that." William and Morgan both smiled.

"Okay, I'm leaving now," their mother said, picking up the basket. "I want you both to try on these uniforms today."

"No," the boys moaned.

"You will try them on," she said firmly. "If any adjustments are needed, I will have to do them before the first day of school. So, I'll be back this afternoon." Their mother stopped in the doorway. "When I come back, I expect to see this place looking a little tidier. There are books all over the floor and dishes that must be taken downstairs."

"What's with Mom?" William said after she had gone.

"She seems stressed," Morgan replied. "I

guess we'll have to humour her by trying on the uniforms later. I'm going to tidy up a bit. Why are there books all over the floor?"

"You threw them there last night," William said.

"I did not," Morgan argued.

"Yeah, you did. It happened while you were acting like a zombie. Don't you remember that?" William asked.

"I know that I was thrown out of bed, and I clearly remember the pounding in my head," Morgan said. "The next thing I can recall is bright light filling the room. I'm guessing that's when you turned on the lamp."

"You were acting really weird before you found the box," William informed him. "That reminds me, where are the crystals?"

"I put everything in my desk drawer," Morgan replied.

"Good thing or Mom might have seen them when she was in the bedroom," William said. "I'm going to call down for some food now, and then we can go over everything from last night to see if we can figure out what we have to do with the crystals."

"Good idea," Morgan agreed. "And while we're waiting for breakfast, I'll put the books back on the shelf."

After the boys had eaten, they studied the crystals and the note for some time, but they were no closer to solving its mysteries than they had been the night before.

"This is so stupid," William said impatiently. "What's the point of leading us to the crystals if we can't figure out what we're supposed to do with them?"

"I don't think we have all the pieces to the puzzle yet," Morgan said. "Maybe we just have to wait until we're given the next clue."

"Oh no, I can't handle another night with you turning into Zeke the Zombie."

"You can't handle it!" Morgan exclaimed. "I'm the victim here."

"And, I'm the sane one trying to figure out what you're doing," William said.

"If it happens tonight, I hope you get to be the zombie," Morgan said. "I'd be happy to be the observer for once."

"This isn't getting us anywhere," William commented. "Let's look at the box again. Maybe it has a secret compartment."

The boys went over every inch of the box, but were unable to find any part that would spring open and reveal something that could solve the mystery. Frustrated, William got up, and clomped out to the sitting room.

Morgan decided to search the Internet for information about crystals. He managed to find a few interesting things on a site called, Crystals of Atlantis. He read aloud: "Some people believe that Atlanteans were an advanced race of people that may have used crystals for healing, rejuvenation, dematerialization, storing information, transmitting matter, and communication. Crystals may have been stored in generators and used as a power source."

While this was all very interesting, it didn't help Morgan understand possible uses for the crystals in the box in his desk. He searched further, and finally found something that grabbed his attention. "Will, come and see this," he yelled to his brother.

"Whatever it is, bring it out here," William replied. "I'm sick of these crutches."

"I can't, it's on the Internet," Morgan said. "I found something about crystals."

"This better be good," William growled, as he shuffled into the bedroom.

"Look at this picture," Morgan said, excitedly. "These crystals look just like ours."

"Some people think that crystals were used in Atlantis thousands of years ago. Listen to this. 'Seed crystals are still being found today. Some believe that there may be a frequency between crystals and people that draws them to each other over space and time. These seed crystals are small, perfectly balanced prisms of four to six inches in length, with centre diameters of one inch. They contain colourful frequencies from clear to pale amethyst. They are powerful, and transmute high energies."

"What does all of that have to do with us?" William asked.

"Well, I think that it's pretty interesting that the size and shape of our crystals seems to be very similar to the description of the Atlantean ones," Morgan replied.

"We need callipers," William said, suddenly.

"What for?" his brother asked.

"To measure these crystals, so we can see if they really are the same size."

"That's a great idea!" Morgan agreed. "But where will we find callipers?"

"I think I have some in that kit I got last Christmas," William said.

"Kit?" Morgan repeated.

"Remember, Grammy Nan sent me that rock tumbling kit when she thought I was interested in becoming a geologist."

"Oh, right." Morgan remembered. "Did you bring it to England?"

"I'm sure I did," William said. "I think it's in

a box with my CDs and computer games." He got off the chair and crawled over to his desk and began to rummage around in a box. "I found them," he said triumphantly, crawling back to his brother.

"Why are you crawling around on the floor?" Morgan asked.

"So I don't have to use the crutches," he replied, dragging himself onto the chair.

"These are exactly what we need!" Morgan exclaimed when he saw the callipers.

William carefully adjusted the small measuring tool. Each of the three crystals was within four to six inches in length and one inch in diameter. He set the crystals down, and smiled at his brother. "They're all the same size as the Atlantean crystals."

"No way!" Morgan cried. He studied each one with renewed interest.

"That doesn't mean that any of this Atlantis stuff is real," William reminded him.

"I know that, but it does mean that our crystals are perfect and probably have some very special purpose," Morgan said thoughtfully.

"I want to know how we find out what that purpose is," William said.

"I guess we have to find more clues," Morgan suggested.

"Where else can we look?" William asked. "We've searched the green book, checked the library shelves, and gone over every inch of this box. Where else can we look?"

"Maybe I missed something in the secret compartment last night," Morgan said, excitedly. He was all set to climb the ladder immediately and search for more clues.

At that moment, the telephone rang. Morgan picked it up. Within a few seconds, he hung up, without having said anything.

"Was it a wrong number?" William asked.

"No, it was Mom," Morgan muttered. "She said she'll be up here at four o'clock for our fitting. She wants us to be wearing our uniforms when she arrives."

"Oh, great," William complained. "Well, I'm not putting on any uniform, so she can just get over it."

"I think you'd better get over it. If you don't put the uniform on, you know she'll put it on for you," Morgan warned him.

"That's not going to happen," William said defiantly. He stood up and adjusted the crutches. "We've got two hours before your inspection, so let's check the bookshelf again." He clomped out of the bedroom.

Morgan placed the crystals in the box and hid

it in the desk, before joining his brother.

"Can you remember where the opening is?" William asked.

"Of course I can," Morgan replied. "I wasn't that clueless last night."

"Just checking," William chuckled. "So, get up there. I'll hold the ladder."

Morgan pushed the ladder halfway down the row and climbed to the top shelf. He carefully removed several books and laid them on the shelf below. He felt along the wooden wall, pushing gently, until he heard a small click. Part of the wall opened and the tiny cupboard was revealed.

"I found it!" he exclaimed, as he stuck his hand in.

"Is there anything in there?" William asked.

"I haven't found anything yet, but it's a lot bigger than I remember," Morgan said. "Do you think you can get me a flashlight?"

"All right, but it will take me a while," William replied. "Will you be okay up there?"

"Yes," Morgan assured him. "I'll keep looking. The opening goes back pretty far."

William returned with a flashlight and handed it to his brother.

Morgan turned it on and shone the light into the dark cavity. "It goes all the way back to the end of this row," he said. Standing on tiptoe,

Morgan pressed his head against the wall to get a clearer view inside the secret compartment. Finally, the light shone on a bulky lump about halfway down. Stretching his arm as far as he could, Morgan was unable to reach the mysterious mass.

"There's something in here," he cried excitedly. "But, I can't quite reach it. I need something to pull it closer."

"Would a ruler be long enough?" William asked.

"That should work," Morgan replied. "There's one in that desk beside you."

After digging around with the ruler, and using it to bring the mass within his reach, Morgan was finally able to get hold of the object. "Yes!" he cried, withdrawing his arm.

"What is it?" William asked.

"Another little book," Morgan answered.

"Throw it down," William said.

"No, I'll bring it down," Morgan said. "It looks quite fragile."

"Just give it to me,"

"No, I'm not going to throw it down," Morgan insisted. "I'm going to look in the compartment one more time, to be sure that I didn't miss anything. Then I'll put the books back and come down." William hobbled angrily over to the sitting area and turned on the television.

"Okay, here's what I found," Morgan said when he'd finished.

"Are you sure you want to share it, Greedy Guts?" William growled.

"Don't be mean," Morgan said. "I have to take all the chances because you hurt your ankle. I should at least get the first look at what I find."

"Take all the chances?" William snorted. "Ooh I forgot, climbing a ladder is so dangerous."

"You can be sarcastic and irascible if you want..."

"I'll show you irascible," William shouted. He threw one of his crutches at Morgan.

Morgan picked it up and leaned it against the television. "If you are finished being hostile, and promise to be more appreciative and civil, then we may peruse the book together," he said pleasantly. He knew exactly how to push his brother's buttons.

"Stop talking like a nerd!" William snarled.

"Do you want to see this book before Mom comes or not?" Morgan asked.

"Yes," William admitted gruffly. "Now, get over here."

Morgan sat next to his brother so they could both look at the little black book. They discovered it was another diary of sorts, written by John Adney. Fortunately, the script was much easier to read than Farold Tyme's had been. The first entry was dated 1857 and began with the same quote that was on the paper in the little box.

Omnis annus centum
Two shall go as one
Across time and distance
So the Mighty One may sleep
Gregor and John Adney went on their journey in 1857
and are grateful to have survived.

Morgan flipped through the rest of the pages. They were all blank.

"Great!" William grumbled. Are we ever going to find something useful?"

"Should I go back up the ladder?" Morgan offered.

"There's no point," William said. "It's almost four o'clock. Mom will be pounding on the door at any minute."

"We better get into our school uniforms," Morgan said. He gave William his other crutch and together, they went to the bedroom. Morgan put the small book in the desk drawer with the crystals, and then he changed his clothes. He smiled when he looked up and saw that William had also put on his uniform.

The boys were in the sitting room, ready and waiting. At exactly four o'clock, there was a knock at the door. Their mother walked in with a rather sheepish grin on her face. Following closely behind her was Janey Burrows.

*****

Asa spent several days struggling to keep Durkin alive. The small man suffered raging fevers and delirium. The stab wound to his chest was not healing, and his burned feet continued to crack and become infected. Several times, the dwarf had stopped breathing and the healer had to resuscitate him.

After five days of constant vigilance, Durkin was finally resting comfortably. Leaving his patient in the care of Camilia, Asa allowed himself some time to sleep. When he awoke several hours later, he went to check on Durkin. Camilia quietly informed him that a note had come from the king. Asa angrily snatched the paper from its envelope. The king's orders would surely endanger Durkin's life again.

Durkin the Messenger
Is hereby ordered to attend a meeting
In the royal chambers
Tomorrow at midday.
Signed: King Ulric of Greywood

Asa was furious. It seemed that the king was determined to kill Durkin. As soon as the healer dared to hope that his friend might recover, unreasonable demands from the king threatened his life again. Asa hastily scribbled a reply.

Durkin unable to attend
Due to grave condition of health
Please advise
Your humble servant, Asa

Camilia ran off to deliver the note. The healer sat at the table with his head in his hands, dreading the king's reply. Ulric wouldn't hesitate to risk Durkin's life again. And he would most likely threaten his life as well.

CHAPTER ELEVEN

Janey, what…" Before Morgan could say another word, Janey began to talk.

"Hello twins, you look smashing!" she said with an appreciative smile. "I expect I'm the last person you thought you'd see today. I'm here to tell you, in person, about a party that is happening at the weekend."

"We aren't interested," William grumbled.

But there was no stopping Janey once she got started talking. "As you know, my parents run the recreation centre. What you don't know is that every September, we have a party on the last Saturday before school starts. Everyone that goes to Wadebridge School will be there, so I thought it would be a great chance for you to meet some of our batch and your mother agrees with me. Right, Mrs. Hanford?"

Their mother didn't get a chance to respond, because Janey had more, much more to say.

"So the party will be on Saturday night. Night isn't exactly correct, since we start in the afternoon with games, and then we have food and music when it gets dark. Your friends Tag and Jack will be there, and I know you'll fit in well with the rest of us. So that's pretty much the top and bottom of it."

"What kind of games?" Morgan asked.

"Football and cricket, out on the pitch," Janey said. "Inside, there will be chess, darts, and snooker. We'll have a good lot of food and music too. The parents bring food and leave it with my friend, Liz. She takes care of setting up all the food. Mark's parents own Pizza Takeaway, and they donate enough pizza to last the night. All the parents go home after the games. Then we dance or listen to the music of my brother, Russell, and his band. I'm sure Katie will be surprised when she hears how good they are." Janey paused for a breath.

Morgan took the opportunity to ask another question. "How long does the party last?"

"Until everyone has gone home," she giggled.

"I won't be there," William said. "I can't

play any games with this ankle."

"Suit yourself," Janey sniffed. "But you can still eat. Plus, you wouldn't be the only one that watches. I think you'd both have a great time."

"It does sound like it might be fun," Morgan said tentatively, looking at William.

"Go if you want," William said. "I'm staying here."

Janey's eyes focused on Morgan, waiting for his response.

"It isn't necessary to decide right this minute," their mother said. "Janey just came up to extend the invitation." She turned to Janey. "Thanks for coming, dear. I think the boys need some time to think it over."

"Of course," Janey said. "We'd be delighted to see you both on Saturday."

"Can you find your own way out?" the twins' mother asked. "I have to make uniform adjustments so the boys will be ready for school on Tuesday."

"Yes, thanks ever so much, Mrs. Hanford," Janey replied. Her red curls bounced off her shoulders as she sailed out of the room.

"Why did you invite her up here?" William asked angrily.

"I didn't exactly invite her," his mom explained. "She came to the door when I was on my way up the stairs. She flew in like a whirlwind, insisting that she had a very important matter to discuss with you boys. Before I knew it, she was following me, talking a mile a minute, and thanking me for inviting her in."

"She's really something," Morgan said, smiling. "I've never met anyone who talks as much as she does. It's really quite amazing."

"Amazing?" William retorted. "More like, annoying."

"That too," Morgan agreed. "But the party does sound like fun."

"I think it would be a great opportunity for you boys to meet some of the kids that you'll be going to school with next week," Mom said.

"Yeah right," William muttered.

"I see one advantage," Morgan stated. "The more kids we get to know, the less time we'll have to spend with Janey Burrows."

"True, but I don't want to be hobbling around on these crutches all night. I'll be bored stiff," William said.

"Let me see what I can do about that," said their father. He stood in the doorway, arms folded, with a big grin on his face. "I saw young Janey leave, and I had to come up to see what chaos she had created this time. She always manages to get you boys in a tizzy," he said.

"No she doesn't," William protested. "Were you about to tell me that I might be able to ditch these crutches by the weekend?"

"Possibly," his dad replied. "If the swelling has gone down, you can start to put weight on your ankle."

"Let me get a look at his uniform before you start your examination," Mom said. It seemed to fit perfectly, so she sent William to change. His father followed him to the bedroom to check his ankle.

Morgan's pant legs were a bit long and the button at the waist needed to be moved. His mother marked the changes with dressmaker's chalk. "Are you going to attend the party?" she asked as she measured the trouser length.

"Maybe," he replied. "I'll go if Will agrees to go with me."

"I think you can talk him into it," she whispered. "It would be more fun than sitting around watching television." She stood back, looking at the pinned-up leg length. "With a few minor adjustments, they should fit perfectly," she said. "You may go and change, but bring the pants back to me."

When Morgan got to the bedroom; their father was supporting William as he tried to put weight on his injured ankle.

"Does that hurt?" Dad asked.

"A bit," William admitted. "But I think I can walk on it."

"That's good. It healed much faster than I thought possible. I'll put the splint back on, and tighten it so that you'll have more support when you walk."

"Won't he need the crutches anymore?" Morgan asked.

"He'll need them when his ankle gets sore or starts to swell, but otherwise..."

"I won't need them," William insisted. "Look, I can walk just fine." Morgan watched his brother limp across the room, gaining confidence with each step.

"Good job," Dad said. "I'll leave the crutches here for a few days. Take your time, but walk on it as much as you can. Elevate your leg every few hours and put ice on it. Morgan, I'd like you to keep an eye on him. I have to go to a meeting tonight, but if William needs anything, you tell your mother and she'll call me."

"William, that's great news," Mom said, as she walked into the bedroom.

"Best news I've had today," he said happily. "It feels good to be off those crutches."

"I'm going to leave too," his mother said.

"Do you boys want to come down and have dinner with us?"

"No, I don't think I'm ready to walk that far," William said. "Maybe tomorrow…"

"That will be fine," Dad said. "I trust you'll take it easy until I return in the morning."

"I'll be careful," William promised. "I don't want to have to use the crutches again."

After their parents had gone, William practiced walking back and forth across the sitting room until his ankle began to throb. "I'll never get over this pain and walk normal," he grumbled. He limped over to his chair and elevated his leg.

"You can't expect your ankle to be back to normal the first time you put weight on it," Morgan said. "I'll get some ice for you. That reminds me, it would bc great to have a flat of Coke in our little fridge. I'm getting tired of juice and milk."

"I keep forgetting about that fridge. A Coke would taste a lot better than that special juice that Jally is always bringing me. I think she spikes it with drugs. I always feel sleepy after I drink it," William complained.

"I doubt that it's spiked with drugs," Morgan said. "But she might add some herbal concoction that has helped you to heal so quickly. Dad seemed pretty surprised that you could already put weight on your ankle."

"I guess I'll rest my ankle, and watch TV until supper arrives," William said.

"I think I'll study the objects we found in the secret compartment again. Maybe I've overlooked some tangible sliver of information that could possibly lead us to a greater understanding of their purpose." Morgan shot a warning glance at his brother, knowing that he was about to make fun of his choice of words again.

"Where's that ice you promised me, professor?" William asked, smiling innocently.

Morgan put several ice cubes into a plastic bag and tied it up. He threw the bag at William on his way to the bedroom.

Morgan took the box out of his desk and carefully laid the three crystals on the black cloth. Beside them, he placed the note written by one of the twins that had built Adney House. He reached into the desk drawer again and withdrew their most recent treasure, the small black diary that was written by John Adney, one hundred years after Wrighton's note. He read the odd quote over and over, trying to grasp the hidden meaning within the words. Suddenly, he jumped up and ran to the library, and took a Latin dictionary off the shelf.

"What's going on?" William asked when he saw his brother racing across the room.

"Nothing," Morgan said, as he dashed back to the bedroom.

"Whatever," William mumbled.

Morgan flipped through the dictionary; mumbling, and scribbling on scraps of paper, as he tried to decipher the first line of the quotes in the two notes. Finally, he had it figured out. Then he read the second line over and over.

"I have an idea," he said aloud. Once again, he jumped up and ran to the library. He located Farold Tyme's green book and quickly found the parts he had previously read. He read the words aloud, on the way back to his desk.

"Tell me what you're doing," William demanded.

"Hang on," Morgan said, as he walked by.

Within a few minutes, he was standing beside his brother, clutching the green book, the black diary, and a scrap of paper. A huge grin spread across his face. "I've figured out the first two lines of the message in the notes we found," he said proudly.

He had William's full attention, so he sat down and began to explain.

"The note in the crystal box and the one in

the black diary from John Adney are the same. Let me go over each line. 'Omnis annus centum' is Latin for 'once every hundred years'. I think the next line, 'Two shall go as one' has something to do with being identical twins."

"How did you come up with that?" William asked dubiously.

"I figured out that many of our twin ancestors seem to have gone on the same journey. In 1657 Farold Tyme wrote about a strange journey that his identical twin brothers had taken. A hundred years later, Wrighton Adney, who also had an identical twin brother, mentions it again. Then, in 1857, another identical twin, John Adney writes the same entry in his diary," Morgan replied. "So, I'm guessing that you and I might be the next ones in line to go on the journey."

"Hold on," said the practical William. "That would be one hundred and fifty years later, what happened to 1957?"

"I thought I had this all figured out," Morgan began. "Let me get the family tree and check the chronology." He went over to the desk and got Grandie's book and turned to the relatives of the 1800s. "Here is the entry for John and Gregor, born in 1844. So if they went on their adventure in 1857, they were..."

"Thirteen," William interjected. "Let's see if all of them were around our age when they took the big trip."

Morgan found the birthdates for the Tyme twins. "Victor and Nevin Tyme were born in 1645."

William already had the green book open to Farold's illegible recollection of his brothers' journey. "According to Old Farold, they went in 1657," he read. "So, they were twelve."

"Okay. We already decided that Wrighton and Marcus were thirteen when they left," Morgan said.

"They went in 1757, and Gregor and John went in 1857, when they were also thirteen. The next twins should have gone in1957," William reminded him. "Who were they?"

"Oh yeah," Morgan said, looking at the ancestral tree. "They were Grandie's babies born in 1945. She told us that they died when they were eight."

"They would have been twelve in 1957," William said.

"So, they would have taken the journey if they had lived," Morgan said. "That's why it has been one hundred and fifty years since anyone has gone." His face paled. "That also means that it really is our turn," he said quietly. "We're supposed to go next."

"Yeah, and we're already at the one hundred and fifty year date," William said.

"We still have to figure out where and how," Morgan said. "The green book says: Though they were mere boys, what they learned from crossing the oak bridge would raise the hair on the necks of scientists and historians alike." Morgan shuddered. "That line really gives me the creeps," he said. His hand shook, as he opened the black diary.

"This quote is the same as the one in the box of crystals. The first line means 'every hundred years' and the next line is 'two shall go as one', as in identical twins." William was about to interject but Morgan held up his hand and continued. "And the third line is, 'across time and distance'."

"Give me the green book for a minute," William said. "I think a key part of Farold's writing is this line, 'what they learned from crossing the oak bridge'. That tells us something about where they went. Did you find out anything about an oak bridge?"

"Actually I forgot about that," Morgan admitted. "I've seen no evidence of an oak bridge around here, nor have I heard anyone mention one. Yet, there is something familiar about that line you just read. Wait, I remember!" he exclaimed. He went over to the library and returned quickly with *'Arthur and Merlin'*, a book he had been reading when they first arrived in England. He sat down and began searching earnestly for a passage that mentioned an oak bridge.

"Finally!" he exclaimed. "I knew it sounded familiar." He began to read. "There are several rituals that may be performed to pass into other worlds; incantations, stone circles, invisibility rituals, and other secret portals. One may enter via secret doorways, wells, stone circles, waterways, fairy grave mounds, or by crossing the oak bridge. All portals are accessed from the present-day world except the oak bridge. In that case, one enters by other means, and crosses the oak bridge just before reaching the other side."

Morgan looked up from the book. "Do you think it's possible that our ancestors travelled to another time?" he gasped.

"That would by my guess," William agreed, turning a page in the green book.

"Remember this quote from Victor and Nevin?"

'Twas a place we did not know
We know not how it came to be

That we two were propelled by tempest winds
Through cold and darkness
To a dense forest where we lay terrored and alone...

"That does sound like they might have travelled through time," Morgan agreed. "I've read about people being sucked into time portals. Their descriptions were similar."

"That also fits in with the third line of the quote about crossing time and distance," William pointed out. "What's next?"

"There's only one more line," Morgan said. "This one is the most confusing of all. 'So the Mighty One may sleep'. What do you think that could mean?"

"I guess we have to figure out who the Mighty One is," William suggested. "You've read lots of books on myths and magic. Has anyone ever been called the Mighty One?"

"I have heard that term used for gods or giants, and sometimes, formidable creatures," Morgan recalled.

"Broleus was a giant," William speculated. "Maybe we have to do something to give him some peace."

"That's a possibility," Morgan said. "It could also be some kind of creature."

"Well, it looks like we're definitely destined

to go on an amazing trip," William said.

"Don't get ahead of yourself," Morgan cautioned. "We have no way of knowing where we'd be going, how we would get there, or what our purpose would be. That doesn't exactly sound amazing. It sounds dangerous. What if we couldn't get back?" he added nervously.

"We'll obviously be able to get back, just like all of our ancestors. As for getting there and our purpose, you'll figure it out like you have everything else. I have faith in you, brother." William said with certainty.

"Thanks for the vote of confidence," Morgan said. "But, even if I can decipher all the clues, I want you to know that I have no intention of leaving the comfort and safety of this reality to go on some preposterous journey to another time, no matter how much it appeals to your sense of adventure."

"You know it will be incredibly cool," William urged. "Besides, I'll be there to protect you from the monsters."

"Very funny!" Morgan said. "Will, I want you to understand something. After the midnight piskie ceremony, I made a decision to not let you talk me into doing anything that I don't want to do, ever again."

"That's fine, but here's something that you

don't understand," William paused and looked at Morgan's chalky face. "This time, you don't have a choice."

*****

An hour later, Camilia returned, accompanied by the king's personal physician.

Asa walked over to greet the unexpected guest. "Lucian, it is a pleasure to welcome you to my humble cottage," he said.

The doctor smiled and shook his hand warmly. "Good to see you, Asa," he said. "I have orders from the king to examine the messenger."

"Of course," Asa said, leading him to Durkin's cot. "He is fighting for his life after being attacked in the forest."

"So I've been told," Lucian said. Carefully, he lifted the cover and began to examine Durkin's injuries. Gently, he cut away the bandages on his chest and feet. He listened to his heart and checked his vital signs. Looking up at Asa, the royal physician shook his head. "He has been brutally beaten. I'm surprised he is still alive. You've done well, my friend." Asa and Lucian dressed Durkin's wounds again. "His feet appear to have been burned," Lucian added. "Is that a result of the beating too?"

"No," Asa replied, looking directly into Lucian's eyes. "That was a reminder of loyalty and obedience from the king." The king's physician shook his head sympathetically.

"King Ulric has requested that I report my findings to him immediately," Lucian said. "You are to accompany me. He wishes to speak with you as well."

Asa glanced nervously at him. "I see," he said weakly. He cleared his throat, and called to Camilia. "Please, stay with Durkin. I must go with Lucian to the palace."

CHAPTER TWELVE

Morgan was shaken by William's comment. He didn't argue because he knew his brother was right. Even if he didn't want to go on the journey, there was no way he could refuse. The night creatures had ways of making him listen. Quietly, he gathered up the books and took them to the bedroom. He laid them on his desk; carefully put everything back into the drawer, and sprawled across his bed.

There was still so much he didn't understand. He thought about the dangers that he and William could encounter on such a bizarre journey. He wondered how he could master his fears and prepare himself for a journey that was completely beyond his comprehension. That thought confused and frightened him even more. He sighed and covered his face with his hands. He felt so vulnerable. Nothing made sense anymore.

He wished he could be more like William who never seemed to worry about what lay ahead. He just dealt with things as they came up. William was always willing to take risks. In fact, he seemed to live for the challenges of the unknown. As very young boys, the twins had been labelled, 'William the Adventurer,' and 'Morgan the Cautious'. He hated that! It had always made him feel that a big medallion was hanging around his neck with the words, 'Caution: Weakness of Character' engraved on it. "I'm a wimp!" he said angrily, turning his face to the wall.

"Morg, come and eat," William yelled from the other room.

Slowly, he dragged himself to a sitting position. Their dinner had arrived, but Morgan certainly didn't feel like eating.

"Morg," William shouted again. "Are you coming?"

"Yeah, I'm coming," he growled.

Morgan moved food around the plate and picked at the vegetables, but he couldn't eat anything. He kept thinking about the inevitable journey.

"Now that I can walk without the crutches, I was thinking maybe we should go to the party on Saturday," William announced.

"Go to the party?" Morgan echoed; his dark mood lifting. "I thought it would take a lot of convincing to get you to agree to go to a party that Janey Burrows was hosting."

"I plan to avoid her," William said. "I'll hang out with Jack and Tag while you keep her occupied. She's obsessed with this twin thing, but you know it's you she likes best."

"I'm not spending time with her," Morgan said firmly. "And you had better not leave me alone with her if she starts hanging around us."

"When she shows up, you'll be on your own," William teased. "She wants to be with you and there's nothing you can do about it. Just think, Katie and Russell, and you and Janey. How sweet is that?"

"You should consider a career in stand-up comedy," Morgan said mockingly.

"Seriously," William said. "Let's go to the party, but I don't want to stay very long."

"Me neither," Morgan agreed.

For the next few days, Morgan tried not to think about their pending excursion. The boys began eating their meals downstairs with the family again. The party and school were the main topics of discussions at dinner. William's ankle continued to heal quickly and he was soon able to walk for longer periods of time without his ankle swelling.

Saturday arrived without the usual rain and fog. The twins had a great time at the party. They were pleased that everyone was so friendly. Most of the kids had heard that they were living at Adney House, and they were anxious to find out all about the interesting old place. The first question everyone asked was, 'Is it haunted?' The boys insisted that it wasn't, regardless of the rumours, but it seemed like no one wanted to believe them.

Russell's band played very well and Katie was thrilled to be associated with one of the musicians. The games had been fun to watch and there was enough pizza for everyone. Janey kept bringing her friends over to meet the twins. She acted as though she had known them forever and led everyone to believe that she was their closest friend. William ignored her and Morgan spent most of the night dodging her.

On Sunday afternoon, Morgan turned again to the mysterious crystals and the diaries. But, he was unable to find any new information or clues that would answer his questions and put his mind at ease. As the days passed without any new messages from beyond, he began to hope that the journey wouldn't really take place after all. He convinced himself that a cruel trick had been played on them by their Adney ancestors. With that thought firmly in his head, Morgan was able to sleep soundly.

Tuesday morning came all too quickly. The boys dragged themselves out of bed at six o'clock and reluctantly prepared for their first day of school. Katie and the twins got a ride to Wadebridge with their father. When he dropped them off at the school, Katie ran off to find Russell, and the twins headed in the opposite direction to avoid running into his sister, Janey.

That evening at dinner, the family discussed the first day of school.

"I got lost going to every class," Katie admitted. "But everyone was friendly and willing to show me the way, so it was rather fun."

"And how was your day?" Dad asked the twins.

"Boring, just like every other first day of school," William grumbled.

"At least we're together for most of our classes," Morgan said.

"Do you know any of your classmates?" their mother asked.

"Tag is in our history class," Morgan replied.

"Janey is in three of our classes," William added. "And that's three too many."

"Oh speaking of Janey," Morgan said. "I had to sit with her at lunch, since I was abandoned by my brother when he saw her walking toward us."

"You could have walked away from her just like I did," William said.

"It was a little difficult, since she grabbed my lunch tray and took off with it," Morgan reminded him. "At least I didn't have to think of things to say. Janey did all of the talking. I ate my lunch and didn't pay much attention to what she was saying. But my ears perked up when she got to the topic of family nicknames. Here is a direct quote from the lips of Miss Janey Burrows: 'I heard that you twins called each other Wim and Mog when you were babies.'"

"What?" William said, dropping his fork. "How did she find that out?"

"I don't know for sure, but my guess is that she heard it from her brother, who in turn heard it from someone in this room," Morgan said. Katie's face turned bright red.

"So what did you say to Janey?" William asked.

"I didn't deny it, but I did offer her a little information that she didn't already have."

"Like what?" William asked.

"I told her what we called Katie when we were small. Apparently she hadn't been told that." Katie's jaw dropped.

"Ah yes, 'Kapie'. Did you tell her why we called her that?" William asked.

"Yes, I thought it only fair that I explain that we couldn't pronounce her name, and we also called her Kapie because she thought she was a girl super-hero, flying around the house wearing a red cape," Morgan replied. "Janey thought it was hilarious and couldn't wait to tell her brother."

"Morgan how could you?" Katie shouted angrily.

"No Katie, how could you?" Morgan retorted. "What you told Russell was private, and it should have stayed in our family."

"Both of you should have remembered that," their mother interjected. "Katie shouldn't have given Russell personal family information, but Morgan, you made it much worse."

"Maybe," Morgan said. "But I was able to fix it so that our pet names will never be mentioned again."

"How did you manage that?" William asked.

"I bluffed her into telling me the Burrow family nicknames," Morgan said proudly.

"But Russell didn't tell me any..." Katie

began.

"Janey didn't know that," Morgan cut in. "So, I said that our names weren't half as weird as the ones she and Russell called each other when they were small. She got all shocked and said, 'Russell told Katie about Wazoo and Puddlepants?' I said, 'No but you just did." She looked like she might die of embarrassment."

"Puddlepants," William was doubled over, laughing. Even Katie began to smile.

"That was my first reaction too," Morgan continued. "But, I could see that she was sorry she had said anything, so I made a deal with her. I promised never to mention their nicknames to any of our friends if she didn't mention ours. She agreed immediately. So that's how it was left. I'm pretty sure it will never come up again."

"I hope this whole thing will never be mentioned again," their father said.

"This is a small town and gossip travels quickly," their mother added. "William, this will never be mentioned again, is that clear?"

"Me?" William protested. "I'm not the one that's telling family secrets. It's Katie and Morgan you should be warning. I just think it's funny."

"Okay, it's over now," Dad said. "Let's finish our dinner."

That night, the boys laughed about the day's events as they crawled into bed. Since they weren't used to getting up so early, they both fell asleep quickly.

At midnight, Morgan was rudely awakened by a familiar tapping noise. Terrified, he curled into a ball, and waited. He began to hear whispering voices all around him. The tapping noise seemed to be coming from within the bedroom. Morgan tried to think beyond the noise, to figure out what was expected of him this time. He covered his head with his pillow, and begged the intruders to stop. When he could no longer bear to be alone with his fear, he called out, "William! William!"

"Morg, what's wrong?" he answered. William got up and went over to Morgan's bed. "I can hear voices," he whispered.

"Calling my name," Morgan said in a quiet, flat voice. "Saying, 'Time is drawing near'. Can you hear the tapping noise, Will?"

"Yeah, it seems to be coming from your desk," William replied. He turned on the lamp, but it cast very little light, because the room was engulfed in swirling, grey mist.

"The fog is back," Morgan stated in the expressionless voice that William referred to as the 'zombie voice'.

"Morgan, snap out of it," William demanded.

"I must do what they say," Morgan replied in a flat tone.

William shook him, trying to rouse him from his stupor. "Wake up, Morg, wake up."

Morgan pushed his brother away and climbed out of bed. Robotically, he walked over to his desk. He turned on the desk lamp. Mechanically, he opened the drawer that held the treasures from the cubby in the wall.

The tapping stopped, and John's black diary flew out of the desk and hit the floor. Morgan picked it up and began turning the pages. He paused, waiting for instructions from the whispering voices. He flipped to the middle of the book and rubbed his hand over several pages. When Morgan held the open book over the lamp, the fog lifted and there was silence in the room. He let out a shuddering sigh that signalled an end to his trance-like state.

William quietly slid off the bed and went to look at the diary pages that Morgan was studying. "A message written in invisible ink!" William exclaimed, looking over his brother's shoulder. "We never considered that old trick. What does it say?"

Morgan's hands trembled as he silently read the brownish print that had been exposed by the light. He handed the book to his brother. "I was hoping that this whole thing was some kind of cruel trick," he said grimly. "But I guess we really are expected to go on this journey."

William quickly read the message. He looked at Morgan, his eyes filled with excitement. "It says that we'll be going on a day called 'Alban Vine'. Do you know when that is?" he asked.

"Yes, I have heard of it," Morgan replied. "It's also called Fall Equinox, and I think it happens on the first day of autumn."

"How do you know that?" William asked. "Never mind, Professor, just tell me when we will leave."

Morgan picked up the calendar on his desk and looked at the fine print that showed the moon phases and special days for the month of September. "We'll be leaving on Sunday, September 23rd," he said quietly. Without another word, he turned off the two lamps and crawled into bed.

"So, you're just going to go to sleep!" William exclaimed, in utter disbelief.

"There's nothing more to discuss," Morgan mumbled from under his quilt.

"What do you mean, there's nothing more to discuss?" William argued.

"I mean, I don't want to talk about it," his brother replied calmly. "I have to get up for school in five hours, and I don't want to think about anything else."

"You are totally in denial," William snapped. In the dark, he stumbled over to his bed. He threw the covers over himself and turned to face the wall, muttering angrily.

Morgan closed his eyes, and tried to quiet his thoughts. But he couldn't stop thinking about the date; Sunday, September 23rd. Just a few weeks away! There were still so many unanswered questions. Where were they going? How would they get there? What preparations were required? And, the most important question of all; Why? Morgan knew that they would be expected to go on the journey, no matter what. He also knew that he had never been more terrified in his life.

*****

Asa waited in the receiving room while Sir Lucian reported the results of Durkin's examination to King Ulric. Before long, a page escorted Asa to the throne-room.

"My physician tells me that your dwarf is indeed 'under the weather', shall we say," the king began. "He also informs me that you have done more than expected to return him to good health."

"I have done what I could," Asa said humbly.

"Be that as it may, the visitors will soon arrive. Since the dwarf is the only one who can receive messages, he must go to the oracle."

"But, that will not be possible!" Asa exclaimed.

Suddenly, a jolt of electricity surged through the healer's body. It almost knocked him to the ground. He was barely able to maintain his balance.

"Do not argue with me," the king said coldly. "I have arranged for Sir Lucian to spend a few days at your cottage, because I cannot bring the dwarf here in his present condition. It would arouse suspicion. Therefore, Lucian will share his expertise and medications to accelerate the recovery. A message will be delivered by the dwarf

in seven days. Is that clear?"

"Yes Majesty," Asa said quietly. He knew that it was impossible for Durkin to recover that quickly, but the healer dared not risk the king's ire by speaking again. Instead, he bowed and backed respectfully out of the room, while trying to deny the incredible pain that was coursing through his body.

CHAPTER THIRTEEN

The twins groaned as their alarm clock rang harshly the next morning. They prepared for school in silence. William was still angry, which didn't bother Morgan. He still wasn't ready to discuss what had happened the previous night. They struggled through the school day, barely able to stay awake.

By three thirty, they were back in the tower and William was settled in front of the television with his ankle propped up on a pillow.

Morgan lay on his bed staring at the cracked plaster patterns in the ceiling. There was so much to think about and so little time. He fell asleep wondering how everything would come together. However, even sleep didn't relieve his stress. He drifted in and out of dreams of bizarre creatures beckoning to him from dense forests veiled in fog.

The demanding ring of the telephone woke him. He stumbled out of bed to answer it.

"Hello dear, dinner is now being served and we request your presence at our table," his mother said pleasantly.

Morgan wasn't in the mood for her lame sense of humour. "Okay Mom," he sighed. "We'll be right down." He told William about the call and they quickly changed out of their school uniforms and headed downstairs for dinner.

On the way down, Morgan said, "I'm sorry I was such a jerk last night. When I can't handle things, I have a tendency to bury my head in the sand, hoping it will just go away. I do understand that there is no choice about going on the journey."

"No, we don't have a choice," William confirmed. "And I think we'd better get it all sorted really soon because we don't have much time."

"Don't have much time for what?" Katie said, joining them on the stairs. They looked at each other, wondering how much their sister had heard.

"None of your business," William growled.

"It is if I make it my business," she teased. "Now tell me what you were talking about or I'll bring it up at dinner."

"For Pete's sake, Katie," Morgan began. "After last night's table conversation, I think we'd better…"

"Better what?" she challenged. "I'm still furious about what you told Janey, so you know that I'm going to find a way to get even. Now tell me what you have to sort out soon because you don't have much time." She folded her arms, and leaned against the banister, waiting for an explanation.

"It's no big deal," William said. "We have a science project and we're having trouble figuring out where to start."

"You worried about homework? Yeah right," she said, studying their faces carefully. "So, you aren't going to tell me the truth. Well, I'll be watching every move you make, so don't get into any trouble or try to leave the country," she said, pushing past them. The boys smiled knowingly at each other. Katie had no idea how close she had come to guessing the truth.

That evening, Morgan pulled out the diary and carefully read the message again. He decided to rewrite it into modern language to see if that would make things any clearer. When he was finished, he sat back in his chair and read the translation aloud:

"You will leave at dusk on the first day of Fall Equinox, one century from today to complete the mission of the Adney twins."

Grandie's boys were supposed to have gone on the last mission around 1956, but they had died; so now it was up to the Hanford twins to fulfill the ancient obligation. He hoped that going fifty years later wouldn't anger anyone in the other world.

"What's up?" William said looking over his shoulder.

"I just rewrote John's note," Morgan replied. He handed the paper to his brother. "Now, we have to figure out the necessary preparations for the trip. I wonder if there's a list of instructions somewhere."

"Maybe more of the diary pages were written in invisible ink," William suggested.

"Good point," Morgan agreed. He turned to the next page and held it over the lamp.

Nothing happened. He tried several pages, but not a single word appeared.

William took the diary and also tried several pages, but he wasn't able to expose any hidden words either. Then he turned back to the brownish words that Morgan had found in the middle of the book and noticed something. "There are Roman numerals at the end of his note," he said. "Maybe that means something."

"LVII is the numeral fifty-seven," Morgan replied. "I assumed that was for the year it was written – 1857."

"Could be a page number," William suggested.

"The pages aren't numbered, but let's count them, just in case you're on to something," Morgan said. He took the diary and carefully counted out the pages. He held pages fifty-six and fifty-seven over the lamp. "You were right!" he exclaimed as small brownish words began to form. He exposed the two pages to the light until no more words seemed to be forming, and then he began to read.

What to Take

- 3 clear crystals in leather pouch
- 2 precious stones each; blue sodalite and red jacinth
(Jacinth to be worn around the neck on a leather cord)
- 2 beeswax candles, flint
- grey clothing

BEWARE OF ANA CHRONISM

On the second page, Morgan found detailed instructions of preparations and procedures to follow.

Instructions for Departure

At dusk on the Eve of Alban Vine, at low tide, assemble at the Bay of Merlyn. Place twelve stones in a circle, equal to the diameter of one body length.

Walking around the outside of the circle, place the following symbols equidistant inside the circle:

North – twig of birch tree
West – two hazelnuts
South – three rowan berries
East – four oak leaves

After cleansing feet with sea water, enter the circle.

Standing side by side in the middle of the circle, make a quarter turn after reciting each line in unison.

Facing North: *Powerful Stag, Protector of the Forest*
Facing West: *Ancient Salmon, Master of the Sea*
Facing South: *Mystic Blackbird, Guardian of Sun and Fire*
Facing East: *Soaring Eagle, Messenger of the Winds*

Sitting in the centre of the circle,
both facing East, say together:

Noble Owl, Twilight Traveller
Please light our way
As we go, two as one
Across time and distance
So the Mighty One may sleep

Morgan handed the book to William and sank back into his computer chair. "This just gets spookier by the day," he said, shaking his head.

"It's going to be a lot of work to get everything ready," William said, studying the instructions. "How much time do we have?"

"We have exactly eighteen days," Morgan said, looking at the calendar.

"That's not much time," William said, closing the diary. "Do you know where to find all of this stuff?"

"No, but Mom knows a lot about plants and trees. We'll get her to help us."

"And how can we do that without raising suspicion? She'll want to know why we're suddenly interested in trees," William pointed out.

"Well, we did tell Katie that we were working on a science project. This could be part of the assignment," Morgan suggested. "Don't worry I'll convince Mom that it's for school. I'm more concerned about those unusual stones we have to take with us."

"Lucky for you, little brother, I know all about stones, and I saw a small shop in town that sells every kind you could imagine."

"Do you think we can find all of the stones and have necklaces of jacinth made in the next two weeks?" Morgan asked.

"Absolutely," William replied confidently. "Tomorrow, we'll stop at the shop on our way home from school. Once we choose the stones, I'll get the storeowner to drill holes in the jacinth and we can use leather shoelaces to make them into necklaces. Finding flint will be easy too."

"There is so much to do and so little time," Morgan complained. "I remember reading somewhere that you can't mess up one thing, not even mispronounce one word, or a chant or magic spell won't work." He went over and sat down on his bed. "It's just so unbelievably difficult. I don't think I can do this, Will."

"Sure you can," William assured him. "Between us, we can get everything ready and still have time to spare. Don't look at the big picture; just take it one step at a time. We can do it, I know we can."

"Saying that doesn't make it any less daunting," Morgan grumbled.

"Well, I just happen to have a plan, so listen up," William said. "After school tomorrow I get off the bus in the village and go to the rock store and choose our stones. You take the bus home, and talk to Mom about our science project. You go with her to find the trees and the stuff that we need from them. You take the samples to the tower. I meet you there with the stones. Voila! Two major parts of the preparations are finished."

"Sounds simple enough," Morgan conceded. "But, are you absolutely sure that you know which stones to get?"

"Of course I do! I'm already familiar with flint, and I know about sodalite because it's Canada's national stone. The store guy can help me find the jacinth," William replied.

"Okay, I'll take care of the four tree symbols," Morgan said. "And, I'll start by looking for pictures on the Internet. I've also been wondering why we have to take those specific stones with us. Does your rocks and minerals book mention superstitions or powers connected to certain stones?"

"No, but I can show you pictures of them," his brother replied. He picked up the book and quickly found coloured pictures of sodalite and jacinth.

"I wonder if it's their colour or their properties that make them crucial to our journey," Morgan said. "I can see that I'm going to have to research powers of the stones, time travel, and spells. I think I'll start with that book that told us about time portals." He jumped up, suddenly eager to explore the world of magic and superstition.

William smiled. "All you need is something to research and you go nuts every time."

After school the next day, William stayed in the village while Morgan went home to seek his mother's help.

"I'd love to go for a walk, and I know just the place to find everything you need," Mom said. "Let's go now, while the sun is shining."

As Morgan followed her down the hill to a small forest below Grandie's house, he rattled on about their imaginary science project.

"There is something I don't understand," his mother began. "If your project has to do with indigenous trees, what is William doing at the 'Gem and Jewels' shop? Aren't you both working on the same assignment?"

"Yes, we are working on the same project," Morgan replied quickly. "He's looking for information and samples of rock formations characteristic of this region."

"It seems a bit strange that he'd be at a commercial outlet that deals with stones from all over the world," Mom said doubtfully. "Why isn't he combing the moor and the caves for rocks?"

"He's planning to do that as well," Morgan said, trying to think of what he should say next. "He's probably hoping that the shopkeeper can give him some ideas about specific rock formations and where to locate them." His mother still looked confused, so he added, "Mom, we both know that Will does his assignments as quickly as possible with minimal amounts of research. So, if someone at the rock store can give him the historical and current information he needs, why not use it to his advantage?" Morgan laughed heartily, hoping to draw his mother's attention away from any more questions about their non-existent science project.

"I agree," Mom said, smiling. "If William spent as much time and energy doing his homework, as he does trying to avoid it, he'd be an honour student. Speaking of homework, let's get back to your part of the project." She walked over to a huge tree. "This, my dear, is the mighty oak," she said, patting its bark affectionately. "And you are standing next to a birch tree. Now, tell me what you need from them."

When they arrived back at the house, Morgan thanked his mother for her help and headed up the stairs. He was pleased that they had found exactly what he needed.

After dinner, the twins finally had a chance to talk. Morgan showed his brother the twigs, leaves, nuts and berries. William gave him one of the deep blue sodalite crystals. He told him that the store manager was putting holes through the jacinth and they would be ready to be picked up the next day. He pulled a pair of leather shoelaces from his pocket, and explained that they would thread the leather through the holes in the jacinth to make them into necklaces.

"The storeowner said something weird, when I told him I wanted to wear the jacinth around my neck," William said. "He asked me if I was planning a special trip, and when I said that I wasn't, he looked over his glasses at me with an odd expression on his face.

Then he asked me who was going with me on my journey."

"And how did you respond to that?" Morgan asked.

"I didn't. I just smiled and said I'd be back to pick up the stones tomorrow."

"I haven't had time to look up the superstitions of these stones," Morgan said. "But I think that I want to do that now. You've piqued my curiosity."

"Well, Professor, I'm glad I was able to peep your curiosity," William teased.

"Pique, not peep," Morgan corrected. "It means to arouse interest." He immediately began searching the Internet. "Here's something," he said excitedly. "Sodalite: Dark blue opaque crystal, often with streaks of calcite. It is usually found in lava flows. It was the gem of the goddess, Venus." He scrolled down to the powers and superstitions section. "It is used for centering, calming, courage, strength, and intellect. It is thought to eliminate fear and awaken the mind. It is a good stone to use for meditation. In ancient times, it was considered to be part of the sapphire family of gemstones, and was known as the stone of September. It is currently, the chosen gemstone of Canada."

"Told you," William reminded him.

"Here's what it says about the other stone," Morgan continued. "Jacinth (Hyacinth): Ancient name for the gemstone, Zircon. In medieval times it was used as an amulet to protect travellers against plague and injury and was used as an antidote to poison. It was known as the stone of mysticism, prophecy, visions, and idealism. Worn over the chest or in a ring, jacinth assured the wearer of success in wars and contests. It was also believed to protect the wearer from phantoms, evil spells, and trickery."

"With these two stones, plus the three clear crystals, we'll have all the protection we'll need for a successful journey through time," William announced confidently.

"Yeah, if these superstitions are based at all on actual powers," Morgan said. "I was just thinking about something else," he added, looking up from the computer screen. "If the shopkeeper knows about these ancient beliefs, no wonder he stared at you oddly."

"Maybe I should find out what he does know," William said.

"No, we don't want to arouse anyone's suspicions," Morgan replied emphatically.

The next day, the boys went into 'Gems and Jewels' to pick up the jacinth. The shop keeper was an unkempt little man with unruly reddish hair, a huge bulbous nose, and a scruffy beard. He looked surprised to see identical twins walk through the door. When he handed William the stones, he stared uncomfortably long and hard at both of them.

"These are perfect," William commented. "Thanks for doing them so quickly."

"You are most welcome," the man replied in a scratchy voice. "It's really not my business, but I'm a bit curious about why you chose jacinth stones to wear."

"I read that it brings people good luck, so I thought it would be cool to wear it," William said, casually.

"They're a lot more than good luck charms and I think you well know that lad," the shopkeeper said, eyeing him suspiciously. "You used the ancient name for zircon, which is odd to begin with. And you have chosen to wear it around your neck." He paused, his runny red eyes darting from one boy to the other. "I know the properties and powers of jacinth, and I have a feeling there is a great deal you aren't telling me. You Adney twins are always up to more than meets the eye."

"How do you know who we are?" Morgan asked nervously. The shopkeeper was making him feel very uncomfortable.

"Your name is on the receipt," he replied quickly.

"Wrong," William sneered. "Our last name is Hanford, so why don't you tell us how you really found out who we are?"

"I-I just know," the man said, busily putting the stones into a bag. "I don't want any trouble. I know that jacinth is the stone of travellers on unusual journeys, and I just wanted to warn you of possible dangers."

"You don't have to warn us about anything," William interrupted rudely. "What we do is none of your business." He stormed angrily out of the store.

Morgan stared at the strange little man as he handed him some money to pay for the work he had done. The shopkeeper leaned over the counter to give him his change.

"Be careful," he hissed. "There are some who will do anything, and I mean anything, to take what you have."

Morgan snatched the coins from his gnarly old hand. He dashed out the door and collided with his brother.

"What's wrong?" William asked when he saw the frightened look on his face.

"Let's get out of here," Morgan replied, running down the road.

William called for him to wait because his injured ankle was slowing him down.

Morgan didn't stop running until he reached the phone booth by the post office. By the time William arrived, he had already called their mother to come and pick them up.

"Tell me what happened in the rock store," William demanded.

"That shopkeeper really freaked me out," Morgan admitted. He told William exactly what the man had said.

"Don't get all paranoid. He's just an old busybody trying to scare us. He doesn't know anything about us, or what we're doing," William assured him.

Morgan took several deep breaths, trying to shake off the nervous churning in his belly. He managed to appear reasonably calm by the time their mother arrived. William tucked the stones into his backpack, so there would be no inquiries about their purchase.

On the way up the hill to Adney House, Mom asked them about school and what they were doing in the village. William muttered something about the rock store.

"Just as I was leaving the house, I had the oddest phone call," she said.

"Who was it?" William asked.

"It was a man from the 'Gems and Jewels' shop. He told me that you boys had been looking at some stones, and he wanted me to let you know that he has an interesting crystal that he forgot to show you. He'd like you to stop in and see it tomorrow." She gave each boy a questioning glance.

*****

Back at his cottage, Asa was relieved to find that the damage from the king's warning jolt had been minimal. Two angry blisters on his right foot and an open wound on the back of his neck seemed to be the extent of his injuries. He muttered bitterly as he dressed his wounds. King Ulric was a fool. He used cruelty to control everyone in Greywood. If only he'd try collaboration rather than coercion, the king would have the same respect that the people had shown his father.

Asa winced as he took his first steps toward Durkin's cot. Camilia kept her eyes on Durkin, bathing his forehead with damp cloths. Asa looked at her inquiringly.

"He is with fever again," she replied softly, stepping aside so the healer could examine him.

Suddenly, there was a knock at the door. Sir Lucian stood in the doorway; a bag in each hand and a bedroll under one arm.

"Come in Lucian," Asa said. "You are always welcome here. 'Tis good to see you again. Please, choose a cot and put your supplies wherever you can find space."

Lucian noticed Asa's injured foot, but he politely chose not to ask about it.

The two men walked over to Durkin's cot. Camilia looked surprised to see that the king's physician was planning to stay with them.

"Sir Lucian has come to help with Durkin's recovery," Asa explained to her.

"I shall be your assistant, Asa," Lucian said humbly. "I have the utmost respect for your healing methods. Durkin would not even be alive, were it not for your skill and dedication."

CHAPTER FOURTEEN

"I don't care what that old man said to Mom," Morgan said pacing back and forth in the tower. "I'm not going back to the store. Not tomorrow! Not ever!"

"He really got to you didn't he?" William said, amused.

"You think this is funny?" Morgan spluttered furiously. "Listen; there is something seriously creepy about that shopkeeper. Why do you suppose he called here?"

"I guess he wants us to go back to the store to see a special crystal," William replied.

"No, that isn't it at all," said his brother. "There is no special crystal. That insidious little man is just trying to lure us there to...to..."

"To what?" William asked. "You are

seriously freaked out by him aren't you?"

"Yeah, I admit that," Morgan said. "And you should be too. There is something ominous about him and his little rock shop. Promise me you won't go there again."

"Why? I'm not scared of him," William bragged.

"Please don't go there," Morgan begged. "That guy's motives are evil. I've had some creepy experiences lately, so trust me when I say that he is not what he seems."

"Okay! I won't go there," William assured him. "But I think you're..."

"You think I'm losing it? Going crazy? Well I don't care what you think, because what I'm feeling is very real," Morgan said. "Besides, we don't want to jeopardize our journey by getting caught up in something with that old..."

"Hey, I said I wouldn't go there, so let's drop it," William said impatiently. "We have a lot more important things to talk about anyway. We've got the stones and the tree samples for the trip, so what's next?"

Morgan was quite willing to change the subject. "I'll get John's diary," Morgan said. He went to the bedroom and returned quickly with the small, black book. "Here's the list," he said, turning to the wrinkled brown pages. "We have three crystals, the sodalite, the jacinth, the leather cord, and the flint. We still need beeswax candles."

"I'm pretty sure regular candles will do," William said.

"No, they won't," Morgan replied. "I looked up the meaning of the warning at the bottom of the list. Ana chronism, or anachronism, means out of harmony with a time period. We can't take anything that doesn't fit with the time and place we'll be going to visit. So if it says beeswax candles, then that's what we have to take. Katie has about fifty candles in her room. She'll know which ones are made of beeswax."

"We aren't going to ask Katie about candles or anything else," William argued. "She's already suspicious of us."

"Then where do you suggest that we'll find them?" Morgan asked.

"We'll buy some in town tomorrow," William said.

"I guess that's a better idea than involving Katie," Morgan agreed. "We'll also need to put all of these supplies in some kind of leather bags."

"Why leather?" William asked. "I'll just take my backpack."

"No anachronisms," Morgan reminded him.

"We can't take flashlights, pocket knives, synthetic fabrics, plastic, or anything else from our world."

"You can take care of the ach-rom...anchor-ims, or whatever they're called, and I'll take care of the candles," William offered.

"Okay," Morgan said, smiling to himself. His brother had always been a man of action, rather than a man of words. "The last thing on the list is grey clothing."

"We have those old grey jogging suits," William reminded him. "And I think we should wear shoes to get down to the bay. We can hide them before we wash our feet."

"Right," Morgan said. "And since we have to leave at dusk, we won't be able to clamour around looking for stones, so I think we should go down to the bay ahead of time and pick out the stones for the circle."

The next few days were spent making the final preparations for their journey. Morgan had found two leather shoulder bags in an old trunk in the storage room, and William had purchased two blue beeswax candles. On Saturday, they had gone to the bay and stacked twelve stones behind a large rock near the shore. They had also found their jogging suits and some old shoes that they could leave at the beach. The boys were ready to go!

When Sunday, September 23rd arrived, William was so excited that he could hardly contain himself. Morgan was so nervous that he could barely function. During breakfast, their mother looked at Morgan's pale, tense face and asked him if he was feeling well.

"I'm fine," Morgan assured her. "I just didn't sleep very well last night."

"I think you just need some fresh air," William suggested.

"Thanks doctor," Morgan said in a sarcastic tone.

Throughout the day, the boys remained in the tower, packing and going over their supply list. They had practiced the circle chant so many times that Morgan knew they couldn't possibly make any mistakes. He gathered his tree samples together and put them carefully into John's diary for safekeeping. He had decided to take the diary with him, just in case they needed some of the information for their return journey. Farold's old journal was returned to the bookshelf. Anything else relating to the trip was safely tucked away in the back of Morgan's desk drawer. He had erased all of the research information from his computer.

William wanted to eat dinner in the tower so

they'd be ready to leave at the first sign of dusk. He rang down to get a tray delivered to their room, but their mother called back a few minutes later, and said that they were not permitted to miss Sunday Family Dinner.

Neither of the boys ate much, which seemed to worry their mother. "You boys don't look well," she said. "William, is your ankle bothering you?"

"Mom, I'm fine," he protested.

"I think you both should do your homework, and get to bed early," she said. "You might be coming down with that flu that's going around."

"We're fine!" Morgan said. "Maybe we just need some fresh air like William suggested this morning."

"Yeah, we could hike around the cliffs for awhile before we do our homework," William said. "If we clear our heads, we'll be able to think better."

Their mother objected at first, but the boys soon persuaded her to let them go. She told them to be back in an hour. The twins thanked her and rushed upstairs to change.

As dusk began to fall, the boys walked leisurely toward the cliffs wearing their grey jogging suits and old canvas shoes. They didn't want to arouse suspicion, but it was all they could do not to dash madly down the hill to Merlin's Cave.

They set up the stone circle exactly as described in the notebook. William had brought his compass, so he gave orders while Morgan placed the tree samples at the north, south, east and west locations.

Morgan suggested that they check each other's bags to be sure that they hadn't forgotten anything and, in William's case, to be sure that there were no anachronisms. In addition to the compass, Morgan found a pocket knife and a watch in his brother's bag.

"I told you not to bring anything that wasn't on the list," he complained. "Now you'll have to hide all of these things somewhere until we get back."

"I'm not leaving them here for someone to steal," William barked. "Besides these are things we'll need, so I'm taking them."

"They have painted plastic parts, and this is a holographic watch," Morgan argued.

"Put them in your shoe, and let's get on with this trip before it gets dark."

William grumbled as he took off his shoes. Out of the corner of his eye, Morgan saw him stuff the three items into the toes of his shoes, before shoving them into a crevice.

They washed their feet with sea water, entered the stone circle, and stood side by side facing north. As William said the first line, Morgan began to tremble.

"Morg, it's okay," his brother said. "I'm right here beside you. You know that we have to do this. Now let's say the chant together."

After taking a deep breath, Morgan nodded, and together they said, "Powerful Stag, Protector of the Forest." The boys said the other three lines as they faced west, south, and east.

Once they were seated side by side, in the centre of the circle, Morgan glanced anxiously at his brother. He could feel William's courage and support reaching out to him. He smiled weakly and grasped William's hand. Together, they recited the rest of the chant they had practiced so many times.

Immediately after they had spoken the last word, a violent wind ripped them from the stone circle and tossed them into the air. Morgan heard a rebel whoop of victory from his brother as they began to hurtle through space. Then, the ear splitting noise of the roaring wind drowned out all other sounds. Somewhere in the back of his mind, Morgan told himself that this must be what it would be like to be caught in a tornado.

The boys were propelled headlong into a

terrifying vortex completely devoid of light.

They pitched aimlessly through a black tunnel. Morgan felt as if his body was being ripped apart by the powerful force that was driving him forward. He clung tightly to the leather bag with one hand and to the stone around his neck with the other. At some point, he thought he felt William grabbing at his shirt, as they slammed into one another on their vicious voyage.

Gradually, the blackness turned to grey and Morgan thought he could see light in the distance. Before long, he was wrenched from the wind tunnel and deposited face down, on solid ground. He was amazed to discover that he was alive and his body was intact. Beneath him, he could see real dirt and moss. When he turned over, he saw sunlight dancing on the leaves of the tallest trees that he had ever seen. "What wondrous land have we just tumbled into?" he asked aloud. He turned his head, expecting to see William lying beside him, but he wasn't there.

Morgan sat up quickly and his world began to spin again. He put his head between his knees, waiting for the wind to take him away. Nothing happened! He opened his eyes and saw that he was still sitting in the same spot in the forest.

Then, Morgan realized that the spinning sensation had been a head rush from sitting up too fast.

He stood up slowly and adjusted his shoulder bag. He rotated one full circle, scanning the area, hoping to see his brother. A sick feeling came over him when he realized that William was nowhere to be seen. He tried calling him, but his voice was no more than a hoarse whisper. Morgan frantically searched the area where he had landed, looking for some sign of his brother.

All at once, Morgan spotted a brown coloured object, tangled in the leaves of a nearby bush. Morgan pulled it out, and was relieved to discover that it was William's leather bag. He slung it over his shoulder and looked around again, hoping to find a brother to go with the bag. Fear mounting, Morgan started walking around aimlessly. He felt completely alone in this strange, quiet place; no animals, no people, and no William.

Suddenly he heard a familiar sound – running water. He desperately wanted a drink and hoped that his brother did too. William was probably already there, lying on his belly, drinking greedily from a stream. Cutting diagonally through the trees, he soon located the stream, but William wasn't there. Dejected,

Morgan fell to his knees, wondering if he would be alone in this uninhabited limbo forever. Angry with himself for having such dismal thoughts, Morgan leaned over the stream and splashed cold water on his face. Then he scooped some into his mouth.

His thirst slaked, he stood up, cleared his throat, and shouted William's name. This time, his voice was stronger and it echoed through the forest. He waited. Nothing! Morgan wasn't sure what to do next. If he wandered too far away, he knew that he would never find his way back to the spot where he had found William's bag. So, he decided it would be best to go back to the place where he had landed.

Once back at the mossy spot, he continued to wander around, calling his brother. Morgan was getting very worried. What if William went through a different time portal? What if he was lying somewhere injured or, worse than that, what if he was dead? He shook off his morbid thoughts and sat down on the ground. Propping himself against a tree trunk, Morgan forced himself to think positive thoughts and focus on useful things. A good place to start would be to figure out how to get out of this place once he did find his brother. Taking out the old diary, he reread every word that was written on the wrinkled pages. Then he remembered something he'd read in Farold's book about crossing an oak bridge. He stood up and looked in all directions, but he couldn't see any bridges.

Suddenly he heard the sound of running feet. He quickly hid behind the tree, wondering what manner of life form might appear. The feet stopped near his hiding spot. The creature was panting heavily, like he'd run a great distance. Morgan peeked cautiously around the tree trunk.

"William!" he shouted. His twin wheeled around and grabbed him by the shoulders.

"There you are, Morg" he said. "I thought you'd landed in some other time." The boys clung together, pounding each other's backs, relieved to be together again.

"I thought the same thing about you," Morgan said. "Where were you?"

"I landed over by that clearing," he said. "I've been looking for you, and I was also looking for my bag."

"Well you found me, and I found your bag," Morgan said. "That was a horrifying trip wasn't it?"

"I thought it was pretty cool, except for the landing," said 'William the Adventurer'.

"You would," laughed Morgan. "Well, we're here now, and we seem to be okay. I'm wondering what we should do next?"

"When I was hunting for you, all I found was an old dirt path and a creek. The weird thing is, there are no people or animals anywhere," William said.

"I know," Morgan agreed. "I found the creek too. Didn't you hear me calling you?"

"I thought I heard a voice when I was running, but when I stopped to listen, I didn't hear anything. I wonder where we are."

"I've been trying to figure that out," Morgan said. "I don't think we've reached our destination though."

"And what makes you think that, Professor?" William teased.

"Remember Farold's account of his brothers' journey? He said they had to cross the Oak Bridge, and since we haven't found any bridge, I don't think we're there yet."

"I might know where the bridge is!" William exclaimed. "When I was at the creek, I walked around a bit and I think I might have seen some kind of wooden structure downstream." He paused and laughed. "Hey, I'm starting to talk like you."

"Yeah, and run like me too," Morgan said. "I noticed that your ankle doesn't seem to be bothering you."

"It's like nothing ever happened to my ankle. I don't have any pain at all," he said.

"Let's find the bridge," Morgan said. "I suddenly have this feeling that we should hurry. I don't know about you, but I don't want to be caught in some 'in-between world' because we wasted too much time."

"Okay, let's go," William agreed, leading the way.

When they got to the stream, the boys saw what did, indeed, seem to be a bridge in the distance. The path was uneven and muddy and William grumbled about not having brought their shoes. Eventually they arrived at a heavy wooden bridge. William started to go across.

"Wait, don't cross the bridge," Morgan warned. "Something's missing."

"What?" William asked impatiently.

"I'm not sure," Morgan said. "But I feel a need for caution, so let's just take it easy."

"First you say we have to hurry," William said. "Now you're saying take it easy. Make up your mind."

"For some reason, I think we have to wait here," Morgan said uncertainly.

"I've been expecting you," someone said from the other side of the bridge.

*****

The fever had finally broken and Durkin was able to sit up and drink clear broth.

"It is good to have you back, my little friend," Asa said affectionately. "The king sent Sir Lucian to help with your recovery. It seems to have worked."

"Thank you Sir," Durkin said, weakly extending his warty little hand to Lucian.

"Don't thank me," Lucian said, shaking his hand. "Asa has done all of the work."

On the seventh day, a soldier arrived with a note from King Ulric, ordering the dwarf to go immediately to the palace with a message from Tawyn.

"I won't allow you to go," Asa said firmly. "You can't possibly walk that far."

"I must go," Durkin replied. "You know I don't have a choice." Asa shook his head.

The soldier said that he had brought a horse and cart for Durkin and Lucian.

A driver took them to the woods and waited while Durkin walked the short distance to the pool. Kneeling down carefully, the messenger received the words of Tawyn. He pulled himself up and hobbled slowly back to the cart.

At the palace, Lucian helped Durkin get up

the stairs and into the king's chamber.

Ulric looked down from his throne and saw the broken, fragile little messenger before him. The king nodded and motioned for him to speak.

"Two as one cross the Oak Bridge and arrive this day at dusk," Durkin said weakly. He bowed and backed away from the throne, nearly collapsing at the door.

Lucian was waiting for him in the foyer. He picked the small messenger up in his arms and carried him to the cart. The royal physician personally drove Durkin back to the healer's cottage.

CHAPTER FIFTEEN

The twins looked across the bridge into a misty forest, but they couldn't see anyone.

"You must cross the Oak Bridge," said the person with the gentle, feminine voice.

"Where are you?" William asked boldly.

"I am there, I am here," she replied. "It is time for you to perform the entry ritual."

"What is the ritual?" Morgan asked, cautiously intrigued by the invisible girl.

"Hold your clear crystals toward the sun," she said.

Morgan rummaged around in his leather bag and pulled out two of the long, clear crystals. He handed one to William and they held them up to the sun. Two brilliant rainbows formed over the bridge and the water.

"You may advance," she said. "When you reach the middle of the bridge, one of you must toss a blue stone into the water. I trust you have brought blue stones."

"We have brought sodalite," Morgan replied, placing the crystals into their pouch.

"Then advance," she urged.

When they reached the centre of the wooden bridge, William showed his blue stone to Morgan and then dropped it into the stream. As it hit the water, a beautiful multi-coloured mist engulfed the boys and the bridge for a few moments before dissipating.

The twins continued across the bridge and stepped into the hazy forest. There, by a giant yew tree, stood the most beautiful lady they had ever seen. She was wearing a white flowing robe and her long black hair cascaded down her back. She smiled and beckoned them to follow her. The twins blindly followed, too dazed to speak.

They moved rapidly through the dank forest, and then up a very steep path on the side of a mountain. The boys were practically running to keep up with her.

After keeping up this pace for some time, William stumbled. "My ankle's killing me, Morg. And it's getting dark." He called out to the woman. "Excuse me, Miss, where are we going? Can we stop for awhile?" She didn't reply. Instead, she continued up the steep, mountainous path. Morgan tried to help his brother by supporting him as they trudged on, afraid to lose sight of their guide.

They arrived at a cave entrance and the woman finally stopped. "We are at the end of the first part of your journey. You will stay here until you have been prepared for your entry to Greywood," the woman said.

"Prepared? Greywood?" William repeated. "What are you talking about?"

"Come," she said, ignoring his questions. Their beautiful guide picked up a stick by the cave entrance. When she tapped it against the stone wall, the entranceway lit up.

Once they had light, the boys could appreciate the uniqueness of the cave. The walls were covered with shiny slabs of stone, and soft warm moss carpeted the floor. They continued along a winding passageway until she led them into a massive room with walls made of beautiful, clear crystal. The room was bathed in soft blue light that radiated from several huge balls that were hanging from a stunning, crystal ceiling.

"Wow!" William whistled. "What is this place?"

"This is the Crystal Chamber, known by few, inhabited by none," she said.

"Why are we here?" Morgan asked.

"As I said, here you will begin preparations for the rest of your journey," she replied.

William groaned, "I'm hungry and my ankle is throbbing."

Once again, she didn't respond to his grumblings. She invited them to sit on a stone bench that surrounded a large marble table, and then she left the room.

"This place is unbelievable," William said.

"It reminds me of Merlin's cave and Broleus, for some reason," Morgan said, looking around. "I keep expecting him to pop out and start talking to us."

"The blue lights," William said. "They're like the one he had on his walking stick."

"I wonder if there is a crystal chamber like this in Merlin's Cave," Morgan said.

"I doubt it," William said. "Otherwise, someone would have discovered it."

The young woman reappeared with an armful of clothing. "These are the clothes you must wear during your stay. The things you are wearing now will remain with me until it is time for you to return to your home," she said. She set the clothes down on the table and left the room again. The boys examined their new clothes. They would be wearing identical outfits; leather pants, white cotton shirts, and leather moccasins. The girl returned shortly with a tray of fruit and cheese and a pitcher of juice.

"What is your name?" William asked.

"I am called Rhiannon," she replied. "It is good to finally meet you, William."

"How did you know his name?" Morgan asked.

"We have been waiting for you," she answered. "We are quite knowledgeable in matters of your family."

"I can imagine," Morgan said. "Many generations of Adney twins have come here before us. We just don't understand why."

"This must be very confusing for you," she said sympathetically. "But it will all be made clear when the time is right. After you have eaten, I will show you where you will be sleeping. Tomorrow your training will begin, and you must be alert at all times."

"Training!" William exclaimed. "What kind of training?"

"Mental and physical training," Rhiannon replied, as she handed them fruit and glasses of nectar, which they quickly devoured without any further discussion.

"Come, I will show you to your living quarters," she said when they were finished.

"Are we staying in this cave?" Morgan asked, picking up the bundle of clothing.

"Yes, this is where you will remain until it is time for you to go to Greywood."

"Will we be here alone?" he asked anxiously, as he followed her.

"You will be very safe here," Rhiannon assured him. She stopped at each room along the stone passageway.

"This is your lavatory," she said as they peered into a room with coral basins. She handed each boy a towel and a disc of clear soap. The next stop was a pantry full of fruit, nuts, cheese and pitchers of various juices. Finally they reached a small room furnished with two wooden cots that were covered with thick down-filled quilts.

"This will be your sleeping area. If you are not warm enough, there are more blankets," she said, pointing to a recess in the wall. "The blue lights will remain on until sunup. Will that bother you?"

"No it's fine," Morgan said. "Are you staying with us?"

"No, I will return in the morning with your tutor," she said.

"But, who will stay here with..." Morgan began. But Rhiannon was no longer in the room. She had vanished into thin air. "Where did she go?" he asked.

William had been examining every nook and cranny of the room and was now settled on one of the cots. "I don't know where she went, but I get this bed," he said.

"Let's wash and put on our new clothes," Morgan suggested.

The boys showered in a warm stone waterfall and then put on the soft leather garments, which fit perfectly. They left their jogging suits and towels on a shelf, and went back to the sleeping area.

William dived under his feather quilt and promptly settled into a comfortable snore.

Morgan was exhausted too. So much had happened and there was so much to absorb.

He sighed heavily as he lay down on the other cot. He found comfort in the steady glow of the blue lights and the stars in the night sky above the crystal ceiling. Within a few minutes, he was asleep.

The twins awoke to a roomful of dancing rainbows. Rays of morning sunlight pierced the crystal dome and scattered into prisms of luminescence. The boys looked at each other and smiled as they shared the wonder of the kaleidoscopic masterpiece.

"Wow," William whistled. "What a way to start the day."

"Carpe diem," Morgan mumbled. "Hey, I just thought of something," he said turning to his brother. "I think I know what Broleus meant when he said, 'When the time comes, carpe diem'. He was talking about this journey. He knew about it and wanted to remind us to seize the day and make the most of whatever happens."

"I doubt it," William said, yawning and stretching.

"No, I'm sure he knew about it," Morgan insisted.

"Well, if he did, then I guess we should do our best to seize the day," William said. "This is the most amazing place I've ever seen. I was studying the crystal formations last night and they look flawless."

"Yeah, this is a really cool cave," Morgan agreed. "But I was just wondering how long we'll have to stay here."

"It's not like we're prisoners," William laughed. "Let's go exploring."

The boys were still dressed in their clothes from the night before, so they jumped out of bed and headed down the corridor. Remembering their precious crystals, Morgan ran back to stash the leather bags under their mattresses, and then caught up with William.

At the main entrance, they ran headlong into a clear crystal barrier across the cave's opening. Both of them bounced backward and landed on the floor.

"What the..." William said, rubbing his forehead.

"What were you saying about not being prisoners?" Morgan muttered, getting up from the mossy floor. They carefully examined the wall. The barrier was impossible to move and they couldn't find any release buttons.

"That's weird," William said. "C'mon, there must be another way out." The twins ran back along the passageway.

As they entered the crystal chamber, they were surprised to see that they had visitors. Rhiannon had returned and had brought someone with her. A very tall man stood beside her. He was wearing a loose fitting shirt, leggings and a long, hooded cloak that hung to his knees. On his feet, he had leather shoes similar to the twins' new shoes.

"Good morning," Rhiannon said. "Come and meet your tutor and guardian." The boys moved cautiously toward them.

"Sir, this is William, Noble Protector, and Morgan, Wise One of the Sea," she said.

The boys glanced at each other, surprised by the strange introduction.

"I would like you to meet Sir Osdruan, Follower of the Sacred Oak," she said to William and Morgan. "He will be staying with you until you go to Greywood."

"Welcome lads," the tall man said, holding out his hand to greet them.

Osdruan was at least seven feet tall with long grey hair that hung down his back. He had thick eyebrows and a kind, weathered face that reminded Morgan of Broleus.

"Nice to meet you, Sir," he said, shaking the man's massive hand.

"How did you get in here?" asked the ever-curious William. "The entrance to the cave is blocked off for some reason. We were just going to look for another way out."

"Well my boy, you wouldn't have found one," Osdruan chuckled. "Now tell me, have you had your morning tea?"

"Not yet," William replied. "But I want to know ..."

"Then come. Let us have tea and something to eat," Osdruan said. "All of your questions will be answered soon enough. We never discuss important matters before we've broken our fast." He smiled as he bit into a piece of apple and reached for his cup.

Morgan openly studied the tutor's worn face as he ate his breakfast. Under the hooded hairy brow, were the most startling blue eyes that he had ever seen.

When they had finished eating, Rhiannon spoke again. "I shall return at midday with your physical training instructor," she said. Then she vanished.

"Hey, she disappeared again!" Morgan exclaimed. "How does she do that?"

"Come lads, we'll clear the table and go to the instruction room," Osdruan said.

"As in classroom?" William mouthed silently to Morgan as they helped gather up the food and dishes. After taking everything to the pantry, the tall man led the boys down a passageway they hadn't seen before. They entered a small library and Osdruan directed the boys to sit at a small wooden table.

"This room is both a classroom and my favourite reading spot," he said, standing next to the table. "Let us begin now. I will start with answers to the questions you have already posed. There is only one entrance to the cave; the one that you used at the time of your arrival. The opening was closed off to protect you from intruders. Rhiannon, Magical Maiden, is exactly that. It is within her power, and hers alone, to move about the earth invisibly. She can also take others with her. That is how we get from place to place when caution is of the essence. No one will know that you are here until you can blend into Greywood inconspicuously. When you have learned our ways and acquired the necessary skills for successful completion of your mission, we will go down to Greywood."

"What exactly is our mission?" William asked.

"Do you remember the last words of your chant in the stone circle? Osdruan asked.

"Across time and distance, so the Mighty One may sleep," Morgan recited proudly.

"Well done!" Osdruan said. "Griswold, Mighty One, is an ancient dragon that has protected Greywood for centuries. Unfortunately, he is on his 'last legs,' as they say. He will die if he does not soon return to his home on Dragon's Isle, where his mate, Faida of the Folded Wings, waits for him." The astonished boys were speechless.

"Now lads, don't look so frightened," he said. "Do you know of Merlyn the Magus?"

The boys nodded mutely.

"At the time of his death, Merlyn was absorbed into the oak tree. However, as he was assimilated, his leather pouch of magic was not. It was found by a villager and taken to the dragon for safekeeping. Over the years, many have fought to possess it, especially when it became apparent that the pouch contained irreversible magic. Griswold was constantly fighting off enemies, particularly the piskies, until members of your family stepped in to help conceal the magician's bag. Do you know of the piskies?" he asked.

Again the boys nodded, waiting for the tale of dragons and wizardry to continue.

"I won't go into all of the details about how your family became involved. Suffice it to say that, without their assistance, the treasure would surely have fallen into the hands of the evil piskies. They would have ruled the world, and that most certainly would have altered the course of history. So, once every centum, identical twins from your family have come here to ensure that Griswold's caverna is secure."

"So, how can my brother and I help the dragon?" William asked, daring to interrupt.

"Your task is to release Griswold from his duties, so that he may go home."

"What about the bag of magic?" William

asked.

"Using seed crystals, you will release it from a special vault and it will be taken to Snowdonia where the enchantments of other sorcerers are kept," he replied.

"Is Snowdonia guarded by a dragon too?" Morgan asked.

"It will be now. Griswold's youngest son will transport Merlyn's bag to Snowdonia, and he will remain there as sole guardian of Merlyn's irreversible magic," Osdruan said.

"What's his name?" William asked excitedly. "Will we get to meet these dragons?"

Osdruan smiled. "His name is Egandor, Fiery Guardian, and yes, you shall have an opportunity to meet both of them."

"Cool!" William exclaimed.

"About the dragons...are they...dangerous?" Morgan asked.

"Absolutely not," Osdruan assured him. "Griswold is looking forward to your visit."

"Good," Morgan said with relief.

The tutor sat down on a chair beside the twins. "That is all we will discuss about your mission at this time," he said. "If you have an unrelated query, voice it now."

"I have another question," Morgan said. "Why does everyone here use such long introductions when meeting one other?"

"Your names define who you are," Osdruan replied. "In other words, you become who you are because of what you are named."

"So, when we're born, the names our parents give us predetermine who and what we will become?" Morgan asked, confused by such a concept.

"I doubt our parents gave it that much thought," William said. "I think they just liked the names, or maybe they named us after relatives."

"Perhaps that is the way it seems," Osdruan said. "But, you must wonder why they liked that name, or why they chose to give you the name of someone else."

"Please tell us more about our mission," William said eagerly.

Osdruan smiled. "I will tell you about some of the preparations. During your stay in the Crystal Chamber, you will learn different styles of self-defence. You will also require some elocution training. Your unusual articulation will set you apart from residents of our community." He saw looks of concern and confusion on the boys' faces. "None of this will be difficult. You will adapt quickly, with assistance from some very gifted individuals," he assured them. "When you have completed your training, you will go to Greywood and meet with our king." He took a deep breath and stood up. "That is enough information for the time being. There is something I would like to show you."

He walked over to the books. Reaching behind one of the shelves, he pressed a button and a hidden wall opened up to expose another passageway. Osdruan took a lantern from a hook inside the doorway and lit it. The boys followed him along the dimly lit corridor. Before long, they came to a steep, narrow staircase. They had climbed up thirty or forty stone stairs before Osdruan finally turned the handle of a heavy oak door. With a great deal of creaking and moaning, the door slowly opened. The boys followed him out of the dank tunnel and into the sunlight. Once their eyes had adjusted to the brightness, they found themselves standing on a huge green field that was enclosed by enormous stones. Morgan and William ran over and looked between the stones. They saw a dense fog covering all but the tallest treetops of the forest that surrounded the crystal cave.

*****

Lucian carried Durkin into Asa's cottage; his face flushed with rage. "I had a good mind to punch our dear king in the face for forcing this desperately ill man to perform such a needless task," he said angrily, as he laid Durkin on his cot. "He knew very well that the visitors were arriving tonight. Confirmation from the oracle was completely unnecessary."

The two healers began to remove Durkin's clothes and shoes. When Lucian saw fresh blood, he became even more furious. "The king will surely kill him!" he cried.

"I... will be ...fine," Durkin gasped.

"Rest now," Asa said, soothingly. He turned to Lucian, the same grim look on his own face. "I am going to bolt the door and let no one from the palace in until Durkin is well," Asa said firmly. "Even if it means I must incur the king's wrath."

"I staunchly support you," Lucian agreed. "Together, we will keep him safe until he is well enough to walk out of here on his own."

"What news is there from the palace?" Asa asked. "Have there been any suspicious movements among the piskies?"

"No, the guards said it has been very quiet since Durkin's beating," Lucian replied.

"Everyone believes the piskies were behind the attack."

"I have no doubt about that," Asa agreed. "But they have no reason to suspect that the visitors have arrived."

"If the piskies know that this is the final Adney mission, then I truly fear for the lads," Lucian said.

CHAPTER SIXTEEN

William whooped with delight when he saw the fog below. "We're above the clouds," he said excitedly. "What is this place, Sir?"

"This is the field that will be used for your physical training," Osdruan replied. "Because of the altitude, no one will see you, so you may come up here whenever you like. There will be neither people nor animals to bother you."

"Is this where our trainer will work with us this afternoon?" Morgan asked.

"Yes," Osdruan replied, looking at the sun overhead. "And it looks as though it is time to go down for our midday meal," he said ushering the boys through the door.

When they walked into the Crystal Chamber,

they saw a man sitting at the table waiting for them. Rhiannon appeared with a tray of hot steaming food.

"That sure smells good," Morgan said.

"Yeah, and I'm really hungry," William agreed.

"Come and meet your physical training instructor," Rhiannon said, setting the tray down. "He will be eating with you today."

The young man stood up to greet them. Like Osdruan, he was very tall. He was wearing leather pants and a cotton shirt, similar to the boys' new garments.

"This is William, Noble Protector, and Morgan, Wise One of the Sea," Rhiannon said to the young man. "And this is Caedel, Warrior Spirit." The boys shook hands with him.

"Good to see you again lad," Osdruan said, clapping him on the back warmly.

"We just saw the field where we'll be training," William said to Caedel.

"What kind of training will we be doing?" Morgan asked.

"Self-defence, sword fighting, archery, martial arts," William suggested.

"Slow down lads. Too many questions," Caedel said, laughing. "You shall learn whatever is deemed necessary."

"First, let us partake of the fine food that Rhiannon has set before us," Osdruan said, guiding the boys toward the table. And it was indeed a fine meal; roast leg of lamb, potatoes, vegetables and steaming cups of tea. It was the first time the boys had been given meat to eat since their arrival, and they savoured every morsel. When they were done, Osdruan stood up.

"Gentlemen, let us retire to the library where Caedel will tell you what he has in mind for you this afternoon," the giant man said. "And thank you for the fine food," he said to Rhiannon. "Will we see you later today?"

"You are most welcome," Rhiannon said. "Yes, I shall return to take Caedel back after the lessons."

When they were all settled in the library, Osdruan asked Caedel to tell the boys about the training he had planned for them.

"My pleasure Sir," the instructor said. "Well lads, I spoke at great length with your tutor before your arrival and we have agreed that you will need some specific strategies to defend yourselves, mainly against creatures that we call piskies."

"We know a bit about the piskies," Morgan said. "We've already seen some of their capabilities when we witnessed a midnight ceremony."

"Then you realize that they are not to be taken lightly," Caedel said.

"Tell us more about them, and why they are such a threat," William urged.

"Sir, perhaps you should explain the piskies," Caedel said, smiling at their tutor.

"They are a race of small people related to the faerie folk," Osdruan began. "They live in caves, rock cairns, or tunnels beneath the earth. These creatures are mischievous and unsociable. They are constantly scouting for unsuspecting wayfarers to rob or torment. They have a penchant for treasure and will go to great lengths to steal one. When the treasure is as special as the one guarded by Griswold, you can well imagine how determined they are to acquire it. Their most formidable characteristic is their shape-shifting capability. They can assume the shape of any animal or human, which makes it nearly impossible to know in what form they may appear. Therefore, Caedel and I feel that it is our obligation to ensure that you lads have the necessary skills to avoid being tricked or captured by them, regardless of the form in which they appear. Fortunately, you already have one of the best defences there is against the piskies."

"Will Rhiannon use invisibility to take us to the dragon?" William asked.

"Unfortunately, she cannot," Osdruan replied. "Because you have come from another time, she will not be able to use invisibility to transport you. However, you lads have an advantage that you are not yet aware you possess." The boys looked confused.

"Let me explain," Osdruan said. "Because you are identical twins, you will hopefully be able to befuddle them enough to escape their treachery. There is no such occurrence as identical siblings in their realm. They never look at their own images in glass or water. They believe that seeing their own reflection will bring misfortune upon them. Therefore, if they see two identical people, they will think that they are looking at a reflection and they will probably flee, lest ill luck should befall them. That was helpful to your ancestors when they visited Greywood." Osdruan paused to take a sip of tea.

"There are other ways to protect yourselves, and ways to identify them. We will discuss that as we go along. Today, Caedel will show you ways to fight them off, whether they choose to take on animal or human form."

"Will the piskies be the only danger?" William asked.

"Oh no, you may also have to deal with people and animals that are not shape-shifting piskies," Osdruan explained.

"I will do my best to prepare you for chance encounters with anyone or anything,"

Caedel assured the boys. "Are you ready for your first lesson?"

"I am," William said, eagerly. He ran to the bookshelf that opened the secret passage to the outdoor field, and then looked over at Osdruan. "May I open the door to the stairs?" The tutor nodded.

The twins raced up the stairs and burst into the warm sunshine. When Caedel arrived, he told them that Osdruan had chosen to stay below.

The boys were anxious to start their self-defence training, but Caedel had other plans. He wanted to test their strength and endurance, so he had them run around the field several times and do a variety of callisthenics. Satisfied with their levels of fitness, he then questioned them about physical activities they were involved in at home. He seemed pleased that they both were good swimmers and had some training in archery.

"You both seem fitly and therefore quite capable of mastering the first lesson. This will be your weapon of choice," he said, handing each of them an unusual sling and several stones that he had taken from his bag. "With your training in archery, I know you will quickly learn to use the sling effectively."

William's face plainly showed disgust and disappointment. "Sling!" he said, rudely throwing it to the ground. "I can't fight off enemies with some old sling."

"You will be very surprised by its accuracy," Caedel replied. William didn't seem at all convinced. "Did you expect to be training with fancy swords?"

"Anything other than slings," William muttered.

"A sling can be carried or concealed in a bag; a sword cannot," Caedel said. "A boy wandering through the woods with a sword in his hand, or at his side, would certainly arouse suspicion. A lad carrying a sling would not."

"I guess I never thought of that," William confessed, picking up the sling.

The slings were not at all like the ones the boys had used at home. These slings were made of two very long pieces of cord that were fastened to each end of a leather strap. Caedel placed a stone on the leather strap and held the two long cords together in his hand. He whirled the sling over his head and let go of one end. The stone flew out, and landed precisely in the middle of a target that had been placed a short distance from where they stood. With practice, the boys soon got the feel for the strange weapon, and many of their whirling stones began pinging against the target.

"Good work lads," Caedel said. "Now, I want both of you to go halfway down the field and wait. When I raise my hand, Morgan will take aim at the target. When I raise my hand a second time, William will take his turn." The boys quickly got into position and began taking turns. It was much more difficult to take aim at such a great distance, but before long, they could hear their stones hitting the target. When all of their stones had been used, they walked back to Caedel.

"You have done well, lads. Practice as often as possible. When you can hit the centre of the target four out of five times, you will be ready to move to the next level."

"When will we have our next lesson?" William asked.

"Very soon," Caedel replied smiling. He walked toward the door to the library. "Coming lads?" he asked.

"I think I'd better keep practicing," Morgan said. "I haven't hit the centre once."

"We'll stay up here for awhile," William added. Caedel nodded and disappeared down the stairs.

The boys continued to hurl stones at the target for several hours. Both of them were getting surprisingly accurate, which encouraged them to keep going. As the sun began to set, the boys finally put their slings down and went back to the library.

When they entered the eating area, Osdruan was already seated at the table talking to a girl with long golden hair. He smiled and signalled the boys to join them.

"So you have completed your first lesson," he said. "I trust your training went well."

"It was okay," William replied.

"I have someone special that I'd like you to meet," Osdruan said, standing to introduce the guest. The girl seemed to be about the same age as the twins.

"Gentlemen, I would like to introduce Pahlaseda, Sage of Forest Voices," Osdruan said. She extended her hand to William, who shook it briefly. Then she smiled at Morgan and his heart began to pound wildly. When she placed her tiny, perfect hand in his, he held it firmly and stared into her large green eyes.

"I am very pleased to meet you," she said in

a soft, lilting voice.

Morgan continued to hold her hand until William nudged him. "And it's a p-pleasure to meet you too," Morgan stammered. She smiled and gently pulled her hand out of his grip. "Oh sorry," he said, realizing that he had been clutching her hand much too long.

"Pahlaseda is a gifted linguist," Osdruan said. "She understands all languages she encounters, including piskie and other faerie dialects."

"Really?" Morgan said, his voice rising to an embarrassingly high squeak. His face turned bright pink, and he looked down at his plate.

"Maybe she can help Morgan with his dialect," William teased.

"And yours as well," Osdruan said quickly. "This young lady has come to alter your speech so that it will be more similar to the vernacular of Greywood."

"We will begin our lesson after tea," Pahlaseda said. "I must admit that I find your dialect most intriguing."

"Tonight? More lessons?" William groaned. "We've had one lesson after another since we arrived. I need a break."

"Time is of the essence," Osdruan said firmly.

Once the three young people were seated in

the library, Osdruan picked up a book and went to the other end of the room, allowing Pahlaseda to take charge of the lesson.

"I would like to begin by hearing you read aloud from a book I have brought, so that I may assess what it will take to modify your speech," she explained. "Who will go first?"

"I'd be happy to read first," Morgan offered gallantly. William sighed loudly, lay back in his chair, and closed his eyes. Morgan read while Pahlaseda listened intently.

"Thank you Morgan," she said after several minutes. "William it is your turn now."

He ignored her and continued to slouch down in the chair with his eyes closed.

Morgan poked him roughly and thrust the book into his lap. "It's your turn to read," he said loudly.

William glared at him angrily, and then sat up and opened the book. He read the shortest paragraph he could find, and then threw the book onto the table.

"You boys speak differently from anyone I have ever met," she said. "But I think I can help you to alter your speech. You will be talking like the rest of us in no time."

"Yeah right," William said in a surly voice. "I don't see that happening."

"It will be very interesting to see how you adjust to your new accent, William," Pahlaseda said. "I am hoping our dialect will add a more amiable and genteel quality to your voice." There was a sound of choked laughter from Osdruan's corner of the room.

William didn't respond to her comment. He just curled up in the chair, and closed his eyes. Morgan smiled at Pahlaseda and then winked at Osdruan. He loved it when his brother got put in his place.

"I must go now, Rhiannon is waiting to take me back to the village," Pahlaseda said. "I shall return in the morning and we will proceed with your linguistic transformation."

"I can't wait to get started," Morgan said, as he walked her to the door.

After she had gone, Osdruan went to sit beside William. "You know lad, it would be wise to think carefully before you speak," he said quietly. "Many people in Greywood possess special powers that you can't even imagine. You would be well advised to curb your tongue before you anger someone, and the power is used against you. I am particularly thinking of King Ulric. He does not take kindly to disrespectful comments. Trust me when I say that you definitely will not want to provoke His Majesty."

Without a word, William stormed out of the room. Osdruan sighed and shook his head. Morgan had heard Osdruan's advice to William. He had been sitting in the tutor's reading chair across the room, listening unobtrusively. He hoped that William would heed Osdruan's words of warning.

True to her word, Pahlaseda was waiting for the twins in the library the next morning. The furniture had been pushed to the sides of the room and a circle of glowing, scented candles took up most of the floor space.

"You've got to be kidding," William muttered. He folded his arms and shook his head.

Pahlaseda looked up and invited the boys to join her. Morgan immediately went into the circle. William remained standing in the doorway. "Come in William," she said, patting a spot on the floor next to her. "I promise you, this will be painless."

"Painless?" William echoed. "That's not what worries me." Reluctantly he went into the circle and sat beside Morgan.

"We will join hands," she began. "I want you to focus on the candle in front of us, and please do not speak until I say. I am going to use a special meditation technique to alter your speech patterns. It will be a temporary change. When you leave Greywood, you will speak as you did before. Are you ready?"

The boys nodded and the three of them joined hands. Immediately, Morgan experienced a warm, tingling sensation in his head. It felt strange, but not painful, and it only lasted for a few moments.

Pahlaseda released their hands and said softly, "The alteration is completed."

"You better not have damaged my brain," William muttered, rubbing his head.

"That is not possible," she said with a smile.

"Will, your voice," Morgan began. "I should say, our voices; we sound British."

"Yeah, we do," William agreed. "How did you do that?" he asked Pahlaseda.

"Meditation and the use of a special power I have been given," she replied.

William's face turned red, and he headed for the secret door behind the books. "I'm going up to the field to practice," he said to Morgan. "See you up there."

Morgan didn't want Pahlaseda to leave. He tried to think of something that might encourage her to stay longer. "Would you like to watch me attempt to hit a target with my sling?" he asked lamely.

"I regret that I cannot," she replied. "But I will see you again. When you come to the village, you will stay at the home of my cousins."

"I hope that will be soon," Morgan said shyly.

"If you work diligently on your preparatory lessons, I shall see you very soon," Pahlaseda said, taking his hand in hers for a brief moment. With a final smile, she ran quickly down the passage. Morgan watched her until she disappeared from sight, and then he went up to join his brother on the field.

The boys practiced for about an hour before Caedel arrived. He was quite impressed that they had been working so hard. After watching several stones bounce off the target, he called them over.

"Gather up your stones, you are ready for a moving target," he announced. "Be alert. If you see someone or something coming toward you, do not hesitate to take careful aim and hit it right between the eyes."

"You mean we'll have to kill real animals or people?" Morgan asked, horrified.

"It will always come down to you or the enemy," Caedel replied simply. "Get ready."

Without further discussion, the boys got into position and gazed into the distance, waiting for something to happen. Morgan's hand shook as he prepared his sling.

Suddenly, out of nowhere, a savage wolf bounded toward them. Morgan was too stunned to react. Luckily, William was ready. He swung his sling around and released the stone. The wolf fell to the ground with a whimper. Blood was oozing from its forehead. The boys looked at each other in disbelief, and started to walk over to the fallen animal.

"Do not approach the animal," Caedel warned as he ran toward them. When he caught up to them, he put his hands on Morgan's shoulders, leaned over, and looked directly into his eyes. "You cannot afford to be afraid," he said firmly. "You must not think about anything but survival. Fortunately, your brother was able to successfully take the creature down. You lads must work together. Use positioning to your advantage." He moved them closer together, back to back. "Use this position when you are not certain which direction the opponent is coming from," Caedel instructed them. "If you have him in your sights, then take up a side by side stance. Most likely, you will have time to hurl just one stone each before the enemy overpowers you."

"I don't think I can kill anything," Morgan confessed.

"Not even to save your own life?" Caedel asked.

"I-I don't think so," he stammered.

"Then do it to save your brother," Caedel said. He stood up and walked back to the end of the field.

Morgan took a deep breath and turned to face William. "I shouldn't have frozen like that. It won't happen again," he promised. "Good thing you were ready. You took that wolf down with one shot, and saved us both. Thanks."

"I was as surprised as you were when he fell to the ground," William admitted.

"Get into position," Caedel yelled from the far end of the field. The boys got ready for the next attack.

Within minutes, a soldier on horseback came galloping toward them, his sword raised.

"Oh no," Morgan whispered, as he readied his sling.

Their stones were released simultaneously, and the horse fell to the ground. The man grabbed his sword and ran toward the boys, cursing and yelling. The twins had just enough time to reload their slings. Two stones hit the man's face. The boys heard screams of anguish, as he dropped to the ground.

"We did it!" William exclaimed.

"I can't believe it," Morgan said. "We sure were lucky that we had enough time to reload when he fell off the horse."

"Yeah, that was a real bonus," his brother said.

"Well done lads," Caedel said, racing up to them. "You are now working as a fine team."

The boys laughed. They were proud of themselves and grateful to be alive. They turned around to examine their victims, but there was no sign of the wolf or the man on horseback. The field was empty; the grass not even disturbed where they had fallen. Confused, the twins looked up at Caedel.

"Where are the bodies?" Morgan asked.

"I know we hit all three of them. They landed right here," William said, checking the ground, where a few moments earlier a wolf, a horse, and a rider had lain bleeding and lifeless. "And all of them were very dead. So tell us what happened to the bodies!"

*****

Over the next few days, Asa and Lucian devoted all of their time to helping Durkin get well and their efforts paid off. Soon the dwarf was eating well and joining in their conversations. He no longer had a fever and his wounds were finally healing. Asa insisted that Durkin stay in bed, despite his objections.

One morning, there was an urgent pounding on the door. Asa reluctantly went to answer it, fearing the king's next demands. Sure enough, there was one of Ulric's soldiers standing in the doorway. He promptly handed the healer a note and left without saying a word.

"Another note from the king," he said, angrily as he closed the door. He threw the folded paper onto the table where the three friends had gathered for morning tea. It was the first time they had allowed Durkin to join them.

"Aren't you going to read the note?" Durkin asked.

"Later," Asa replied. "We will finish our tea before we bow to the king's orders."

Lucian and Durkin agreed. They picked up their cups and resumed their conversation. After the table was cleared, Asa unfolded the paper and read aloud:

By order of His Royal Highness

The King's Physician, Asa the Healer
And Durkin the Messenger
Will meet with His Majesty,
In the Royal Chambers
Today at midday

Signed: HRH, Ulric of Greywood

CHAPTER SEVENTEEN

Caedel scuffed his foot along the ground where the bodies should have been.

"So where are the bodies?" William said angrily.

It took a few moments before the instructor replied. "There are no bodies."

"I can see that," William retorted. "Where did they go?"

"There never were any bodies," Caedel confessed.

"But we hit them with our stones," Morgan argued. "We both saw them fall and we saw the blood."

"There were no bodies," he repeated. "I created them for the lesson."

"You created them?" William echoed. "Are you saying they weren't real?"

"That is exactly what I am saying," Caedel said. "They were an illusion."

"I'm confused," William said. "An illusion? What do you mean?"

"I have the ability to create such images. I used my powers to make your lesson more realistic." Caedel paused. The boys waited with puzzled expressions on their faces.

Caedel spoke again. "If I had told you ahead of time that it was an illusion, you would not have taken the attacks seriously. I had to see how you would react when faced with, what you perceived as, a life-threatening situation."

"But how did you..." Morgan began.

"Don't bother asking," William interjected angrily. "I'm done with all of this. We should never have come here in the first place."

"That sounds strange coming from you," Morgan said. "You're the one who couldn't wait to get here, and you forced me to come."

"Yeah, well maybe I was expecting a real adventure, not some hocus-pocus from a bunch of...of...sorcerers," William barked. He threw down his sling and disappeared through the oak door.

Morgan noted that his brother's comments

sounded even more offensive when spoken with his newly acquired British accent. "I'm sorry he was rude," Morgan apologized. "My brother hates to be tricked."

"No worries lad," Caedel said. "I am sorry that your brother saw it as deception. I regret that I had to create the illusion without telling you first, but it was all part of the lesson. Do you understand?

"No, actually I don't," Morgan replied. "While I don't agree with my brother's rudeness, I do agree with his reaction. I don't understand why you felt you had to trick us into believing the attackers were real." He took a deep breath before continuing. "My brother and I did not come here by choice. We are here to honour a commitment made by our ancestors, hundreds of years ago. We need all of the self-defence training you can offer us, so that we might survive long enough to fulfill a promise they made. I think you should have understood that, and trusted us to take the training seriously." Morgan turned and walked away, leaving Caedel red-faced and speechless.

Back in their sleeping quarters, the boys went over the events of the last few days. William complained about everything that had happened since their arrival. He was ready to go home and abandon the mission all together.

"That isn't possible," Morgan reminded him. "We have no idea how to transport ourselves back. Besides, we have a commitment to help the dragon."

"Don't be stupid, Morg," William snapped. "There is no dragon. It's just another illusion to teach us some kind of lesson. None of this is real."

"The piskies are real," Morgan reminded him. "We saw them on the beach, and we know what they did to Tag. And let's not forget Broleus in the cave. He was real."

"Are you sure?" William asked.

"If none of this was real, then I seriously doubt that generation after generation of Adney twins would have taken this journey, and then secretly written about it." Morgan began pacing the floor, trying to think of something else to say that would convince his brother that this wasn't some kind of foolish trick. "There is one thing I do know for sure. Those awful things that happened to me in the tower – they were very real."

"I know that," William admitted. Angrily, he ran his hand through his hair. "I just hate all of this voodoo stuff," he continued. "They're trying to change us, Morg. We don't even talk like ourselves anymore. Of course that wouldn't bother you, since you're totally in love with the girl that put the spell on us."

"I'm not in love with anyone," Morgan said defensively. "And they aren't trying to change who we are, they're just trying to help us fit into their world so that we can complete the mission without drawing undue attention to ourselves."

"Whatever," William muttered. He lay down on his cot and turned his back to his brother. Their conversation was obviously over.

Morgan decided he should talk to Osdruan. He went to the library, knocked once, and entered. The candle circle was gone and the furniture had been moved back into place; something he hadn't noticed on his way back from the field. Osdruan was sitting near the door, reading a book.

"How was your training session?" the tutor inquired.

"Don't ask," Morgan said, sliding onto the chair next to him.

"I heard a great commotion on the stairs and a lot of shouting," Osdruan said. "Do you wish to tell me what happened?"

Morgan told him all about the illusions that Caedel had created and how that news had affected William.

"So, your brother no longer believes in the mission?" he asked.

"No. He doesn't believe any of this is real, including the dragon," Morgan said.

"Let me assure you that Griswold, The Mighty One, is very authentic," Osdruan said.

"I know that," "Morgan acknowledged. "I think William knows it too. But right now, he's angry about being tricked. If he knew how to go back to our time, my brother would be on his way home. That's how furious he is."

"Would you like me to talk to him?" Osdruan asked.

"Maybe later, after he's had some time to calm down," Morgan replied. "I just wanted to talk to you about it. Besides, I still have some questions of my own."

"Absolutely, you may ask me anything," the tutor declared.

"If so many of your people have different magical powers, why haven't the people of Greywood been able to trick the piskies and rescue the dragon?"

"Long ago, when the bag of magic was found and taken to the dragon, the piskies learned about it and tried to steal the bag many times. If it had not been for Griswold's vigilance, and his fire-breathing powers, they would have succeeded. Because they were unable to obtain the treasure, the piskies captured some of our people and held them for ransom. Negotiations went on between our king and the piskie leaders. They wanted Merlyn's magic, so they threatened to kill the prisoners. It was a difficult decision. Of course, King Cedric, an ancestor of our present king, said that the recovery of the prisoners was his primary concern, especially since one of the prisoners was his son Ragan, heir to the throne. It is true that many of our people had special powers, but they could not use them, because the piskies had threatened to kill Prince Ragan, and have his head delivered to the king on a platter if anyone used sorcery.

The elders of Greywood convinced the king that there were only two choices. They had to either get rid of the treasure, or find a way to trick the piskies into thinking that they had. Since there was no way to dispose of the bag of magic, and nowhere else to safely hide it, King Cedric chose the latter. However, finding a way to trick them into believing that Griswold no longer had the treasure was more difficult than anyone had ever imagined. All of the king's advisors worked diligently to come up with a plan.

Then one morning, two men walked into our

village. They were identical twins, passing through on a hunting trip. Our chief advisor realized immediately that they were the solution to our dilemma.

The hunters had also had problems with piskies during their travels. The piskies had stolen their food while they slept, tried to make off with their weapons, and waylaid them several times. Since the men certainly felt no fondness for them, they readily agreed to help deceive the little blighters.

The king's advisors knew that piskies never look at their own reflections, and they also knew that identical twins do not exist in the piskie realm. So, a plan was devised whereby the piskies would be completely confused by the activities of these two identical beings. And it worked. The king's men were able to save the prisoners, and the Adney twins stayed on to help make the dragon's cave a more secure place for the treasure.

When the hunters left, they promised the king that every hundred years, identical Adney twins would come to fortify the cave, thus keeping the piskies from ever acquiring Merlyn's bag."

"But how could they have known that twins would be born into our family every hundred years?" Morgan asked.

"Foresight, special powers, perhaps. I don't know, but Adney twins have continued to come every hundred years, except for this time. It has been one hundred and fifty years since the last twins came to Greywood."

"There were twins born that would have come fifty years ago," Morgan explained. "Unfortunately, they died when they were eight years old. I guess that's why my brother and I are here instead."

"We were aware of their untimely deaths. That must have been most difficult for your great-grandmother," Osdruan said.

Morgan was surprised, once again, that the people of Greywood seemed to know so much about the Adney family. But, he decided to change the subject. He still had so many questions for Osdruan about the mission to save Griswold.

"Why have boys always been sent since that first time?" Morgan asked. "William and I discovered that all of the Adney twins that have come to Greywood were only twelve or thirteen years old."

"The advisors may have suggested that young lads would not be as likely to arouse the piskies' suspicions," Osdruan suggested. "Or, the decision may have been based on an ancient belief that children possess unique strengths and capabilities that enable them to tolerate the journey more easily. However, I understand that this is to be the last mission for the Adney twins, and I believe that you two are the best lads of the lot."

"Thank you Sir," Morgan said, smiling. "When do you think we will be ready to go to Greywood to complete this final mission?"

"I will have news of that this evening," Osdruan replied. "Go now and see if your brother has been able to deal with his doubts."

"But, I still have more questions," Morgan said eagerly.

"Your insatiable curiosity is refreshing," Osdruan said, placing his hand affectionately on Morgan's shoulder. "However, I must leave for a short time. I invite you to seek answers this evening, when we meet to discuss your journey to Greywood."

"Of course," Morgan said. "William and I will see you then."

After lunch, Morgan convinced his brother to go with him to the field. They found their slings on a stone by the oak door. Morgan picked one up and went to the practice area. William leaned over the wall, looking down at the forest for a very long time.

Morgan was relieved when his brother finally picked up the other sling and joined him for target practice.

"Tell me the truth," William said. "Do you really believe there is a dragon?"

"Yes, I really believe there is a dragon," Morgan said. "Before lunch, Osdruan was telling me all about the dragon, the bag of magic, and the piskies. He said that the very first Adney twins were adults. They helped get the king's son back from the piskies."

"And you believed that?" William sneered. "It's seems funny that it was never mentioned in any of the books that we found in the tower."

"Be as skeptical as you like, but I believe Osdruan," Morgan said. "You can ask him about it at the meeting tonight."

"Why are we having another meeting?" William asked.

"He wants to tell us about our trip to Greywood," Morgan stated. "I think we might be going soon. Osdruan said we could ask him whatever we want to know about the mission. So, Pyrrho, you can voice your opinions and pose your questions tonight. Come on, I challenge you to a duel by slingshot."

"Who is Peero?" William asked, as they

positioned themselves near the targets.

"He was a Greek philosopher known as the founder of skepticism," Morgan replied.

"Well Professor, you might know a lot about words, but I can kick your sit-upon at slingshots. Come on then, let's have a go," his brother challenged.

"You sound ever so British," Morgan teased. "Not half bad... mate."

"Don't be such a nelly," William said, in the broadest accent he could muster.

"Let the games begin," Morgan announced.

They distracted each other with their teasing and joking around so much during their game, that in the end, neither twin was sure who had won.

That evening, the boys met with Osdruan in the library. He had surprising news for them. "Today, I attended an assembly of King Ulric and his advisors," he said. "We are all in agreement that it is time for you to go to Greywood."

"When?" Morgan asked nervously.

"Tomorrow morning, Nesta, Wise Traveller, will take you to the village, and you will stay with her family," Osdruan stated. "It will not seem unusual that you should arrive with her, since Nesta often takes visitors to stay with them. I have been given other clothing for you to wear, to ensure that you do not look so much like identical twins while you are staying in Greywood. When it is time for you to go to the dragon's caverna, you will change back into your identical clothes, which will help you to outwit the piskies.

"How long will we stay? William asked.

"Until you have completed your mission," Osdruan replied.

"It feels like we've been here for a long time," Morgan said. "I can't imagine what's going on at home, since our parents discovered that we're missing."

"They will not have missed you," Osdruan stated. "You have taken a journey that overrides time. You will get back almost before you left. Everything will be exactly as it was upon your departure."

"How is that possible?" William asked.

"Wormhole!" Morgan said suddenly. "Remember that program about time travel?"

"Yeah, it was about quantum tunnelling," William recalled.

"Thinking about what happened to us, I wonder if quantum mechanics might be a more accurate explanation," Morgan said.

"Of course! Parallel universes that can interact with one another," William agreed.

"There are many theories and names for the

phenomenon," Osdruan said. "Just understand that it does exist, regardless of what it is called or how it is explained.

Let us focus now on what will happen when you get to the village. You are to be introduced as Nesta's cousins. She will help you with the details. I will also be in the village if you should need me. Tomorrow afternoon, we will meet with the king and his advisors to discuss the plans for your journey to Griswold's caverna. Oh, and one final thing, you must never speak of this Crystal Chamber to anyone," he said solemnly. The boys both promised him that they would never mention it. Smiling at them, Osdruan asked if they had any more questions or concerns about Greywood.

"All of the questions I had planned to ask seem unimportant now that we are going to Greywood tomorrow," Morgan said. "But I must admit that I am nervous."

"Well I'm ready," William said, jumping up. "I've been a bit frustrated and skeptical," he said, smiling at Morgan. "But, now I can't wait to get on with the mission."

"That's the spirit lad," Osdruan said. "Carpe-Diem!"

"Seize the day!" Morgan shouted, raising an imaginary sword. "Sir, you remind me of

Broleus," he said, laughing.

Osdruan grabbed Morgan's arm. "What did you say?" he gasped.

*****

Lucian, Asa and Durkin made the trek to the palace and arrived precisely at noon. They waited for an hour before being escorted to the king. He was seated on his throne and his advisors were sitting at a long table next to him. The two healers and the small messenger nodded respectfully as they passed the advisors on their way to the throne. They knelt before the king, and Ulric motioned for them to rise.

"I see that our messenger has fully recovered from his injuries," the king said, smiling at Lucian and Asa. "Your healing skills are impressive. I am pleased to welcome my physician back to the palace," he said, nodding to Lucian. "Asa, my treasurer will reimburse you for expenses incurred while administering to Durkin."

"And now little messenger, it is good to see you again. My soldiers have looked into the matter of your attack. Unfortunately, they were unable to make any arrests. However, to ensure your safety, a guard will accompany you until someone has been arrested." Asa and Durkin bowed their heads in stunned silence.

"Our guests arrive today. Durkin, since you were the last one to see the dragon, I would like

you to be present at our meeting with them," the king continued. "I have had a room prepared for you." The three of them were then dismissed.

"I can't believe what just happened in there," Asa said, once they were outside.

"That was a grand performance for the advisors," Lucian declared.

"Maybe the king regrets his past treatment of us," Durkin suggested.

"Don't be naïve," Asa said laughing. "Ulric is not one to regret anything. He is just acting the part of the good son of King Frederick to impress the elders."

CHAPTER EIGHTEEN

Sir, you remind me of Broleus," Morgan repeated. "We met him in Merlin's Cave when we were exploring."

"You met him?" Osdruan seemed to be shocked. "I did not realize that he..."

"Not only did we meet him," William interrupted. "I was hurt and he used this energy transfer thing to take away the pain in my ankle."

"Yes, yes, energy transfer," Osdruan mumbled. "I am just ... It has been so long."

"You know Broleus too!" Morgan exclaimed.

"Yes, he is also a follower of the Ancient Oak," Osdruan said quietly. He slowly sank into a chair by the door, obviously shaken by news of his friend. He stared off into space for several minutes. When he looked at the twins, his eyes were damp with tears. “I am sorry lads, but it has been a very long time since anyone has spoken of my dear friend, Broleus. I am very surprised that you have made his acquaintance. Please tell me all that you know about him. Did he seem well?”

The boys assured him that Broleus was doing well and they took turns telling him all about their meeting in Merlin’s Cave. When they were finished, Osdruan wiped his eyes.

“Thank you lads,” he said softly. “It is good to know that he is well.”

“Sir, will you please tell us more about Broleus?” Morgan asked gently.

Osdruan looked from one boy to the other. He seemed to be trying to decide whether or not to talk about his old friend. Finally he smiled and settled himself comfortably.

“Broleus of the Blue Rose has been a close friend of mine for as long as I can remember. We entered the Order as young lads and were as close as any brothers could be. After our training, we were sent to different areas, but we were always able to see one another from time to time. When I was assigned to Greywood after the treasure was found, and Broleus was sent to guard the cave of Merlyn, we were no longer able to keep in touch with one another. I have not seen him for a very long time. The fact that you have met him, and can tell me that he is well, certainly warms my heart."

"But how did he get to our century?" William asked.

"He did not get to your century," Osdruan replied. "He has been there since the death of Merlyn. He guards the secrets of the cave."

"But Merlin died around 500 AD," Morgan said. "That's over 1500 years ago."

"Only by your measurement of time," Osdruan said.

"But how do you…" Morgan began.

"It's probably different with magicians and wizards," William interjected. "Sir, I'd like to know more about 'The Order of the Ancient Oak'. Is it some kind of religion?"

"It is a way of life for a chosen few," Osdruan explained, heaving his massive body out of the chair. "But I am not permitted to discuss the ways of our Order. And, it is time to prepare for your journey to Greywood."

Morgan reluctantly followed him out of the room. There were always so many things left unsaid, and questions that were never fully answered, in this strange place.

"Be sure to pack your slings and your crystals," Osdruan reminded them. "And most importantly, never remove the jacinth stones from your necks." Without any further explanation, Osdruan walked away.

When they got to their bedroom, the boys saw the new outfits that Osdruan had told them about.

"Hey, we won't look exactly the same," William said. The colours are different and we have caps to wear."

"Let's not forget to pack the clothes we're wearing," Morgan said. "We'll be expected to wear identical outfits when we go to meet the dragon. Is your bag packed?"

"I've got everything except my sling," William said.

"Me too," Morgan said. "But I don't want to go up to the field in the dark. We can get them in the morning."

"Suits me," William agreed. "Are you sure you have all of the crystals?"

"I'll check again," Morgan said, drawing the small pouch from his bag. "I have three clear crystals and one blue sodalite. And we are both wearing our jacinth stones."

"Why do you think Osdruan warned us not to take them off?" William asked, rubbing the smooth fiery gem that hung around his neck.

"Perhaps it's because of its protective properties," Morgan suggested. "Or maybe we'll need it for some reason when we get to the dragon's cave."

"I just hope there really is a dragon and this hasn't all been another plot to trick us," William muttered as he sat down on his cot.

"Time to sleep, Pyrhho," Morgan said with a chuckle. "You'll need all of your strength to fight off the dragon if he turns on us."

At dawn the next morning, Osdruan awakened the twins to tell them that he was leaving. He also said that Nesta would be meeting them outside the cave within the hour. The boys got up and bathed one last time in the waterfall shower. After they were dressed in their similar, but not identical, outfits, William went to the field to get their slings while Morgan packed their other clothes.

With bags over their shoulders and apples in their hands, the twins headed along the passageway to the cave entrance. When they stepped outside, they heard the glass door snap into place, closing off the cave.

Before long, the boys noticed a figure coming up the hill toward them. Instinctively, William picked up a stone and reached into his bag for his sling.

"It's probably our guide, Nesta," Morgan said, as a girl about their age came into view. They watched her climb the steep hill effortlessly. She had a walking stick at her side. Nesta was wearing a green cotton shift over light coloured leggings. Brown curls tumbled recklessly around her freckled face.

"You must be my new cousins," she said, smiling. "I'm Nesta."

"I'm William," he said, extending his hand to her. "And this is my brother, Morgan."

"Yes, of course," Nesta said, shaking Morgan's hand. "I have heard all about you from my cousin, Pahlaseda." He felt his cheeks flush.

"Now it is time to go down to the village," she said. With Nesta in the lead, they began their downhill trek to Greywood.

As they walked along, their guide told them a bit about the people of her community and gave them details about her family, so they would fit in as her cousins. She had an older brother named Jarvis who was well-known for his mastery with spears. Nesta explained that they would be introduced as the children of her mother's brother who lived in the industrial village of Helston.

"Should anyone ask, you are both training to

be tin craftsmen," she said.

"Great!" William chuckled. "I hope no one asks us to demonstrate our skills."

After hiking for a few hours, Nesta suggested that they rest in the shade of the trees and drink from a nearby stream.

They were just getting comfortable, when a tall man came crashing through the trees brandishing a huge stick. Before the twins could get their slings, Nesta had grabbed her walking staff and was advancing toward him. The boys backed away, as Nesta and the stranger engaged in battle. They swung their sticks and expertly fended off each other's blows. After several minutes, they seemed to come to an agreement. They nodded, stepped back and lowered their weapons. They walked over to the twins, grinning broadly. "This is my brother Jarvis, Gifted Spear Fighter," Nesta said. He closely resembled Nesta, but he was taller, and he had a deep angry scar down one side of his face and neck.

"Hi Jarvis, I'm sure glad that you aren't the enemy," Morgan said, laughing.

"That was an interesting method of fighting," William said. "It reminds me of fencing. But it seems a lot more brutal."

"There certainly are things you must know,

to avoid being killed," Jarvis said. "With this stick, I could sever a man's jugular vein through the collar of a heavy coat." He paused to take a drink from a flask at his side. "Would you like to learn how to use a fighting staff?"

"Definitely," William replied excitedly. "We've been trained to use slings, but I think that a stick would be a more useful weapon."

"A staff is the best choice for hand to hand combat," Jarvis said. "But a sling is a good weapon to take down an enemy when he is farther away, especially an animal."

"There will be opportunities for teaching them about stick-fighting later," Nesta said impatiently. "We must be on our way. We are expected in Greywood by midday."

Reluctantly, the boys gathered their things together, had another drink from the stream, and then continued their descent into Greywood. Nesta and William walked in front with their brothers following closely behind.

"You fought well against your brother," William said to Nesta. "I'm impressed. How did you learn to fight like that?"

"Everything that she knows, she learned from me," Jarvis said, before Nesta had a chance to answer. "And I admit that she is almost as good as I am."

"I am as good as you are... maybe better," Nesta said.

"You are not!" Jarvis scoffed. "Because you are a girl, I do not fight as hard."

"You have never given me a whit of consideration because I am a girl," Nesta protested. "And I have the scars to prove it. As a matter of fact, I seem to remember coming to your aid once or twice," she added proudly.

"That is surely true," her brother admitted, rubbing the scar on his face and neck.

"Oh Jarvis, I did not intend to remind you of that awful day," Nesta apologized.

"No worries Nessy. I don't mind telling the lads about it," he assured her. They stopped to listen to Jarvis's story.

"My sister and I had gone on a short trip to visit friends who live a few days' travel from our home. We had taken our horses and we were having a race across the moor. When I got to the road, I looked back to see where Nessy was. All at once, I felt my horse go out from under me, and I landed face down in the dirt. I scrambled to my feet and straight away, I knew that I was being attacked by a wretched freebooter."

"What's a freebooter?" William asked.

"A lawless adventurer and robber," Jarvis explained. He took a drink from his flask and cleared his throat. "Before I could defend myself, he had slashed my face and neck.

Then, just in the nick of time, Nessy and her horse galloped down the road toward us. She came up behind the freebooter and, before he could react, Nessy leaned down from her horse and delivered him a smart blow to his head with her stick. He fell to the ground beside me, completely unconscious. So, thanks to my well-trained and powerful sister, I am here to relate the tale."

"Do not be sarcastic," Nesta said. She glanced at William. "It is very difficult for my brother to admit that he has ever needed my help, because he has always looked after me." She turned back to the path. "Just across the wold is our Greywood."

They left the woods and headed across a vast, open field. When they arrived in Greywood, they had to make their way through a small crowd of curious villagers who had come to welcome Nesta and Jarvis home. Someone asked about the strangers with her, but Nesta and the boys just smiled and kept walking. When they arrived home, Mertas the Seamstress, and Smythe the Farrier hugged the children and invited Morgan and William into their cottage.

Their home was small, but functional. There

was one main room with a fireplace and cooking area at one end. Several chairs and a wooden table were the only pieces of furniture. Beyond the main room, there was a lavatory and two sleeping rooms. Jarvis took the twins into one of the rooms. Half of the tiny room was separated by a heavy curtain. Nesta's sleeping area was on the other side of the curtain. He showed them two cots that had been added to the cramped space that the twins would share with him.

Jarvis opened a door next to his bed, and the boys followed him into an odd little courtyard. It looked like another bedroom, but it had no roof. The space was empty except for a tall post and a gigantic tree with smooth grey bark and glossy leaves. The twins looked at Jarvis for an explanation. He smiled and gave a low whistle. From high up in the tree, there was rustling and a short barking sound. Suddenly a massive, brown bird flew down and perched on the post. The boys stepped back in surprise.

"This is Adelar, Noble Eagle," Jarvis said proudly.

"You have a golden eagle for a pet?" William asked in disbelief.

"He is not really a pet," Jarvis replied. "Adelar chose us."

"What do you mean?" Morgan asked.

"On one of my treks around the countryside with Nessy, this incredible bird began to fly alongside us. Whenever we stopped, he waited in a nearby tree. He stayed with us for about three days and then flew off. After we had been home for awhile, I saw him in this tree and he has lived with us since that day."

"Does he come and go whenever he pleases?" Morgan asked.

"He remains here most of the time," he replied. "When Nessy travels, he tries to go with her. She usually lets him go along, but sometimes she asks him to stay behind."

"She can communicate with an eagle?" William asked.

"Yes, I am not sure how she does it," Jarvis said. "He seems to understand a few things I say to him, but my sister and Adelar can communicate without speaking."

"Why did you say that he chose you?" Morgan asked.

"He is a familiar," Jarvis replied. "Have you heard of that?"

"Is a familiar like an animal guide or protector?" Morgan said.

"That's right. An eagle represents wisdom, swiftness, and spirit," Jarvis said. "And his keen sense of sight guides us."

"Has he ever had to protect either of you?" William asked.

"Yes, he lets out a high piercing sound as a warning, and swoops down in front of us if he senses danger." Jarvis said. "Unfortunately, the day that I was attacked was one of the days that Nesta told him to stay home. The horse she was riding gets very nervous when Adelar is with us." He rubbed the scar on his face.

"Morg, do you remember that kid back home who went everywhere with a crow on his shoulder?" William asked.

"Yeah, his name was Fletcher," Morgan replied. "Could that crow have been his familiar?" he asked Jarvis.

"Very likely," Jarvis agreed. "A crow represents boldness, and prophecy. They are great protectors and are also capable of shape-shifting."

"That's amazing," Morgan said. "It would be great to have a familiar."

"Yeah, we could sure use one on the journey we're about to take," William said.

"Please say no more," Jarvis cautioned. "We are not permitted to know about your mission or your homeland."

"Why?" William asked.

"If we do not have information, then no one

can force us or trick us into revealing information about you," he said. "It is for your protection as well as ours."

For some reason, Jarvis's words left Morgan feeling alone and vulnerable. He glanced at William, who nodded, and changed the subject.

"What was this courtyard used for originally?" William asked.

"It was a place to shelter our livestock," Jarvis said. "When we no longer kept cows and chickens, I took most of the roof off and opened it up for Adelar."

"Was that tree always in here?" Morgan asked, noting its amazing size.

"Yes, the room was built around it," Jarvis said, smiling. "It is a silver beech tree so we could not chop it down. Many people believe that this kind of tree holds ancient and forgotten wisdom. My father said that cutting it down would surely bring misfortune upon us." Adelar screeched and looked toward the doorway. Nesta had come to tell them it was time to eat.

During the noon meal, the twins learned that Mertas was a palace seamstress and Smythe was the appointed blacksmith for the king. When they had finished eating, Smythe informed the twins that he would be taking them to the palace. There was to be a meeting with the king and his advisors regarding their mission.

During the long walk up the hill to the castle, Smythe told them what he knew about its structure. “It is a simple castle, small by anyone’s terms. Known as a motte-and-bailey castle, it is not much more than a few fortified keeps surrounded by this hill and a stone curtain wall. We have never had many battles, but we do have barracks filled with soldiers, catapults, and ballistae, if we are ever threatened.”

“Does the castle have a drawbridge?” Morgan asked.

“No it does not. There never was a moat,” he said. “But we have a well-guarded gatehouse and the surrounding walls are nearly twenty feet high.”

“Is there a dungeon?” William asked.

“Yes, but I doubt that the king will throw you down there,” Smythe said, grinning.

“Will we get to see it?” William persisted.

“Oh no lad,” he replied. “You won’t be taken on a tour of the place. You are just here for a meeting. It will be held in the Great Hall in the centre of the main keep.”

When they got to the top of the rise, they stopped to take in the view. They could barely see Greywood now; low clouds shadowed the valley. Behind the huge wall in front of them, the castle towers eerily poked through the swirling grey mist.

The three of them walked through the outer gate. “We will not be going through the inner gate,” Smythe said. “Since you are supposed to be my nephews, we will go through the postern by the stables where I work.”

A guard approached them as they entered the courtyard. “Who have ye brought along then, Smithy?” he asked.

“These are my nephews from Helston,” Smythe replied. “They are to meet with His Majesty and the advisors at half one.” The guard nodded and told the boys to follow him.

Once they were inside the main part of the castle, the guard shoved them roughly through a doorway, and pushed them onto a bench. “Wait here,” he growled.

“Morgan was so nervous, he could hardly breathe. He leaned forward, closed his eyes and took several deep breaths, trying to regain his composure. When he looked up, he could see William across the room rummaging around in the bookshelves. “William, come over here,” Morgan whispered urgently. “You’re going to get us into trouble.”

“Everything is so old,” William said, as he studied a huge painting. “Look at this dude with the curly wig and tight pants."

Morgan went to look at the portrait. "It must be one of the king's ancestors. It says 'Frederick I' on the plaque," Morgan said. Changing the subject, he asked, "Will, are you scared about the meeting?"

"Nope," William replied, walking over to a tall ornate cabinet filled with silver and china trinkets.

Morgan saw him pull at the knob to open the glass door. "Stop!" he hissed.

"Gentlemen," said a deep voice. The surprised boys wheeled around and saw a portly man with a long, waxed moustache standing in the doorway. "Follow me," he declared.

*****

Durkin paced restlessly around the small tower room that had been assigned to him. He was still confused by the king's sudden change in behaviour. Asa had said that the king's words weren't genuine and Ulric had just been putting on an act for the elders. Asa was Durkin's truest friend and he had always believed whatever the healer said. But he was not so sure this time. Perhaps the king really did regret his cruelty. Besides, Durkin knew how much King Ulric hated to be disobeyed. When he had gone to see Griswold without His Majesty's permission, Durkin knew that he would have to pay. He had deserved King Ulric's punishment. But Asa had said that everyone should be treated with respect and that no one deserved that kind of cruelty. Could that be true?

"I shall not waste time trying to understand His Majesty," Durkin said aloud. "I am just a messenger for the oracle, what do I know about kings and such?" He winced painfully as he put on his leather shoes. His feet still hurt considerably.

When the tower bell tolled the hour, Durkin remembered that he had not eaten. Just as he was wondering if anyone would bring him food, there was a knock at the door. There stood a small girl with a tray of bread, cheese and tea. He thanked her as she placed it on a small wooden table by the door. Durkin took his time eating; he was savouring every bite. He sipped the tea slowly, feeling full and relaxed.

Within a short time, a page arrived to escort Durkin to the Great Hall for the meeting. He was anxious to meet the Adney lads. He truly hoped they would be able to complete their task and set Griswold free.

CHAPTER NINETEEN

The boys silently followed the man with the moustache into a massive room that was the size of the football field at Wadebridge School. Ornate velvet seated chairs were evenly spaced along each side of the room from one end to the other. At the far end of the room, the boys could see a throne on a carpeted dais. Woven hangings covered every inch of wall space and heavy drapes framed each window. Because of the overcast day, and the poor lighting, it took a few minutes for the boys' eyes to adjust to the dimness. Morgan sighed with relief when he saw a familiar figure approaching them.

"Come lads, The Royal Council is waiting to discuss your mission," Osdruan said with a warm smile. The boys followed their tutor to a table near the throne. He introduced them to a man with a very long white beard. His name was Ellersby, the Elder, and he seemed to be the chairperson. Going around the table, they met the other council members.

Morgan was pleased to see that the only woman on the council was someone he and William already knew - Rhiannon, Magical Maiden. When they were introduced to a very small man next to her, Durkin, the Messenger, Morgan gasped. He knew immediately that he was the troll that he and William had seen in the blue tide pool at Merlin's cave. A broad, toothy grin spread across the messenger's warty face as he also seemed to recognize them. Osdruan took his seat, and the boys sat beside him.

The meeting was called to order and each of the councillors had a turn to ask the boys questions. Morgan was surprised that everyone at the table seemed to already know so much about them and their family.

"The council members will offer you items and information that will be useful to you on your expedition," the chairman said. "We will begin with Chartar, the Mapmaker."

By the end of the meeting, Morgan and William had received a compass and a map of the route to Griswold's cave from Chartar, as well as useful information about the ways of the piskies from Mendel, the Scholar, who had studied them for many years. Using Chartar's map, Branard, Man of Proven Courage alerted them to possible dangers and circled places on the map where it would be safe for them to bed down along the way. He also told the boys that they would learn the basics of stick fighting from Jarvis, Gifted Spear Fighter. Geary, the Changeable, talked about shape-shifting and gave the twins clues that would help them to recognize a piskie that had changed its form. Durkin, the Messenger, gave them information about Griswold, since he had been the last one to see the dragon. He told them that they should be able to communicate with the dragon telepathically. He discussed Griswold's ill state of health and emphasized that it was imperative that the boys begin their journey as soon as possible. Rhiannon had briefly described the interior of the dragon's cave and warned the boys about a cave nymph, Perinina, the Dream Weaver, who would hypnotize anyone who looked directly into her eyes. Rhiannon said that Perinina was very protective of Griswold, and told them they would be safe as long as they didn't make eye contact. Osdruan invited the boys to his cottage the next day so that he could help them with their final preparations.

Morgan's mind was reeling from so many names to remember and so much information to process.

Suddenly, the doors at the side of the room were flung open and the king and a page entered. Once King Ulric was seated on his throne, the page walked over and whispered something to Ellersby.

The chairman stood. "Our meeting is now adjourned. His Majesty would like the visitors and Durkin to remain." Osdruan smiled warmly at the twins as he left the room.

Morgan's throat constricted with fear when he and William were told to follow Durkin to the throne. He felt insignificant and nervous as he stood before Greywood's ruler.

"Messenger, introduce the guests," King Ulric said impatiently.

Durkin bowed. "Sire, allow me to present William, Noble Protector and Morgan, Wise One of the Sea."

"Come forward lads," the king said more kindly. They moved ahead a few paces.

King Ulric looked at the twins, studying them carefully. "I was told that you would come 'two as one' and I can surely see that you are identical. Now, speak of your mission," he demanded.

Morgan was too timid to speak, so he glanced at William.

"We have come to free Griswold and the people of Greywood," William said boldly.

"Are you prepared to accomplish such a formidable task?" the king asked.

"Yes, Sire," William replied confidently.

"Other boy," Ulric said rudely. "Are you also prepared for this mission?"

"Y-Yes Sire," Morgan stammered hoarsely.

"You do not sound prepared," the king said scornfully. "You sound terrified. Fear is an enemy more deadly than anything you might encounter along the way, and it will certainly destroy your chances of completing the mission successfully. The downfall of Griswold, the people of Greywood, and your brother, will be on your head if you succumb to fear. Are you prepared for that?" Morgan hung his head in shame.

"Wait a minute! My brother is the reason we are here," William said defensively. "He's the one who convinced me that family obligations have to be met. So don't..." Suddenly William gasped and grabbed his cheek. Durkin touched Morgan's arm as a warning not to speak or move.

"You may be your brother's keeper where you come from," the king said coldly. "But in Greywood, he is on his own. And, you will speak only when I give you permission. Is that understood?"

"Yes, Sire," William replied contritely. He placed his hands at his sides and bowed.

Morgan could see that his brother's cheek was badly burned. A huge welt had already formed.

"Messenger," the king snapped. "Have you anything else to say?"

"No Sire," Durkin replied nervously.

"Then be off!" the king hissed angrily.

The twins followed Durkin as he bowed and backed away from the throne. As they were walking toward the exit, Morgan heard the king mutter, "Sending boys to do a man's job…Idiotae!"

Once they were safely outside, Morgan said, "Let me see your face, Will." He looked closely at the huge blister on his face. "What happened in there?" he asked Durkin.

"Your brother received one of His Majesty's powerful, and often deadly, bolts of energy because he spoke out of turn," the small messenger said sympathetically.

"But that's ridiculous! It's so unbelievably

cruel," Morgan spluttered.

"Did that ever happen to you?" William asked, cupping his hand over the burn.

"Many times," Durkin said quietly. "Last time, he... but I never thought he would do that to a young visitor who has come here to help us."

"We need a doctor for William," Morgan said.

"My friend Asa the Healer, will give him something to ease the pain," Durkin offered.

"No, I'll be fine," William said. "We're meeting our uncle at the stables. Please, take us to him."

"Of course," Durkin said. The boys followed him across the misty courtyard.

Durkin hobbled along, stooped over, leaning heavily on a walking stick. Morgan wondered how the small man, who barely came to his shoulder, had become so crippled.

Smythe was cleaning one of the horse stalls when they walked in. "Well lads, how was your meeting with..." He stopped mid-sentence when he saw William's swollen face. "What happened?" he asked, staring at the boy's cheek in shocked disbelief.

"The king thought I was a coward and he took offence when William tried to defend me," Morgan said.

"I am Durkin, Messenger of the Oracle," the

small man said, stepping up to Smythe.

"Yes, I have heard of you," Smythe said, shaking Durkin's hand absently as he continued to stare at William. "I do not understand why the king would hurt a lad."

"When the king gets angry he lashes out, especially when he feels that he is being defied," Durkin said, trying to explain. "I do not think he meant…"

"Are you defending that maniac?" Morgan interjected.

"I just want to get out of here," William said weakly. "I feel kind of sick." Morgan barely managed to catch his brother as he fell limply against him.

William awoke, moaning painfully. A tall man was leaning over him, putting some cream on his face. He struggled to push the man away. Morgan could see that the cream was making the pain worse. He sat beside William, whispering words of comfort to him.

"I am almost done lad," Asa, the Healer, said. "I am trying to ease your pain."

William continued to thrash about. "No, no, you're causing my pain," he moaned.

"Will, lie still," Morgan said loudly. "We're at Jarvis and Nesta's house. Asa is a doctor, and he's trying to help you." Morgan's words seemed to have a calming effect on William. He relaxed a bit and opened his eyes.

"How did I get here?" he asked.

"After you fainted, Smythe borrowed a horse and cart to bring us back here while Durkin went to get Asa," Morgan explained. William looked from his brother to Asa, and then reached up to touch his cheek. The healer gently pushed his hand down.

"Please give the poultice time to ease the pain and swelling," Asa said. "You have quite a serious burn, but I think it will heal quickly."

"Thank you," William said, smiling sleepily. "I think your magic is already beginning to work." He closed his eyes again.

"He will rest more comfortably now," Asa said to Morgan. "I shall return this evening to check on him."

When Asa returned later that evening, he found his patient playing a game of chess with Jarvis. "You must be feeling much better," he said.

"Thanks to you," William said. "I don't know what you put on my face, but it sure worked. It doesn't really hurt at all."

Asa looked closely at the burn. "I am very pleased," he said. "I will leave this small vial of herbal cream. Put some on the burn tonight and again in the morning. And try to stay out of direct sunlight for a few days."

"That shouldn't be a problem," William said. "It always seems to be foggy in this valley. Doesn't the sun ever shine in Greywood?"

"Not much at this time of year," Jarvis replied. "Spring and summer are sunnier."

"I will be off then," Asa said. "Look after yourself, and send someone for me if you need more medication."

"I will, and thanks again," William said. "Hopefully, I won't need anything."

"You should be fine, as long as you stay away from the palace," Asa said, chuckling.

"Trust me, I don't plan to visit your king ever again," William assured him.

The next morning, Osdruan arrived to take the boys to his cottage. He frowned when he saw the welt on William's face but he didn't say anything. Instead, he turned to Mertas. "I shall have your nephews back within the hour."

Osdruan's cottage wasn't far away. It was similar to Smythe's home, but smaller. When they walked in, they saw Durkin seated at the table in the main room.

"Durkin wanted to see for himself that you are up for the journey," Osdruan said.

"I'm fine now," William said as the dwarf

hobbled toward them. "I guess I must have fainted or something."

"I want you to know that I understand how horridly painful your injury was. I have had personal experiences with the king's wrath." He looked at his feet briefly. "I wish that I could have said or done something to prevent it from happening, but I was afraid of making things worse by increasing His Majesty's anger."

"You couldn't have done anything," William said. "I shouldn't have spoken to the king like that. I have a habit of running off at the mouth sometimes."

Osdruan and Morgan smiled knowingly at one another. Everyone crowded around the table and Morgan spread out the map that Chartar had given them. Osdruan and Durkin explained the route carefully to the twins and answered their questions.

During the discussion, Morgan abruptly left the table and went to sit by the fire. He soon felt Osdruan's hand on his shoulder.

"What is it lad?" he asked.

"I discovered yesterday that the king has no faith in our ability to carry out this mission," Morgan said. "He thinks I'm a coward and that Will is too impulsive. As we were leaving, I heard him muttering something about 'sending boys to do a man's job' and he's probably right. I admit that I'm afraid. What if we fail? What will happen to us and to all of you? Seriously, I don't think I can go through with this mission."

Osdruan gently assured Morgan that their expedition would, indeed, be successful. He spoke about generations of Adney twins who had fulfilled their obligations, and reminded him that they had all been about his age. Osdruan said that he and William were well prepared and more capable than any of the others that had come to Greywood.

William went over to talk to his brother. "C'mon Morg, let's prove the old king wrong. Think how cool it will be to throw that in his miserable face," he suggested.

"It would be, if we really could succeed," Morgan said doubtfully.

"We can do it," William argued. "Remember that day when I fell in Merlin's cave? You knew exactly what to do to take care of me. With your brains and my courage, we can do anything."

Morgan grinned at his brother's lack of modesty. He looked up at Osdruan and saw an encouraging smile. Morgan knew he didn't have a choice. He had to go through with the mission. With a sigh, he stood up and the three of them returned to the table to continue going over the map.

"This would be so much easier if Rhiannon could take us to the dragon," William said.

"I truly wish that were possible," Osdruan said. "But I know you lads will be fine. Jarvis will teach you hand to hand combat and, when you are ready to begin your journey, Nesta will accompany you as far as Blanford."

"Is that where we'll cross the river?" William asked, looking at the map.

"Yes," Osdruan replied. "From there, you will be on your own. Study the map at frequent intervals and you will find your way without any problem."

"Do you know when we can expect to be on our way?" Morgan asked.

"Yes I do," Osdruan answered with a smile. "Remember, time is of the essence. You will leave in five days." He looked at Morgan's stricken face. "Come now lad, do not look so worried. I have faith that you'll be ready in five days. And, with Asa's help, William's face will be completely healed. Then, once again, you will look exactly alike and you will be able to fool the piskies as you go forth, two as one."

Morgan didn't feel as confident as Osdruan and William seemed to be, but he planned to do his part to make this journey a success. He rolled up the map and put it into his bag.

When they arrived back at Smythe's cottage, Jarvis gave Morgan and William fighting staffs that he had made for them. The sticks were of perfect length and weight.

Over the next few days, the twins quickly learned the basics of stick fighting. Jarvis was pleased with their progress. By the fourth day, the twins were able to hold their instructor off when they fought two-on-one.

"Well done!" Nesta shouted as she watched from the sidelines. "You really had Jarvis working hard."

"I guess we'll be okay as long as we can fight, two against one," Morgan said.

"Let us celebrate your mastery," Nesta suggested. "I say we should go to Pahlaseda's home. Her mum makes the best fried fish and mushy peas you will ever taste." Morgan and William agreed that it was a great idea.

"I have other plans," Jarvis said. "But you three go on then. I will tell Mum not to expect you at evening meal."

An hour later, the four of them were sitting around the table enjoying delicious food and laughing with their new friends. Morgan was happy to have a few hours to focus on something other than the pending journey.

The next morning, Mertas woke the boys at the crack of dawn. They stumbled to the table. In the semi-darkness, they ate cheese and bread and drank tall mugs of milk.

Mertas came over to the table, carrying two grey cloaks. "I made these for you," she said. "They will shed the rain and should keep you warm at night." She showed them large inside pockets that were filled with bread, cheese, and apples.

"Thanks so much," Morgan said, throwing the cloak over his shoulders. It was made of heavy wool and he knew that it was exactly what they would need for the cold, damp nights ahead.

"This is a wonderful gift," William added.

"It is time for us to leave," Nesta announced. "We must be on our way to Blanford."

Morgan's stomach lurched as he realized that he and William would soon be trekking across unfamiliar land by themselves, to complete a journey that had started five hundred years ago. He forced himself not to think of the dangers that lay ahead.

The boys had carefully packed their things the night before. In the morning, they had remembered to put on their outfits that were identical. They had left the second set of clothes on the cots in Jarvis's room. Nesta and the twins stopped at the door to say good-bye to Mertas. She handed each of them a flask of water.

"We'll be back before you know it," William said cheerfully.

"Look after each other," she said, hugging them.

The three travellers picked up their walking sticks and started down the road.

"Godspeed," Mertas whispered softly, as she closed the door.

*****

Durkin watched Nesta and the twins pass his window very early that misty morning. He was relieved that Griswold would finally be able to go home. He was certain that his son, Egandor would guard Merlyn's bag with his life. True, the young dragon would have to travel from cave to cave protecting the treasures of other sorcerers as well. Fortunately, he could use the connecting inner passageways that had been sculpted by the Race of Giants thousands of years ago. Everyone would rest easier, knowing that the secrets of Merlyn would be secure forever.

On the other hand, he was very worried about the lads who had come so far to save the bag of magic and free the mighty Griswold. A monumental undertaking! He had offered to accompany them on their mission, but the Royal Council had refused because of his age and his injuries. Bah! What did they know? Durkin would have guarded the boys with his life.

He understood family loyalty, but this would be the riskiest journey any Adney twins had taken. If the piskies had somehow discovered this was their last chance to get the bag of irreversible magic...

The messenger reassured himself that the

boys' identical appearance was their best weapon against the miserable little beasts. Also, the lads had been prepared for this journey by the most highly skilled and the wisest of Greywood.

Durkin sighed despondently as his mind turned to another, darker concern for the twins. He knew their journey would be fraught with other dangers too; dangers no one had dared to mention.

CHAPTER TWENTY

The walk to Blanford was damp and dreary. The boys were already grateful for the grey cloaks that kept them warm and dry. The three of them walked along for several hours before Nesta finally suggested that they should rest in a small shelter near the road and have something to eat.

Once settled in some hollowed out rocks, Nesta pulled a candle from her bag and lit it with her flint. She then placed it in the dirt and the three of them crowded around the candle. It gave off more heat than Morgan would have thought possible, and the flickering flame was comforting.

"You should use only candles for light and heat," Nesta said. "Fires draw unwanted eyes and are difficult to extinguish in an emergency.

Did you bring candles and flint?"

The boys dug deeply into the bottom of their bags and managed to locate both items.

"Maybe we should practice using the flint," Morgan suggested.

William thought that it was unnecessary, but Nesta agreed with Morgan. She had him sit right beside her as she showed him how to get a spark. Morgan tried, but couldn't get his flint to work. She leaned over and guided his hand the next time he tried and sure enough, the candle burst into flame. William suddenly became interested in practicing too. Nesta smiled and leaned over to help him. They ate some of the bread and cheese in their pockets and soon were rested and ready to move on.

The rain stopped as the day wore on and the sun even peaked out of the mist from time to time. By mid-afternoon, they arrived at a river.

"Here we are," Nesta said. "This is Blanford."

"I don't see any houses. There's nothing here but a river," William said.

"Blanford is not a village," Nesta giggled. "It is just a river crossing. Originally, it was called 'Grey Haired One's River Crossing', named for the old man that built the bridge."

"It doesn't look very safe," Morgan said

looking at the crudely built structure.

"No one has ever fallen through," Nesta replied. "And this is the only way across, unless you want to swim." Anyone could see that swimming wasn't an option. The river was far too turbulent.

William walked part way across the bridge. "It's okay Morg," he shouted above the roar of the roiling river.

"We should fill our flasks with water," Nesta said to Morgan.

"Why do you travel around the countryside all the time?" Morgan asked.

"I carry messages and packages from village to village," she replied.

"Seems a rather risky job for a young girl," he suggested.

"It is my chosen career and I have been well trained for it," Nesta said. "I enjoy spending time with my friends and acquaintances, and I am rewarded every time I see the joy on their faces when I give them news of their loved ones."

William returned from his inspection of the bridge. "It is perfectly safe for us to cross," he announced. "It will be dark soon," he said to Nesta. "It won't be safe for you to go all the way home tonight."

"I am not going home, I have friends about

an hour down stream," she said. "And I have Adelar for guidance and protection."

"But the eagle didn't come with us," Morgan said.

"He has been following us all day," Nesta said. She whistled softly. The eagle swooped down from a tall pine tree and landed on a stump near them.

"We didn't hear or see him the entire time," William said. "Where was he?"

"He flew above the fog," she replied. "He did not have any reason to make his presence known."

"He is a powerful guide," Morgan said. "Do you think he would accompany us?"

"He is exactly what you need, but his loyalty to me is very strong," Nesta said, stroking Adelar's feathered head.

"Have you ever been to Griswold's cave?" William asked.

"No," she replied. We are not permitted to cross Blanford Bridge without permission from the king."

"Your king is so…" William began.

"Things are as they must be," Nesta said quietly.

"We should get going if we are to find our first stopover before dark," Morgan interjected.

"As Osdruan would say, 'time is of the essence'."

"I will meet you at this spot in four days," Nesta offered. "Then we can walk back to Greywood together and celebrate the success of your mission."

"Dead-on!" William exclaimed.

"I'm not sure I like your choice of words when we're about to start off on a perilous adventure," Morgan said, frowning.

"Everything is sure to go well, and you will arrive back here before me," Nesta said.

"Let's promise that we'll wait for each other, no matter what," Morgan suggested. The three of them placed their hands, one on top of the other, in a friendly pledge.

"I am off then," Nesta said. As she headed downstream, she waved to them. "Be safe and follow your map," she reminded them.

The boys waved and watched her disappear into the mist.

"Are you ready to go?" Morgan asked with more confidence than he felt.

"Sure," William replied eagerly. "Let the adventure begin!"

Side by side, they crossed the bridge and walked into a dense forest of majestic trees with glorious autumn leaves waving in the breeze. The boys were so focused on the trees that they failed to notice a log across the path. They both tripped over it and fell. The boys laughed as they picked themselves up and adjusted their gear.

As they started down the path, William unexpectedly stopped and pointed at something. A small grey cat sat leisurely grooming itself in the middle of the path.

"Shape-shifting piskie," William whispered, grasping his walking stick tightly. The cat looked up at him with huge, green eyes, arched its back, and stretched. Then, very casually, the cat walked toward the boys.

"Looks like a regular cat," Morgan whispered. The cat sat down several feet in front of them, and studied them with a mesmerizing stare.

"A regular cat wouldn't be in a forest in the middle of nowhere," William said.

"Wait," Morgan said sharply, as William raised his stick. "She's not a piskie."

"How do you know that?" William asked.

Morgan was staring into her green eyes. "Because she just told me," he replied in a flat tone. William grabbed his brother by the shoulders.

"Stop looking into the cat's eyes. It's hypnotizing you," he said, shaking him.

"She's not hypnotizing me," Morgan

snapped, twisting out of his brother's grasp. "Her name is Sephonee, Companion at the Crossroads. She says we may call her Seffie."

"So, you can suddenly talk to cats, and you're telling me you're not hypnotized," William argued. "Forget about the cat. Let's get going."

"We could take her with us," Morgan suggested. The cat rubbed against his leg.

"We don't have time to take care of a cat," William said impatiently. "We have to find a campsite before dark." He headed down the path.

Morgan stroked her smooth coat and she began to purr. "I have to go now, Seffie," he said regretfully. "I hope to see you again." He gave the cat a final pat on the head, and ran to catch up to William.

Using the map, the boys easily found the place where they had been advised to spend the first night. They camped in a large hollow willow tree that was lined with layers of dried leaves. It was just large enough for the two of them to lie curled next to one another, wrapped in their woollen cloaks. They fell asleep almost immediately. The journey had been long.

A short time later, Morgan awoke because he felt something warm around his neck. Slowly, he reached up to grab whatever was choking him. His hand sank into a warm, furry mass. He sat up quickly. Even in the dark, he recognized those huge eyes. "Seffie," he whispered with relief. The cat stretched across him, and began to purr contentedly. The two of them curled up together and went back to sleep.

In the morning, Morgan awoke and looked for the cat. She was gone. He crawled out of the shelter and peered up and down the path.

"What are you doing?" William asked sleepily.

"Looking for Seffie," Morgan replied.

"Don't start with the stray cat," William grumbled, as he crawled out of their lair.

"She was sleeping with us last night," Morgan said. "I wonder where she went."

"It was just a dream," William said. "You don't even know what's real and what isn't anymore."

"Oh, she was real," Morgan assured him.

"C'mon, let's eat something and check the map," William said.

The boys munched on apples as they checked their itinerary. Chartar, the Map Maker, had divided the map into sections, indicating how far the boys should travel each day.

"Today we'll travel east through these woods, and across a field," William said, tracing the route with his finger. "And then we head slightly south into another forest."

"And it looks like we cross a small stream before getting to our next campsite which isn't far from a cairn of rocks," Morgan added. "What are these little squiggly marks here and there on the map, especially on the last leg of the journey?"

"Branard, the guy who knew so much about piskies, said those are places where the piskies have been known to hang out," William said.

"There are three spots marked on the path we take today," Morgan said nervously.

"That doesn't mean we'll see any piskies; we just have to pay close attention." William said. "So, you'll have to stop thinking about the cat and focus on the trip."

"I think I know that," Morgan retorted. "And don't forget that we always have to stick together, looking exactly the same, to confuse the piskies. So if I wear my cloak, you'll have to wear yours too," he reminded his twin.

"What did that other person on the council say about fooling the piskies by doing something to our clothes?" William asked.

"Oh yeah," Morgan replied. "His name was Mendal. He said we should wear our shirts inside out."

"That sounds pretty silly. He must have been

joking," William said.

"Mendel didn't seem like a person who would joke about anything. I think we should try it. Maybe it'll help," Morgan reasoned. He took his shirt off and put it on inside out and then folded his arms, waiting for William to do the same. Finally with a disgruntled snort, William changed his shirt.

"C'mon let's get going," he grumbled.

By the time the sun was overhead, the twins were halfway across the field. It was very hot, so they stopped for a rest. Morgan insisted they check the map to be sure they weren't stopping near a piskie dwelling. They had already passed the first squiggle on the map without incident, but it paid to be vigilant. According to the map, the area they were in didn't seem to be a piskie haunt, so they sat against an old stump and ate some bread and cheese and had a drink from their flasks.

As they were getting ready to move on, William suddenly threw his things down and grabbed his sling. "There's something coming this way," he said as he loaded a stone in his sling.

Morgan looked up and saw a huge wolf charging toward them. He quickly readied his sling and stood beside his brother. When the snarling wolf was within range, they both swung their slings around and let go of the stones. The wolf stumbled and hit the ground.

The twins grabbed their things and ran to the spot where the animal had fallen.

William held his fighting stick over the wolf, just in case he was still alive. Blood oozed from the creature's lifeless body. "We nailed him," he said proudly. "And this time there's a body to prove it."

"Yeah," Morgan said sadly. "He sure is beautiful. I wonder what he was doing out here at this time of day."

"Maybe he was heading home after a wild night of killing," his brother suggested.

"What should we do with him?" Morgan asked.

"Nothing, we have to get going," William replied.

"We can't just leave him here," Morgan protested. "We have to do something."

"There's no time," William insisted. "Come on!"

Within a few hours, the boys had reached the edge of the forest that they would follow for the rest of their journey. They sank into the mossy shade of the first trees they saw. It felt good to finally be cool after their long trek across the open grassland. William pulled the map out again.

"Based on how long it took to cross the field, I think we're about one or two hours from our next campsite," he said.

"We seem to be making pretty good time," Morgan said, lying back to rest his head on his bag. "Where is our next source of water?"

"Our next source of water would be called a stream. It isn't far from here so we should find it within the hour. Does that suit you, Professor?" William teased.

"That will do nicely," Morgan replied with an exaggerated British accent. "We must be on our way. Remember, time is of the essence."

They walked deeper and deeper into the forest. Huge conifers flanked the path. Before long, they spotted a pile of rocks neatly stacked against one another.

"Here's the pile of rocks that was marked on the map," William announced.

"There's supposed to be a stream nearby," Morgan reminded him. Sure enough, it wasn't long before they were greedily drinking the cool water. After filling their flasks, they checked the map again.

"We're almost at our next camping spot," William said.

"And we have a piskie haunt close by," Morgan added, looking over his shoulder.

"We haven't had any problems with them so far," William assured him.

"I know, but we're getting closer to the dragon's lair," Morgan pointed out. "I expect they'll show themselves anytime now, so let's be sure to stick together and be as two as one as possible."

They proceeded down the path, watching for any unusual movements. From time to time, Morgan was sure he saw a grey cat walking among the trees.

It was dusk when the boys finally arrived at their campsite. According to the map, they were supposed to spend the night under a yew tree. They found the huge tree with out any problem.

"I think we should spend the night up there," William said pointing toward the upper boughs of the tree. "The piskies wouldn't get us if we slept up there."

"Osdruan said that the leaves and fruit seeds of the yew are poisonous," Morgan said.

"We'll be sleeping up there, not eating," William said sarcastically.

"We could fall out of the tree in the middle of the night," Morgan retorted.

"Okay, scaredy cat, why don't you sleep down

here with the piskies," William said in a surly tone. "I'll be safely snoring up in the tree."

"You seem to be forgetting that we have to stay together," Morgan reminded him.

"Okay then, I guess you'll be sleeping in the tree," William retorted. He threw down his cloak and stick, and climbed the tree.

Morgan could see his brother settling himself in the branches of the tree. He knew William would regret not taking his cloak, but Morgan was too angry to worry about him.

Since he was determined not to spend the night in a tree, he wandered over to an old oak tree and settled among some large plant leaves that covered the tree's huge, twisted roots. He wriggled into a comfortable position, feeling sure that he had chosen a safer spot to spend the night. As Morgan drifted off to sleep, wrapped in his woollen cape, he felt a certain satisfaction knowing that William was going to be very cold up in the tree.

Sometime later, he was awakened by a rustling sound near the yew tree. It was a dark, moonless night, so he couldn't see anything, but he hoped the noise was coming from William. Maybe he was on his way over to the oak tree.

The rustling noise continued, but William didn't appear. Morgan tried to yell for help, but, he was unable to make a sound. He sat up and tried to get to his feet, but his legs were completely numb. His heart began pounding against his shirt. He couldn't get up and he couldn't speak. What was happening?

Morgan looked over at the yew tree, hoping to see his brother climbing down from his perch. Instead, he saw a light near the tree. At first, he thought William had lit a candle. But, he soon realized the light was coming from a small firebrand. He could vaguely see tiny people rummaging through William's things at the base of the yew. Piskies!

He tried to shout a warning, but he was still unable to speak. Again, he struggled to get up. Something was tied around his legs! He reached down and felt something cold, thick, and sinewy wrapped tightly around his ankles. When he reached down and touched the binding tendrils, Morgan could feel a strange pulsing sensation within the fibres. Desperate to be free of the disgusting tendrils that seemed to be alive, he yanked with all of his strength. From somewhere beneath him, an agonizing scream pierced the night air. Terrified, he released his hold. The screaming stopped.

Within seconds, the piskies were standing in front of Morgan. In the glow of the small torch, he could see seven sets of piggy little eyes staring at him.

"Mandragora, mandragora," they chanted, as they laughed and pointed at him. Then they ran off, singing, "No more brother, no more brother."

That was the last sound that Morgan heard. The night became still and eerily quiet.

All of a sudden, he was forced to the ground. As he lay on his back, unable to move, he could feel the pulsing fibres slithering across his entire body. Hypnotic voices began whispering from the ground beneath him. The throbbing tendrils enveloped him, and the lyrical voices got into his head and lured him down...down...deep into the bowels of the earth.

*****

Durkin was jolted out of a sound sleep. He sat up in his bed, sweating and gasping for air. He had heard screaming – ominous banshee screaming. Durkin jumped out of bed and threw on his clothes. He paced back and forth in his room in the grey light of dawn. He was overcome with a feeling of foreboding. Then it came to him. Something had happened to the lads!

Durkin lit a torch from the embers in his fireplace. He had to get to the pool. Tawyn would show him what had happened.

He left his cottage and walked through the trees as quickly as he could. Kneeling before the pool, he shone his torch on the water.

Immediately the dark water began to swirl and he clearly saw piskies laughing and pointing at something. He could faintly hear them saying, "Manda...manda'.

The sound faded and the image in the pool shifted to a yew tree. A boy was rapidly climbing down the tree and running toward the piskies.

"Just one boy," Durkin murmured. "Where is the other?" The water rippled and he saw broad leaves of a low-growing plant, covering the base of an oak tree. He was overwhelmed with a deep feeling of dread. "Oh no!" he gasped.

"Mandragora..."

Durkin closed his eyes and then opened them quickly. He checked the pool image, hoping that he had been mistaken. Again, he saw thick, large leaves of a plant that he knew well.

Then, a new image appeared; one boy sitting on the grass with his arms wrapped around his knees. Beside him sat a small grey cat.

CHAPTER TWENTY-ONE

Morgan dreamed that he was falling into a deep, dark hole. He couldn't see anything, but he could feel snakes grabbing him; squeezing the life from him. He forced himself to wake up. Indeed, he could see nothing, and he couldn't move. He quickly realized that the squeezing was not caused by snakes. It was the same pulsing tubers that he had felt before. As they slithered across his face, Morgan clamped his mouth shut and shook his head from side to side, but the tendrils forced his lips apart. A bitter, repulsive liquid filled his mouth, and an excruciating pain bored into his eyes.

The next time he awoke, Morgan felt something clawing at him, tearing the ropey tubers from his body. Soon, he was free, and he felt himself being lifted up. He tried to open his eyes, to see who was helping him, but his efforts only intensified the searing pain that was pounding behind his eyes. He thought of Seffie, and the pain began to ease. He felt himself leaving all pain and fear behind, as he succumbed to the darkness.

Morgan was awakened by the sound of his brother's voice.

"Morgan, please wake up," William begged. "Lady Grey, what is wrong with him?"

"Your brother's heart still beats, but he has suffered a great trauma," she replied.

Morgan felt himself being lowered gently to the ground. He could hear William talking to someone. He fought to clear his head. He tried to speak, but his raw throat refused to respond. Morgan let out a painful moan.

"He's waking up," his brother said. "You're safe now, Morg. Open your eyes."

Morgan felt his eyelids flutter, but he couldn't open them enough to see William.

"He will soon begin to react to the shock that his body has experienced," a woman said. "We must keep him warm. Do you have blankets?"

"No, but we have wool cloaks," William replied. "I'll get them."

Within a few minutes, Morgan felt his leather bag being lifted off his shoulder, and placed under his head. Then he felt the warmth of the soft woollen cloaks as they were wrapped around him.

"What happened? Where did you find him?" his brother was asking the woman.

"He was taken by the Mandragora," she replied.

"I heard the piskies shouting that word last night," William said. "Then I heard horrible screaming. Who is Mad-a-gora?"

"Mandragora is a poisonous plant with strangling roots. The plant lures people into its clutches to feed on their life energy, so that it can grow and multiply. It feeds only at night, and one body can satisfy it for a very long time.

Morgan didn't know what she was talking about, but her voice seemed familiar. He tried to remember who it could be, but he couldn't think clearly. He decided to focus on his brother's conversation with her. If he could hear her voice again, maybe he would remember.

"Where is this gross plant?" William asked.

"Usually under oak trees," she replied. "Go over to the tree where I found your brother, and look at the plant growing at the base. Memorize its appearance so that you never forget it. The mandragora is sensitive to light, so it is harmless during the day."

Morgan's stomach began to churn painfully. He groaned.

"Hush now, your brother is coming back," the lady said softly.

"Morg, I'm here," William said, gently patting his leg. "Lady Grey, I went over to the plant. It seems to be alive. I think I could hear it breathing. "

"Mysterious voices emanate from the plants at night," she said. "They whisper in a way that entices humans into their clutches. If anyone tugs at their roots, they shriek loudly, as though they are in great pain."

Morgan remembered the voices he'd heard in the night. He cried out, as he thought about being trapped underground. His body began to convulse.

"He is ridding himself of the foul poisons," Lady Grey said. "This is good. New blood and life force will soon fill his body."

The spasms stopped and Morgan lay still; exhausted from the seizure. He was very thirsty. He tried to tell them that he needed water, but all he could do was smack his lips together and swallow hard.

"William, your brother must have fresh

water. Go quickly," the lady said.

Soon Morgan felt water dribbling into the corner of his mouth. Eagerly, he drank as much as he could. He felt the pain in his throat subside, so he tried again to talk.

"Will," he gasped, reaching for his brother.

"I'm right here," William said, taking his hand and holding it tightly.

Morgan relaxed immediately. To his surprise, he could now remember where he'd heard that lady's voice before. It sounded like the voice the grey cat used when she spoke to him in his head. "Seffie, Seffie," he said weakly.

"The cat was here, and she'll be back soon," William assured him. "Just rest now."

Morgan opened his eyes, but saw only darkness. "Still night?" he rasped. His throat felt raw and painful. He struggled to sit up, so that he could see his brother's face.

"No, it's morning," William replied, helping his brother to a sitting position. "See the sun shining through the trees?"

"Can't see," Morgan cried, beginning to panic. "My eyes! Can't see!" He clawed at his eyes, trying to force them to see again.

"This happens to some people when they return from the mandragora," the lady said.

Morgan heard the cat's voice again. She was

speaking aloud. She wasn't just thoughts in his head. "Seffie?" he croaked.

"Calm down," William replied. "Lady Grey is here with us."

"No, Seffie," he argued. "Where is she?"

"The cat really isn't here," William said. "Lady Grey is the one who saved you."

"Ropes! Get them off me," Morgan shouted hoarsely, grabbing at his legs.

"Hang on, you're just tangled in the capes," William said, quickly removing them. He held his brother's head against his chest. "You're okay now."

Morgan relaxed for a moment. Then, he began to feel very sick to his stomach. He squirmed away from William and leaned over to vomit. Mud, leaves and chunks of tuberous roots poured from Morgan's mouth, onto the grass.

"Water," Morgan spluttered, spitting out the last bits of mud.

After rinsing his mouth, and resting for a short time, Morgan asked his brother to help him stand up. He was still a bit dizzy and weak, but he felt much better.

"We must get help for your brother, as soon as possible," Lady Grey said to William. "If you can support him, I will carry your things and lead the way. Granny Gingergrace lives nearby. She has special medications that will make him whole again."

"I don't think my brother is well enough to go anywhere yet," William said.

"If Will helps me, I think I can make it," Morgan said to the lady with Seffie's voice. "Can your granny cure my blindness?" he asked.

"She has cures for many things, I know she will do her best," she assured him. "Are you are certain that you are able to travel?" Morgan nodded.

They hadn't gone far, when Lady Grey led them off the main path. It was difficult for Morgan to trudge over the uneven ground, but William patiently guided and supported him. After several stops, for Morgan to catch his breath and drink some water, the three of them arrived at a small earthen dwelling beneath a hill. William helped his brother down several stone steps that led to a little wooden door.

Before they could knock, the door opened, and a tiny old woman, with a very large nose and long white hair, greeted them. "Welcome, wayfarers, I am called Granny Gingergrace," she said kindly.

As they entered her house, Morgan noticed interesting aromas and he could hear a tea kettle whistling. He suddenly began to feel ill and very weak. When he let go of William, he stumbled and almost fell.

"Take your brother to the cot," she said to William. "He must lie down."

"It is wonderful to see you again, Lady Grey. I have made tea for you and William," she said, shuffling across the dirt floor to a small stove. "Please sit down. You must be worn out too."

When William and Lady Grey were settled at the tiny table, sipping tea, Granny Gingergrace went back to the stove and poured some pleasant smelling herbs into a cup and carried it over to Morgan. She held his head so he could take a few sips of the infusion. Granny laid him down again, and carefully removed his shirt. There were several red, ropey blisters across Morgan's neck, chest, and arms.

"Aro gard nam?" Granny Gingergrace asked, looking at Lady Grey. She nodded. "Eesot elbat ons ieh?" Again, Lady Grey nodded. The old woman muttered to herself as she left his bedside and walked across the room with his muddy shirt in her hand.

"What did the granny say to you?" William asked Lady Grey.

"She asked me if the mandragora had caused his blindness," she answered.

"What language was she speaking?" he

asked.

"She spoke the ancient language of our people," Lady Grey replied.

The old woman walked by the table with two basins of warm water and some clean rags. An odd, pungent smell wafted through the room. William wrinkled his nose and mouthed the words, 'What's that?' Lady Grey just smiled at him.

Granny Gingergrace placed one of the warm, damp cloths on Morgan's eyes. After gently cleaning most of the dirt from his body, she put warm poultices on the angry blisters. Morgan lay very still, allowing Granny to take care of him. She gathered up the cup and the basins and set them on the back of the stove to keep warm.

"You must stay here tonight," she said to William. "Your brother needs to rest."

"But we have to go to the dragon's cave," he said. "We're already behind schedule."

Morgan wanted to agree with William, but he couldn't seem to say anything. He was getting very sleepy, in spite of his strong desire to get on with the mission.

"You will go there in the morning," Granny said firmly.

"Will Morgan be alright by then? Can you cure his blindness?" William asked.

"He will recover, but I do not know if he will see again," she replied. When she saw the look of concern on William's face, she added, "Of course, I will do all that I can."

"It is time for me to leave," Lady Grey said, rising from her chair.

"You can't leave us now," William said. "How will we find Griswold's cave?"

"You will follow your map. If you give it to me, I will show you the way," she said.

He handed her the map and she traced the route with one of her long slender fingers. "It is not marked on here, but this is Granny Gingergrace's house," she said, pointing to a spot just off the main trail. "Go back to the place where we left the path. Once you are on the main path again, continue to follow the directions on your map. It is not far from here." On her way to the door, Lady Grey stopped to talk to Morgan.

"Granny Gingergrace is the best healer I know," she said. "I believe she will be able to make you well."

Morgan reached his hand out to her. "Thank you for saving me," he said hoarsely."

She took his hand in hers and held it gently. "I will see you again, my friend. I wish you and your brother a very safe journey." Lady Grey put his hand down and briefly brushed a long, slender finger across his cheek.

Morgan could hear the two women talking outside. He listened intently, wondering if they were talking about his recovery, but he was unable to make out what they were saying. He took a deep breath and settled into a comfortable slumber.

While he slept, he returned time and time again to his terrifying ordeal with the mandragora. His mind reeled as he groped for control and mastery of the overwhelming panic that was choking the life from him again. Slowly his head began to clear and he awoke. Morgan tried to open his eyes, but the wet cloth was covering them. As he reached up to remove it, Granny spoke to him gently.

"There you go lad, do not be afraid. Let me remove the poultice and we shall see if your sight has returned." Carefully, she took the warm cloth from his eyes.

Morgan put his hands on his damp face and slowly opened his eyes. He could see nothing! "I'm still blind," he said despondently. "Where is my brother?"

"I'm right here," William said, rushing to his side. "Don't worry, you'll be able see again soon. Granny Gingergrace will find a way to help you get well."

Morgan reached up and grabbed his brother's shirt. "Don't leave me."

"I'm not going anywhere," William said. "We're going to stay here tonight. Now, drink some of her special tea so you can get stronger." He helped Morgan to sit.

After a few sips of the infusion, Morgan pushed it aside. "Will, promise me you won't go to the dragon's cave without me."

"I won't," William confirmed. "I'll sleep on the floor right beside you." Again, he put the cup to Morgan's mouth.

After drinking a little more tea, Morgan began to relax. But he continued to hold on to his brother's shirt as he drifted off to sleep.

*****

Durkin sat down on the shore. His hands were shaking. Felis Silvestris! At least the grey cat was there. She would find the other boy, unless the mandragora had... Just thinking that something fatal may have happened to one of the boys, was more than he could bear.

In desperation, he turned his attention again to the oracle. "Please show me two lads," he whispered. He saw nothing. Dejected, Durkin sank to the grass beside the pool and closed his eyes. He felt helpless and exhausted.

When he opened his eyes, sunlight was dancing on the pool. Durkin dragged his stiff, old body to the edge of the water, angry that he had fallen asleep.

What he saw in the water this time filled him with deep sadness. Griswold was alone, just inside the cave's entrance. He seemed to be drained of all energy and hope.

"Too late," moaned the dragon. "Mandragora has taken one. Now, I shall die."

"Hang on!" Durkin urged. "The lads will come, I know they will."

A miserable, misty sigh escaped from the dragon's once fiery nostrils and tears fell from his tired, yellow eyes.

The water rippled again and Durkin saw a familiar scene. Mounds of earthen homes reminded him that he was looking at his own village of long ago. He saw a tiny old woman with long white hair standing in a doorway. Granny Gingergrace! To his great surprise, and relief, he also saw two identical boys leaving Granny's hillside dwelling. There they were, both of them, walking toward the dragon's lair. Would they make it in time? Perhaps...

CHAPTER TWENTY-TWO

The next morning, the twins began the last leg of their journey. Granny Gingergrace had not been able to restore Morgan's vision. Panic and arguments had ensued between the boys. William didn't feel that Morgan was well enough to go to Griswold's cave. Morgan insisted that he was fine. The arguments ended with Granny's insistence that they must go together, as instructed, to complete their mission. She gave William a small bag and told him to ask Griswold if he would allow the boys to fill it with a healing substance called sanguis siccarum draco.

"I'm sorry Ma'am, I can't do that," William said politely, but firmly. "I don't know what that stuff is, or where to find it. I'm worried about getting my brother to Griswold's cave, I can't handle anything else."

"Let me explain," Granny Gingergrace said patiently. "I feel certain that Griswold will offer some to you. Just place it in the bag, and bring it back to me." She handed him a second small bag. "This is a gift for Griswold. Please give it to him."

"What is that sangi stuff? William asked as he took the small bags from her.

"Dried dragon's blood," she replied. With no further explanation, she went into her house and closed the door.

"Dried dragon's blood," he repeated.

"Don't worry about it," Morgan said, taking William's arm. "I think it must be important or Granny wouldn't have asked you to get it. Let's go, Griswold is waiting for us." He pushed his brother forward, so that William could lead the way through the tangled underbrush.

The day was already very warm, so they walked at an easy pace. After an hour or so, they sat down under a shady tree to rest.

"Do you think I'll ever be able to see again?" Morgan asked.

"Of course you will. I'm sure Granny has some more healing tricks up her sleeve."

"The cloth she put on my eyes didn't seem to

help much," Morgan reminded him.

"Didn't help much?" William cried. "Does that mean you can see something?"

"I think I can tell if we're in the sun or the shade," Morgan said.

"Good!" William exclaimed. "Then you'll definitely get your vision back."

"You're just saying that, because you're as scared as I am," Morgan said. "But, I do appreciate your positive attitude. Now look at the map and tell me how much further it is to the cave."

William took the map from his bag and studied it silently. He walked out to the middle of the path and stopped, looking at the map and then at the trail. "Morg, the map shows two big yew trees in a clearing, just before we climb up to the cave," he shouted. "I can see the trees just ahead of us. I think we're almost there." He helped Morgan to his feet. Arm in arm, they hurried to the clearing.

"We're standing right below the cave," William announced.

"Is it a long way up to the entrance?" Morgan asked.

"No, and the path kind of angles up gradually, so it's not going to be a steep climb for you. Are you ready?" William asked eagerly.

"Let's adjust our gear first," Morgan suggested. "I don't want to trip over my cloak."

"Here, let me take them," William offered, throwing both cloaks over his arm. "Your bag seems fine, and you've got your walking stick, so let's go."

The twins made the short climb to the cave and stopped in front of the entrance.

"Do we just walk right in?" William asked.

"We're supposed to wait here, the entrance is blocked," Morgan said.

"How do you know that?" William said. "Oh, I suppose you can communicate with the dragon in your head, like you did with the grey cat."

Before Morgan could respond, a misty spray began pouring out of the cave. William pulled his brother away from the entrance. When nothing else happened, he let go of Morgan and took a few steps forward. Suddenly, flames shot out of the cave, knocking William down. He jumped up, shocked but not injured.

"What's going on?" Morgan cried.

"A fire!" William exclaimed. "I'm okay but our cloaks are on fire." He quickly began stamping out the flames. Suddenly three piskies popped out from under the burning cloaks, screeching and running for their lives.

"Piskies were hiding in our cloaks," William

shouted excitedly. "And they were still smoking when they hit the bushes. The dragon must have known they were inside the pockets." William took the cloaks over to Morgan. "There wasn't much damage, but the smell of the burnt wool is pretty disgusting."

"Don't talk!" Morgan interrupted. "I'm getting a message in my head."

"From the dragon?" William asked.

"Yes, but I won't be able to hear what he's saying if you keep talking," Morgan replied. He sat on the ground and held his head in his hands as he had done in the tower room at Adney House. "We are invited to enter," he said. "Griswold welcomes us."

William helped Morgan to his feet, and the two of them walked cautiously into the dark cave. Glowing quartz crystals lined the walkway. The boys stopped abruptly when they heard a scurrying noise behind them. William whirled around with his walking stick ready for an attack.

"What's that noise? What's happening?" Morgan asked.

"There's a little glowing fairy flying toward us," William said.

"I am Perinina, the Dream Weaver," she squeaked in a high-pitched voice.

Morgan grabbed William's arm. "Don't look into her eyes," he whispered.

"I have come to guide you to The Mighty One," she squeaked.

"Please, lead the way," William said, without looking directly at her. The tiny girl flew past. They followed her along the passageway and into an enormous crystal room. She flew over to the massive dragon, circled him once, and then disappeared.

"We're standing in front of the dragon now," William whispered. "He's really big."

"What's he doing?" Morgan asked.

"He's lying on the ground. His eyes are closed and he's not moving," William said.

Without warning, Morgan let go of William's arm and walked toward the dragon confidently, as though his sight had miraculously returned.

"At last you have arrived," the dragon said telepathically to Morgan.

"I am Morgan, Wise One of the Sea. I have come with my twin brother, William, Noble Protector," he said to the dragon. Morgan couldn't see Griswold's grateful smile.

"I was dying, but thankfully you have come," the dragon whispered in Morgan's head. "I knew that Mandragora had you in her clutches. I am very pleased to see that you survived. Most people do not. However, I did not know that you had lost your vision." Griswold's eyes filled with tears. "Step closer. Place your fingers on my eye water and then touch your eyes." Morgan leaned over and touched the surprisingly soft face.

"Morgan, don't get so close," William warned. "What are you doing?"

"It's okay. Griswold is trying to help me see again," Morgan replied. He placed his fingers gently on the reptile's tears and then touched his own eyes. The dragon tears caused Morgan to blink several times.

"I can see!" he exclaimed, looking around. His eyes rested on the elegant dragon.

Griswold's massive body almost filled the entire cave. The dragon had a large flat head with a very long jaw. Several sharp teeth were visible. He also had heavily lidded yellow eyes and large, curled nostrils. A flowing crest on top of his head, trailed back toward his neck. Huge, bat-like wings lay folded against his back. Griswold's body was covered with triangular, green and gold, iridescent scales. Powerful claws extended from each of his four feet. Morgan knelt in reverence to the mighty dragon.

Turning his attention away from the magnificent creature, Morgan focused on the beauty and vastness of the crystal lined cave.

Along each wall, quartz crystals provided soft, glowing light. Finally, his eyes rested on William. It was such a relief to see his brother again. They both smiled broadly.

"This cure for your blindness is only temporary," the dragon said telepathically to Morgan. "To restore your vision permanently, you will need a potion that is best prepared by the magical hands of the Granddame Gingin Gratia. Your brother must have brought a small bag that she sent with him. Fill it now with sanguis siccarum draco."

Morgan relayed the message to William, and the two of them waited for Griswold to let them know where they would find the dried blood. The dragon looked at the earthen floor beneath him. The boys followed his gaze, and saw tiny reddish brown stones that were hardly noticeable in the dirt. They looked at Griswold. When he nodded, they filled the small pouch with the red stones, and William put it back into his shoulder bag.

"Now it is time to complete your task. I trust that you have brought crystals that will open the chamber containing the Magick of the Magus," Griswold said silently. Morgan removed three seed crystals from his bag and showed them to the dragon.

"Yes, those are exactly what we need. Now,

you must listen very carefully. There is an alcove in the wall behind you. Once you are in there, stand very close together, with William on your right, facing the wall between us."

Morgan told William what the dragon had said, and the two of them walked into the recessed area and faced the wall between them and Griswold.

"Now, hold one crystal in your left hand, and have William hold one in his right hand. The third crystal should be in your right hand, Morgan, which is to remain loosely at your side for the time being. Next, both of you must extend your arms holding the crystals toward the wall at forty-five degree angles to your heads. Your arms and bodies should form a triangle. The point where your crystals meet will create a polychromous spot on the wall." The boys gasped as a rainbow coloured circle formed on the wall in front of them.

"With your eyes on the circle, carefully touch the centre with the pointed end of the third crystal that is in your right hand, Morgan."

Slowly Morgan raised his right arm and touched the circle with the third crystal. The boys jumped back, when the crystal was instantly absorbed into the wall.

"Do not move!" the dragon shouted into

Morgan's head.

Morgan grabbed William's arm and indicated that they must stand very still. Slowly, a hidden door slid open, exposing a tiny compartment that glowed with a faint blue light. Resting on a single shelf was a tattered, leather bag. A blue crystal ball was suspended above it. Beams from the ball encased the bag in a pyramid of light. Morgan and William looked at each other in disbelief. William reached forward to take the bag.

"I'll take that," a deep voice said. The boys wheeled around and stood face to face with another dragon. They knew immediately it was not Griswold. For one thing, he spoke aloud. Both boys could hear him. Also, his eyes were fiery red and his scales were a solid golden colour. This dragon seemed much younger. Morgan knew that he must be Griswold's son.

"Do not touch anything in the vault," he instructed them. "I am Egandor, Fiery Defender, and I have come for the bag of Merlyn."

"Of course," William said, stepping back. "We were just... we're..."

"You need not explain," Egandor said. "I must take the bag, and go quickly."

"We understand," Morgan said, finally daring to speak.

"My father and I are eternally grateful to you and the Adney twains before you. Because of your family, Merlyn's magic will finally be safely concealed with the treasures of other ancient ones," Egandor said, bowing his head in appreciation.

"We are honoured to have been able to help," Morgan said.

"Thank you," the dragon said. "Forgive me, but I must be on my way. Please return to the main hall. My father waits to bid you farewell."

The boys moved away from the crystal recess. Because of Egandor's size, they had to step over his huge tail to get past him. Holding the bag of magic protectively against his scaly body, Egandor followed them into the main room.

Without warning, a small orange dragon swooped into the cave, screeching as he flew toward them. His beady green eyes scanned the room. He chose his target and flames shot from his nostrils. He was aiming directly at Egandor!

"Go back!" Egandor shouted to the boys.

Morgan and William quickly ducked into the alcove. Once they were safely inside, the boys looked into the vault where Merlin's bag had been. The blue crystal ball was gone, and the shelf was completely bare. Looking more closely, Morgan saw that there was now only a thin layer of clear crystal between the wall and the main room. Crowding close together, the boys were able to watch the horrific dragon fight through the tiny window.

As the small dragon charged at Egandor, a bolt of fire blasted from Griswold's nostrils. The flames shot through the air and hit the intruder. Fire ripped through one of its wings, and the creature plunged to the ground.

Some kind of communication seemed to take place between Griswold and his son. With a nod of his massive head, Egandor sprayed the intruder with a frosty vapour. The small dragon lay paralyzed on the ground. His beady eyes were the only part of him that could move. And those evil green eyes seemed to be focused on the twins.

"He's going to come after us," Morgan whispered.

"He can't hurt us. Egandor froze him with some kind of gas," William said, staring back at the dragon. "Why does he look so familiar?"

"I'm sure we've never seen him before today, so I don't think…" Morgan stopped mid-sentence when he saw Egandor making his way to the other side of the cave.

The crystal wall next to Griswold suddenly opened, revealing a dark passage. Egandor and the bag of magic quickly disappeared into the darkness, and the wall closed.

Griswold then turned his attention to the small dragon. He was beginning to come back to life. Griswold's huge, yellow eyes bored into the beady little green eyes. The small dragon's head began to shake back and forth, as though he was in pain or trying to break some kind of spell. Then, the creature opened his mouth and let out a hideous screech. At that same moment, Griswold released a torrent of fire. The small dragon instantly disintegrated into a pile of grey ash.

"Wow!" William whispered. "That was incredible!"

"That little dragon just came out of nowhere," Morgan said. He was stunned by the events that had just happened, but his thoughts were interrupted by a message from the Mighty One. "Griswold wants us to come out now," he said to his brother.

The boys walked carefully around the ashes and went over to Griswold.

"Ask him what that fight was all about," William whispered.

"I regret the events that you had to witness, and I am relieved that you are both safe," Griswold said telepathically to Morgan.

"Sir we are thankful that you and your son were not hurt and the treasure is safe,"

Morgan said aloud. "Where did that dragon come from, and what did he want?"

"My son and I have no idea where he came from. We have never seen a dragonet of that species before. I tried to force information from him when he was beginning to recover from the shot of cold vapour that Egandor had given him. He refused to reveal anything, so it was necessary to end his existence," he replied.

While Morgan was conversing with Griswold, William wandered over to study the pile of ashes that had once been the small dragon. Abruptly, he jumped up and ran back to the others. "Hey, Morg, I just remembered why that dragon looked familiar," he said excitedly. "The night we watched the piskie ceremony, the head guy morphed into a dragon. That dragon," he said pointing to the ashes, "looked just like him."

"You're right!" Morgan agreed. "I forgot about that piskie." Turning to Griswold, he asked him if that dragon could possibly have come from the caves near Adney House.

"It is indeed possible, and most likely that is exactly who he was," Griswold told him. "The piskies have been a problem ever since Merlyn's bag was brought to me. They are very gifted shape-shifters, but until now, I have never known them to be able to take on a form such as this."

"Tell me what he said," William insisted.

Morgan related what Griswold had told him.

"That's why he was showing the other piskies that he could morph into a dragon," William suggested. "He probably knew that this was their last chance to snatch the bag. He was perfecting his transformation, so he could follow us and grab the magic from Egandor. Ask Griswold what he thinks about my brilliant theory?"

Morgan and Griswold had a brief conversation. "We both agree with your theory and we think you are absolutely brilliant for figuring it out," Morgan said, smiling.

"Yes!" William exclaimed, proudly.

The dragon interrupted Morgan's thoughts once again. "It is time for all of us to leave. Time is of the essence."

"That's what Osdruan always says," Morgan said aloud, so that William could know part of the conversation. "We would like to stay, but I know that it is time for us to go."

"Wait, I have a gift for Griswold," William said, rummaging around in his bag. He pulled out a small cloth pouch. "Granny said to give this to you." He placed the bag on the ground in front of the dragon.

"She is very thoughtful," Griswold told Morgan. "The Granddame Gingin Gratia has sent special seeds to give me strength for my long journey. Please express my gratitude when you see her." He looked from one boy to the other. "Your mission has been completed. You are courageous, loyal lads and you did a magnificent job."

After Morgan relayed the message to his brother, they both thanked the dragon and bowed respectfully.

"Perinina will accompany you to the entrance," Griswold communicated to Morgan. "When you leave, my caverna will be closed forever." He sighed sadly. "If you lads should ever choose to visit Ynys Wyth, my homeland, I will surely welcome you."

"Thank you," Morgan said softly.

Outside the cave, Morgan told William about Griswold's invitation to visit him at Ynys Wyth.

"Osdruan said he was going to Dragon's Isle," William said. "Where's Unus Ooth?"

"Maybe it's another name for Dragon's Isle," Morgan replied absently, focusing his attention on the countryside below the cave. "We must have been with Griswold for a long time, it's already getting dark. We'd better hurry to

Granny Gingergrace's house."

"We have lots of time," William said. "It's only mid-afternoon."

"So the blindness returns," Morgan grumbled miserably. "Well, at least I got to see Griswold."

"Yeah, and the dragon fight," William said enthusiastically. "We never expected to see a dragon fight. That little guy sure was gutsy to try to take on Griswold and Egandor." He continued talking as he guided Morgan down the hill and along the path.

Morgan smiled, aware that William's lively chatter was for his benefit, so that he wouldn't think about his failing vision. Morgan didn't tell his brother that his vision was completely gone, long before they arrived at the cottage.

Granny Gingergrace was waiting for them in the doorway of her earthen home. She looked very sad, when she noticed that Morgan was still unable to see.

William handed her the bag of dried dragon's blood and Granny quickly set about preparing a potion, while William helped Morgan get comfortable on the cot by the door.

As the infusion boiled, a foul odour filled the room. Morgan hoped that he wouldn't be expected to swallow something that smelled like blood and dirt.

Granny handed a cupful of the dark brown mixture to William, and told him to help his brother drink the liquid. He held the cup to Morgan's mouth.

"I can't drink it," Morgan said, pushing the cup away.

Granny sat down beside Morgan. "I regret there is no other way to get this infusion into your body. You must drink this entire cupful, because it is the only way to heal your body permanently and restore your vision," she said. She put the cup to his lips.

Reluctantly, Morgan nodded and accepted the drink. He quickly gulped down as much as he could. He tried not to taste or smell the disgusting potion. When the cup was empty, he had to consciously force himself not to vomit. Granny immediately gave him a mint to suck on, which did help take away the dreadful taste in his mouth.

*****

Durkin looked into the pool one more time. The water rippled and he saw King Ulric's face, twisted in pain. As the image cleared, he saw him clutch his chest and fall to the floor. Durkin had to get to the castle. Something was terribly wrong. He hurried to Rhiannon's cottage. The magic maiden took him quickly and invisibly to the palace.

Durkin went directly to Lucian's room and told him of the vision. They rushed to the king's chamber. They found Ulric lying on the floor, gasping for air. Lucian and Durkin were able to get King Ulric back into his bed.

After a brief examination, Lucian scribbled a few words on a piece of paper, handed it to a page, and told him to send someone to fetch Asa, the Healer.

"Is it his heart?" Durkin asked. Lucian nodded. "What can I do to help?"

"Climb up here and rub his hands and feet to get circulation to his extremities," the physician replied. Lucian massaged the king's chest while they waited for the forest healer to arrive. Since Asa was the only one who had a supply of the forbidden mistletoe, he would know the exact combination of herbs that should be given to the

king. Mistletoe was the best aid for heart conditions, but it was also the deadliest.

Asa arrived and quickly mixed several herbs together in a cup. After drinking a concoction of foxglove, willow, and mistletoe berries, King Ulric fell asleep and was soon breathing more evenly. Lucian checked his heart rate every hour.

Durkin and the healers sipped tea and talked quietly through the night, while they waited for the king to awaken.

CHAPTER TWENTY-THREE

Early the next morning, Morgan awoke feeling much stronger. He called across the room to his brother. William got up quickly and went over to Morgan's cot. Granny was sitting beside Morgan and they were both grinning happily.

"The dragon's blood worked! I can see again!" Morgan exclaimed. "And Granny Gingergrace is sure that my vision has been restored permanently this time." He got up and began to dance around the room, laughing and singing: "Oh, it's great to be alive. Granny is a genius. I'm so happy, I could cry."

"Wow, that's great news," William said, giving his brother a quick hug. "I knew all along that Granny would be able to help you get your vision back. Granny, you are the best healer ever," he said to the little old woman.

"Thank you, my dear, but it was the dragon's blood that did the healing," she said modestly.

"Well, I'm grateful for everything that you have done for me," Morgan said. "Lady Grey was right when she said you would be the one that could make me well."

Granny patted his arm affectionately. "It's been wonderful to have two wise and courageous young men, such as you and your brother, stop with me awhile. But, now that you are well, you lads must be on your way to Greywood."

"I have my vision back, and I'm ready to go," Morgan said gathering his things together. "I hope Nesta hasn't given up on us."

"She'll be there to meet us at Blanford," William assured him.

Granny stopped them as they were about to rush out the door. "Wait," she cried above their excited chatter. "I want to remind you of a few things before you set out. Please get back to Blanford as quickly as you can. Watch out for the piskies, and be more careful about staying together."

"We promise to be two as one, all the way back to Greywood, right, Will?" Morgan said. When there was no response from his brother,

Morgan looked at him questioningly.

"What happened to you with the Mandragora was my fault," William confessed.

"I was the one who chose to sleep under the oak tree," Morgan reminded him.

"I know, but I tried to bully you into doing what I wanted, and you paid the price," William said. "Since that night, I've spent every waking minute remembering that it was my fault that the piskies found us, my fault that you were sucked into the ground, and my fault that you went blind."

"Both of you made a few rash decisions," Granny interjected. "But that is in the past."

She looked fondly at each boy. "You must put aside your feelings of guilt and remorse. Both of you know what you have to do to be safe." Granny said, as she handed each of them a bag of food and a full flask of water.

The boys thanked her again. William went outside, but Morgan stayed back.

"There is no way that I can express my appreciation for all that you have done for me," he said seriously, as he hugged the tiny old woman. "Thank you for everything."

"You are very welcome," Granny replied.

"May I ask you something before I leave?" Morgan asked her.

"Of course," she said.

"Why did Griswold call you 'the Granddame Gingin Gratia'?"

Granny smiled. "That is my given name. It means Gracious Grand Dame of the Healing Ginger Root," she explained. "It is such a long name that, over the years, it has been shortened to Granny Gingergrace."

"I like your full name," Morgan said. "I feel privileged to have been cured by such a gracious healer."

"You are very sweet," Granny said, wiping a tear from her eye. "Go quickly, now," she added, rushing him out the door.

The boys turned and waved to her as they approached the main path. They continued along the familiar trail without talking for some time. They were both lost in their own thoughts. When they arrived at the oak tree that was surrounded by the seemingly innocuous mandrake plants, Morgan stopped and turned to William.

"It doesn't look scary in the daylight," he said.

"Even though Lady Grey said it's harmless during the day, it still gives me the creeps," William admitted.

"Tell me about Lady Grey," Morgan said.

"She just appeared with you in her arms. You looked dead," William said hoarsely.

Morgan shuddered, remembering how frightened he had been. "But where did she come from?" he asked. "What did she look like?"

"I don't know where she came from," William admitted. "She was tall and thin with long greyish, blonde hair and big green eyes."

"I wish I could have seen her," Morgan said, regretfully. "It was very dark and cold under the earth," he said, looking at the plants and remembering the horrifying roots that had wrapped around his body. "I was sure that I was going to die, so I finally quit struggling and waited for my life to be over. The next thing I knew, someone was tearing the tubers from my body and lifting me up. I couldn't see who it was, and I didn't know where I was being taken. But, I do recall thinking about Seffie for some reason, and that made me feel safe."

"That cat was waiting with me by the road for awhile after you disappeared," William said. "And then she just left. The piskies arrived and pretended that they wanted to help find you. They tried to get me to let them hold my leather bag, while I went to search for you by the oak tree. They kept screaming, 'Mandragora'. I was sure they had killed you. What the piskies really wanted was my jacinth and my leather bag. When I refused to give them anything, they all crowded around, pushing and threatening me with a torch. All of a sudden, Seffie appeared out of nowhere. She was snarling and running toward us. That cat scared the pants off those guys. They took one look at her, and started running as fast as their chubby little legs could go. I waited for Seffie to come back. When she didn't show up, I continued to search for you. I thought you had disappeared forever. Then, Lady Grey arrived with you in her arms."

"That night was scary and awful for both of us," Morgan said.

At that moment, the twins heard a scuffling noise, and saw the mandrake leaves start to move. Without a word, they tore down the path at top speed, not stopping until they were out of the forest. By the time the boys reached an open field, they were breathless and weak. Morgan collapsed on the ground, panting.

William sat down beside him. "I didn't know we could run that fast, or for that long," he panted. He took his bag from his shoulder, drank some water, and then took out the map. "I can't believe it. We're already at the field we crossed after we left Blanford."

"We are?" Morgan said breathlessly. He sat

up and looked at the map. "We must have run for almost an hour. No wonder I'm so exhausted." He dropped back to the ground. "Let's not move another inch until tomorrow morning."

"That sounds like a good idea," William agreed. "But I think we should find some shelter first. According to the map, there's a piskie mound near those rocks over there, and let's not forget about the wolf we had to kill the last time we were here."

"How about you find a spot and I wait here until you get back?" Morgan suggested.

"No way!" William said. "This time, we're sticking together. Get up and follow me."

Morgan groaned, as he struggled to his feet. When they stepped onto the path, they were startled to see a tall, scruffy man with wiry red hair, and green eyes. William quickly grabbed his stick and approached the man.

The stranger smiled at him. "Are you lads in need of a place to spend the night?" he asked, looking directly into William's eyes. "May I offer my humble cottage?" William dropped his stick and advanced toward the man, bewitched by his glowing eyes.

"That is very kind of you," William said in an oddly mechanical voice.

His brother's voice snapped Morgan into

action. He grabbed his fighting stick and ran to William's side. "Thanks, but we won't need your assistance," he stated bluntly. "C'mon Will, let's go," he coaxed, pulling at his brother's shirt.

William shrugged him off. "Don't be rude, Brother," he droned. "We accept your kind offer, Sir. Lead the way." The stranger continued to hold William's gaze as he backed away from the path.

A choking fear swept over Morgan when he suddenly realized that this stranger was a shape-shifting piskie. He positioned himself protectively in front of William and swung his staff at the stranger's head.

The tall man snatched the stick from Morgan, and glared at him with fiery eyes. "You miserable little urchin," he hissed angrily. He threw the stick to the ground and grabbed Morgan by the throat. Morgan kicked at him and waved his arms as he hung in mid-air.

Once the piskie's visual hold was broken, William regained his senses. He grabbed Morgan's fighting stick and whacked the piskie across the back. The furious piskie continued to hold Morgan by the throat, as he turned and grabbed William. Grasping a boy in each hand, the piskie brought them close to his face. He looked from one boy to the other and his face went pale. He dropped the twins instantly and began to bellow, "Kithen! Kithen!"

Suddenly, piskies came from all directions! They began hurling stones at the boys. William and Morgan curled up on the ground, trying to protect themselves. The piskies kept up the volley of rocks. Luckily, many of the stones missed their mark.

Just when there seemed to be no hope for an end to the attack, there was a tremendous roar from the trees above them. The piskies stopped dead in their tracks. Morgan and William peeked out from under their arms to see what was happening.

A huge wildcat leapt down from a tree and landed on the tall man. Terrified, the rest of the piskies dropped their stones and ran down the path, yelling, 'Felis Silvestris!' The cat clawed at the stranger relentlessly. His arms and face were soon covered in blood. The man fought hard, and finally shook free of the cat's claws. As he tried to escape, the cat attacked again, biting him savagely and tearing a huge chunk of flesh from the back of his leg. Somehow, the dishevelled shape-shifter managed to get to his feet. He stumbled down the path, with blood oozing from the gaping wound on his leg.

In the silence that followed, the twins got to

their feet. There were stones scattered everywhere, and the ground was soaked in blood. The piskies were gone and so was the large cat.

"That guy was a shape-shifting piskie," William said.

"I know, and he was hypnotizing you so that you'd go with him," Morgan hinted.

"Yeah, thanks for your help. I guess I finally got a turn to be the zombie," William chuckled. "What do you think he wanted?"

"Maybe the jacinth or the crystals that we still have," Morgan replied. "Did you recognize him?"

"No, I barely remember his face. I was hypnotized most of the time," William reminded him. "Who cares about him?" I loved that big cat. It just about killed him."

"I'm sure glad it came to our rescue," Morgan said. "I don't think we could have fought off all those piskies by ourselves."

"I think they were trying to kill us," William said

"I bet they were trying to get rid of us," Morgan agreed. "They probably thought we'd bring them bad fortune because we're identical."

"Probably," William agreed. "Now that we know this is definitely a piskie hangout, we'd better look for a safer place to sleep."

They hunted around for a long time. Finally, they located a large hollow log that was dry and seemed to be uninhabited. Since it was already getting dark, they crawled into the log and unloaded their gear. They lit a candle, and ate some of the food that Granny had given them. After blowing out the candle, they wrapped themselves in their singed cloaks that still smelled smoky, and settled in for the night.

William turned over and noticed two glowing eyes at the far end of the log.

"We have company," he whispered, reaching for his fighting stick.

"It's just Seffie," Morgan said with a yawn. "She's been waiting for us." The small grey cat walked over them and sniffed their cloaks.

"Ask her if she knows the big cat that just saved our butts," William suggested.

"She isn't talking. She's already purring under my cloak," Morgan said.

"Can you really talk to her, or are you making that up?" William asked.

"I'm not making it up," Morgan said defensively. "I use thought transfer, just like I did with Griswold. You should try it. I'm sure you can communicate with her."

"What do I have to do?" William asked.

"Just open your mind, and listen for her

thoughts," Morgan said.

"Easy for you to say," his twin replied. He yawned loudly. "Maybe I'll try tomorrow. Seffie's already asleep, and I'm going to do the same."

The next morning, the boys began their trek to Blanford. They had carefully examined their belongings several times to ensure that no piskies were tucked away in their things. Seffie accompanied them across the field. She jumped through the long grass and, every now and then, she found a small rodent to pounce on. Morgan suggested that William try to clear his mind to receive thoughts from her.

William agreed to try, but he hadn't succeeded. "Maybe Seffie doesn't feel like talking to me just yet," he said. Morgan urged him to keep trying.

By mid-afternoon, the twins crossed the bridge at Blanford. Nesta and her eagle were sitting by the water.

"At last," she said, getting up. "Did you lose your map?"

"Nothing as ordinary as that," William replied. "We'll tell you all about it on the way back to Greywood."

"How long have you been waiting for us?" Morgan asked.

"I arrived yesterday. I've been very worried about you," she admitted.

"Sorry, it took us so long," William said.

"And thanks for waiting," Morgan added. He told Nesta about the small grey cat that had befriended them, but when he turned to introduce her, Seffie was nowhere to be seen.

On the way home, Nesta heard all about the mishaps that had befallen the boys on their journey. She seemed eager for them to talk about their adventures, now that their mission had been completed. When their tale was told, she hugged them and said she was relieved that they had survived.

As darkness fell, the three children saw a candle flickering in Smythe's window. The eagle screeched loudly as they neared the cottage. Jarvis came out to greet them.

Mertas and Smythe welcomed them home, and sat with them as they wolfed down warm stew and fresh bread, until they couldn't eat another bite.

Smythe stood up and cleared his throat. "There is news of the king," he said. "He recently suffered a heart attack."

"Is he dead?" William asked.

"No, but it was a very serious attack," Smythe said. "Sir Lucian and Asa are caring for him. Durkin came by earlier to inform us that the king wishes to see you lads. Durkin and Sir Osdruan will escort you to the castle tomorrow at half-ten."

"I won't visit the king ever again," William announced. "Not after what he did to me the last time."

"You have no choice," Smythe stated. "Besides, he cannot hurt you, he is too ill."

"Is he well enough to see us?" Morgan asked. Smythe nodded.

"What does he want?" William asked angrily. Smythe shook his head and shrugged.

"Let's not think about that now," Jarvis said. "You are all home, safe and sound. It's time to celebrate!"

The three travellers agreed. That evening, they went with Jarvis to his friend's cottage. Several young people from the village had gathered for an evening of fun and music. Jarvis introduced his cousins, William and Morgan, to his friends. The twins had a great time.

It was difficult for the boys to get up the next morning. They were still exhausted from the previous day's activities, and neither of them was looking forward to another visit with the crotchety old king.

Just before ten thirty, Osdruan and Durkin

arrived to take them to the castle. They all rode together in a horse-drawn cart that had been provided by the king. Osdruan asked them about their journey, and the boys told them all about their adventure.

"I was relieved to see that the grey cat was watching over you," Durkin said.

"You know about Seffie?" Morgan exclaimed.

Osdruan grinned. "Seffie is it then?" he said. "You must be very special if she allows you to use her pet name."

"What do you know about her?" Morgan asked eagerly.

"She is known as Sephonee, Companion at the Crossroads. No one has seen her for many years. You should feel very honoured that she chose to accompany you."

"Some folks call her Felis Silvestris, Cat of the Wood," Durkin added.

"That's what the piskies shouted when she pounced on them," William said excitedly.

"Yes, that is a name the piskies know and fear," Durkin said with a smile. "People in my village call her Lady Grey."

The twins were stunned. "But...but...that's the name of the lady who saved Morgan," William stammered.

"Of course," Osdruan affirmed. "Did you not

realize that she was a shape-shifter?"

"No way!" William shouted. "I can't believe it!"

"I thought I recognized her voice when I was blind," Morgan said.

"And that's why you kept asking me where Seffie was," William added.

After a few minutes, the boys related the story of the small dragon that had invaded Griswold's cave. "And thanks to Will's brilliance we were able to figure out where the dragon had come from," Morgan said, proudly. "He recognized the dragon. It was the one that we had seen the night of the piskie ceremony. Griswold said that he hadn't seen a piskie transformed into a dragon before. He called it a dragonet."

"Nor have I," Osdruan admitted. "They must have worked for many centuries to accomplish such a shape-shifting. I suppose they knew that your visit would be their last chance to get the bag of irreversible magic."

"That's exactly the same theory I had," William said.

Osdruan smiled. "Then, we are both very clever," he said. Their discussion came to an abrupt end when the horse and cart pulled into the castle courtyard.

The boys waited nervously in the salon, next to the king's bedroom, while Durkin went in to see if His Majesty was ready to receive them. He returned quickly with Asa by his side.

"It is good to see you again, lads," Asa said. "Please come in."

The twins were told to sit on two high stools at the foot of the king's bed. Ulric was barely visible amid a mountain of quilts and pillows. Morgan was shocked by his appearance. He had become a frail, old man with wild, white hair that was sticking out in every direction.

"Welcome back," the king croaked. "I have heard of your treacherous pilgrimage to the dragon's cave. Congratulations on the success of your mission. You should be proud of your tenacity and fortitude." The king winced as he cleared his throat.

"I wanted to see for myself that you were both fitly," the king continued. "I wish to thank you for all that you and your forefathers have done for my people." He looked from one boy to the other, waiting for one of them to speak.

"We just did what we had to do for Griswold, and for all of us," William said modestly, avoiding the king's eyes. For a few minutes, no one spoke.

"Are you feeling better, Sire?" Morgan asked, trying to break the awkward silence.

"I have the best physicians in the world, so I am improving quickly," Ulric said. "And my family has been taking good care of me as well."

"Your family?" William echoed. "I didn't know that you had a family."

"Yes, I have a family," King Ulric said. "I no longer have a wife, but I do have two beautiful daughters. They have been living with my sister at our summer palace. But, now they are here to see that I closely follow the orders of my physicians." The king suddenly began to cough and gasp for air. Lucian and Asa rushed to his side while Durkin quickly ushered the boys out of the room.

Osdruan was sitting at a small table downstairs, and he invited them to join him. He asked about the king's condition, and they told him what had happened.

"I just don't understand why he was so nice to us today," William said.

"According to many of his subjects, King Ulric has mellowed considerably since his attack. Perhaps he actually is trying to mend his ways," Osdruan said.

"I believe the heart attack gave him a terrible fright," Durkin said.

"Or, he realized that he's human, and can die just like the rest of us," William added.

"I think it's strange that no one has ever mentioned his family," Morgan said.

"He has never acknowledged them publicly," Osdruan said. "The king's wife died giving birth to the second child, and the girls were sent to live with his sister."

"Some people say that he was furious when neither of the children were sons, so he ordered the girls out of his sight," Durkin said quietly. "But, based on what he said this morning, it would seem that he is going to allow them to be part of his life again."

"I wouldn't be surprised if the princesses insist on moving in with him permanently," Osdruan speculated. "The oldest one is a grown girl of fifteen years and one day she could rule Greywood. I expect that she will want to claim her birthright."

"I hope she rules with a kinder hand," Morgan said.

"We shall see," Osdruan said. "Now lads, we must go back to Smythe's cottage. It is time for you to return to your homeland. Rhiannon will come for you later today."

"So soon?" William asked. "I thought we'd have more time to talk with you and have some fun with our new friends."

"Now that your mission has been completed,

it is imperative that you leave post-haste," Osdruan said. "Time is of the ess..."

"I know, time is of the essence," William said, smiling.

"But we love the people of Greywood," Morgan said. "It will be hard to leave."

"Which is precisely why you must go now," Osdruan said quietly. "Remaining with us is not an option." He pushed away from the table and the boys silently followed him to the cart that would take them back to Smythe's cottage.

Durkin was not going back to the village with them. He was going to stay at the castle to help Lucian and Asa. Sadly, William shook the tiny man's gnarled hand. When Morgan hugged Durkin, he realized just how difficult it would be to leave Greywood.

On the ride down to Smythe's home, they talked more about their visit with Griswold.

"Did our ancestors build that crystal vault in the dragon's cave?" Morgan asked.

"The first Adney twins and Griswold designed and built it together," he replied.

"Was the crystal already there, or did they have to haul the stones in?" William asked.

"Griswold produced the crystal in all of our caves," Osdruan informed them.

"What do you mean?" William asked. A

confused frown creased his brow.

"Crystal is congealed dragon's breath. It can only be made by fire-breathing dragons. Griswold belongs to the air dragon species. He is of the firedrake clan," Osdruan stated.

"Wow!" William exclaimed. "That's the coolest thing I've ever heard."

"So fire-breathing dragons must have lived in almost every country, since crystals are found in all parts of the world," Morgan concluded.

"I only know about our firedrakes," Osdruan said. "Since dragons originated in Atlantis, I would imagine they fled to many countries after the fall of the Ancient Empire." The boys sat staring at Osdruan. Their eyes were as huge as saucers.

"I've always wanted to know more about Atlantis," Morgan admitted.

"I want to go there," William said excitedly.

"For now, the only journey you will be taking is the one back to your home," Osdruan said.

The wagon pulled up in front of Smythe's cottage and the boys jumped down.

"Will we see you before we leave?" Morgan asked.

"Yes, once you have said farewell to Smythe and his family, come to my cottage," Osdruan said. "From there, Rhiannon will take you to the Oak Bridge."

*****

Durkin made his way up the stairs, to a small room in the castle where he had been staying since the king's attack. There was a pot of tea and warm biscuits waiting for him. He sat down at the small wooden table, and let his mind wander as he sipped his tea. What would it be like in Greywood with no more worries about piskies and treasures? And no more Adney twins to ever visit Greywood again? It was fitting that Griswold would be reunited with Faida. He was old and tired and deserved time with his family on Ynys Wyth. However, the dragon had been part of Greywood for so long that it wouldn't be the same without him.

What would become of the Adney twins after they left Greywood? Their lives had been changed forever. Durkin was grateful that he would be able to track them visually for awhile, thanks to the oracle. But he would always wonder what they were thinking and doing. Perhaps he could visit them one day.

And what of Greywood? Things were changing quickly. Would there still be a need for an old messenger of the oracle? The boys' stories of Granny Gingergrace and Lady Grey had reminded him how much he missed Granny, and the rest of his family. If King Ulric would permit him to go back to his village, perhaps Durkin could stay there for the rest of his life. Rhiannon could always fetch him, if the king should ever need him.

An urgent knock at the door roused him from his daydream. He set his cup down, and reluctantly went to the door.

Alas, he was still very much a king's servant.

CHAPTER TWENTY-FOUR

With heavy hearts, the twins walked slowly down the road, in the rain, to Osdruan's hut for the last time. It had been unbelievably difficult to say good-bye to the Smythe family and Pahlaseda. The grey cat had appeared again and had chosen to walk along with them. But even her presence didn't ease their sadness, because they knew they would have to leave her too. They arrived at their tutor's house feeling very depressed.

"Come, come lads, you look as miserable as this dreary day," Osdruan said when he saw their glum faces. "I believe we have time for tea." The boys sat by the fire, quietly sipping tea and drying their damp clothes.

"This will be our last chance to talk,"

Osdruan said. "Tell me lads, now that all is said and done, what are your thoughts about your journey to Greywood and your mission?"

"I'm grateful to be alive and I think I've changed," Morgan replied thoughtfully. "Since my capture by the mandragora, and my blindness, I feel like I can face anything."

"How did you survive that?" the tutor asked. "Where did your courage come from?"

"I was ready to give up and let the mandragora keep me," Morgan said. "But, when I heard Seffie's voice in my head, I seemed to gain strength and hope. After that ordeal, I was strong enough to cope with my blindness, and brave enough to help Will escape from the shape-shifting piskie. I'm proud of myself."

"And well you should be," Osdruan replied. "Now you know that there is nothing you cannot master. Remember that always." He turned to William.

"I didn't change at all," he said quickly.

Osdruan laughed softly. "I believe you've changed a great deal," he said. "For one thing, you are no longer so eager to rush into things without forethought, and I sense that perhaps you are more sensitive."

"Are you saying that I've turned into a wimp? Because I haven't," William said defensively.

"I'm not scared of anything."

"I can only guess at the meaning of the word 'wimp'," the tutor replied. "I am not saying that you are not brave. Quite the contrary; I think you now possess the true meaning of courage: Readiness to face danger and adversity with valour and sensitivity."

"Whatever that means," William grumbled. "I can never understand what you're saying. It's like you talk in riddles or something."

Again, Osdruan chuckled. "I see that you still have the need for everything to be explained in black and white terms," he said. "But I think you have also come to accept many things that cannot be explained so simply. For instance, do you now accept the existence of dragons, piskies, mandragora plants, and shape-shifters?"

"I pretty much have to accept that, since they are real," William admitted.

"So you can accept that reality even though there is no logical explanation for it?" he asked. William shrugged.

Osdruan smiled and nodded. "Ah then, you have learned that something that cannot be explained logically, can still exist if you experience it. You have reached an important threshold in your life."

"There you go again with the riddles,"

William said good-naturedly. They all laughed.

"Permit an old man to have the final word on this matter," Osdruan said. "As time passes, and the reality of what happened here begins to blur, allow yourselves to remember the truth in what you saw. Learn to see not only with your eyes, but with your hearts and spirits as well. And leave a window open to all possibilities."

"Can you give me the short version of that?" William asked.

"Of course," the tutor said patiently. "You believe in all things that you can see with your eyes. But there are other things that you will be able to see because you believe with your heart."

"Hey, I think I get that!" William cried.

Osdruan smiled. "I have so enjoyed getting to know you lads." He stood up and walked over to his roughly-hewn table. "But now we must prepare for your return to Adney House. First of all, you must take with you only that which you brought to Greywood," he stated. "So I must ask you to give me the map, the compass, the cloaks, and anything else that was given to you during your brief stay with us." Sadly, the boys handed him their things.

"What about our clothes?" William asked.

"Rhiannon will discuss the exchange of clothing with you, Osdruan said.

At that moment, there was a knock at the door. Rhiannon had arrived.

"So our time together comes to an end," the tutor said. "Let us pledge to never forget one another." The twins looked up at the gigantic man and nodded solemnly. "And if you should see my friend Broleus again, please extend my warmest wishes." He put his arm on each boy's shoulder and walked them to the door.

As they started down the path with Rhiannon, the boys turned and waved to their trusted friend. Words couldn't express the gratitude and sadness that was in their hearts, but they knew that Osdruan understood.

Rhiannon led them down a path that was different from the one they had taken with Nesta. As before, she spoke very little and her rapid pace had the boys practically running. It was still raining lightly, and a mist had once again settled over the valley.

"Aren't we going to the Crystal Cave to get our clothes?" William asked.

"They have been taken to a cottage we will visit along the way," she answered.

"But why aren't we going back to the Crystal Cave?" William demanded.

"This route is shorter," Rhiannon replied, matter-of-factly.

They soon arrived at a small cottage. She led them inside, and gave them their jogging suits. The boys went into an adjoining room to change. No one seemed to be home, and Rhiannon didn't offer any information about the house or its owners.

A short time later, the magical princess was rushing them out the door. "You must cross the Oak Bridge before dusk," she explained as they hurried along.

The rain had finally stopped and the sun was peeking out from behind the clouds.

"The bridge is in the next clearing," she said, pointing ahead.

When they got to the small glade, Rhiannon began to take items from a worn bag she was carrying. She set a blue candle into a hole on a flat, metal dish. Placing it on the ground, she quickly gathered oak leaves and blue morning glory flowers. Rhiannon surrounded the candle with the leaves and flowers. Then, she lit the candle and stood up.

"Don't we have to make a stone circle?" Morgan asked, as he and William watched the strange preparations.

"No, I will do the incantation," Rhiannon said. "Stand together across from me, facing the bridge. Have your blue stone ready to invoke the rainbow essence as you cross. I will indicate when you are to move toward the bridge."

The twins nodded and got into position. Morgan held the remaining blue sodalite stone in his hand. Rhiannon looked the boys over carefully. They stood together wearing their grey jogging suits. Their feet were bare and they had their leather bags across their shoulders. Everything seemed to be in order, so Rhiannon began the chant:

Stone of the Earth	She placed a silver stone on the metal plate.
Emerald leaf of the Oak	She let a leaf fall to the plate.
Bluestar of the Sky	She held her arms up, a blue flower in each hand.
Take Two as One at Birth	She placed a blue flower on each boy's head.

As the flower touched his head, Morgan felt a surge of warm energy pass through his body. Rhiannon gently pushed the boys forward, and they stepped onto the bridge. As instructed, they stopped halfway across, and Morgan tossed the blue stone into the water.

Twin rainbows formed over the bridge and the boys crossed to the other side.

They stopped and looked back at the magical maiden, unsure of what to do next. She told them to hold their clear crystals toward the sun. Morgan quickly found the two Atlantean crystals in his bag and handed one to his brother. Facing Rhiannon, they raised the crystals up, toward the sun. She continued with the incantation:

With crystals of the Ancient Shore
Blackbird of Fire and Sun
Return the Two as One
To the limen of Evermore

The candle in front of Rhiannon suddenly burst into a gigantic flame that encircled her. A shimmering aura of blue light outlined her body. The fire didn't seem to touch her.

That was the last thing the boys saw, as they were immediately sucked into a familiar black vortex and began tumbling recklessly through the dark tunnels of time.

Morgan curled into a ball and wrapped his arms around his legs as a roaring wind propelled him through space. He felt himself hurtling toward a light that he could see, far in the distance. As he came out of the tunnel, he tumbled toward the Earth and landed on his backside with a jolt. He opened his eyes slowly; afraid of what he might see.

He whooped with joy when he saw that he was sitting in the very same stone circle that he and William had created in front of Merlin's cave. Morgan stood on wobbly legs and looked around for his brother, then burst into laughter when he spotted him.

William was lying flat on his back in a tide pool. "Help me," he said indignantly. "I'm stuck in quicksand or something."

"You are not," Morgan chuckled. "You're lying in a tide pool."

William's clothes were completely soaked with sand and water. He made a squishing noise as he walked stiff-legged on the cuffs of his sweatpants toward the rocks where they had hidden their things when they left for Greywood. "Let's find our shoes and stuff and get out of here," he muttered. "I'm soaked." He walked up the hill, holding his pant legs to avoid falling. "What time is it?" he asked.

"You're the one with the watch," Morgan replied. "Remember, I left mine at home."

"Can you reach into my bag and get it out?" he asked. "I'm too cold and wet."

"According to your watch, it is seven fifty-eight, September twenty-first," Morgan stated. "That's exactly the same time as it was when we left."

"So, Osdruan was right about overriding time," William said. "That's cool!"

"And Pahlaseda was right about our voices changing back," Morgan said.

As they neared Adney House, William suggested they should use the secret staircase, so he wouldn't have to explain his wet clothes. They were almost at the kitchen entrance when Morgan stopped abruptly.

"Now what?" William asked impatiently, as he bumped into his brother.

Morgan pointed to a rosebush by the door. "Glowing eyes," he whispered.

A small grey cat with large emerald eyes emerged from under the bush. She stretched leisurely, and walked toward them.

*****

Once again, Durkin knelt before the pool. As it rippled, he crossed his chubby fingers, hoping to see that the Adney twins arrived home safely. He was not disappointed. He saw two boys sleeping soundly in their beds. On the quilt of one bed, a small grey cat was curled up in the curve of one boy's legs. Durkin sat back on the grass and laughed.

With Sephonee, Companion at the Crossroads, to watch over them, the lads would be kept out of harm's way. It was a fitting gift for two boys who had willingly risked their lives to save a dragon and his people.

Durkin's step was a little lighter and he held his head a little higher, as he walked up the path. This was one message he couldn't wait to deliver to King Ulric. He had been very surprised when the king had insisted that he go to the pool and wait, 'for days if necessary', for confirmation that the twins had arrived home safely.

The king's amiable attitude continued to surprise everyone. He no longer dealt out lethal blows, or barked orders like a tyrant. He seemed to truly enjoy having his daughters fussing over him day and night. Maybe the attack had healed a part of his heart that had long been broken.

Durkin no longer wondered about what had caused the metamorphosis; he just hoped it would last.

"Everything happens for a reason," Durkin said aloud as he stroked his mare's velvety nose. She had been an unexpected gift from the king. The small messenger climbed onto his wagon and grinned proudly, as he clicked his tongue and directed his horse toward the castle.